OTHER WINTERS,
OTHER SPRINGS

By Flora Sandstrom

THE MIDWIFE OF PONT CLERY

THE VIRTUOUS WOMEN OF PONT CLERY

Flora Sandstrom

OTHER WINTERS, OTHER SPRINGS

CLEVELAND AND NEW YORK

THE WORLD PUBLISHING COMPANY

PUBLISHED BY THE WORLD PUBLISHING COMPANY

2231 WEST 110TH STREET, CLEVELAND 2, OHIO

LIBRARY OF CONGRESS CATALOG CARD NUMBER: 63-14783

FIRST EDITION

wp863

OTHER WINTERS,
OTHER SPRINGS

1

THE FARMHOUSE was single-storied, built of wood. Once it had been painted ocher-red, with green shutters, but the color had been mellowed and faded by time till it melted softly into a summer landscape. Now it was almost obliterated by snow which smoothed its outline and ran like silver down the frail young trunks of the naked birches in the near-by plantation. Snow smoothed out the ruts and hollows in the road which straggled to the village of Porvesi, a typical Finnish village with its scattered groups of houses and farms strung at intervals among the fields or on the edge of the forest.

The forest was mainly spruce, pine, and birch. In winter it had a savage quality, dark and brooding. There was silence. The sound of the wind in the pines was muffled by snow, and it was no longer possible to tell the difference between the music made by the wind soughing in the pines and the music made by the wind in the birches. The silence was profound. A lonely traveler on his skis might remember the ancient tales of powerful spirits, both good and evil, which haunted the forest. He might feel their presence. The sudden, gliding form of a lynx silhouetted against the snow might cause him to shiver with more than mortal fear as he quickened his pace.

In such moments he might remember, with his blood rather than his brain, that once all regions had their abiding spirits —the forest, the lake, the *sauna,* the byre, the hearth. So his forefathers had believed, part as they were of this remoteness of lake and forest, bred to solitude, Nature their god and their foe. Rooted here, bound by wind, snow, water, forest, and granite rock, man could not triumph. He was instead hewn and fashioned by this cruel, lyrical omnipotence. Here man was awed but fearless, here he knew his own strength and his own littleness.

On the edge of the forest, some twenty-five miles from Porvesi and the nearest dwelling, Erik Vainen had built his wooden house and established his farm. It had been a "cold" farm: that is to say with his own hands he had cleared the forest, wrenching from it a space for his own habitation. In 1940 he had been among the first refugees from southern Karelia, when after the Winter War, it had become a Russian province. He had wandered with his wife Kirsti and five-year-old son Kaarlo and a few hastily packed belongings to this remote hamlet of Porvesi, near central Finland. He had chosen Porvesi because of it remoteness. He had left behind him in southern Karelia a small farmhouse with red-ochered walls, a barn, outbuildings, a *sauna,* a birch plantation, and field and pasture land. Here, wrested from this forest, stood his farm, his barn, his *sauna,* his precious plantation of birch, and a few acres of land. At the outset, with only one bulldozer shared by three hamlets to help him, the forest had still found Erik a relentless adversary, a man not lacking in that granite in the character which the Finns call *sisu.* With a state grant sufficient to buy some tools and equipment, Erik had worked from dawn to dark. Those days had been days of privation and hardship and Kirsti had pined for Karelia, where everyone had been gay, yet slowly and surely satisfaction had crept into their lives. He had been twenty-eight then, strong and hard of body, and Kirsti twenty-three, with wide gray eyes, her body supple and strong. When Erik thought of those days he thought of Kirsti's body big with child, cool and fresh from the lake, or brown from the long days of summer sun. He thought of the taste of new-made bread, the splitting of white wood with an ax, the whir of a loom, the voice of a child gathering wild strawberries in the woods. For the end of everything is a distillation of memories.

Tenacious as they were of their own hard-won acres, the people of Porvesi had regarded Erik with hostility in those early days. But when he had chosen his remote place and begun to tear his sustenance from the forest, they had given him help and good will. They were men whose land was identified with themselves, part of themselves, but Erik Vainen had not coveted their land or expected from them anything that they could not give. The accident of time and place had rendered him, like thousands of others, homeless and dispossessed, but it was clear from the start that Erik Vainen sought neither the protection, the property, nor the companionship of the hamlet.

"We will begin from the beginning," he had told Kirsti. "We will make our home here."

Kirsti had gazed at one tall pine and thought of the labor of felling that one tree. The air was aromatic. From where they stood they could see the shimmer of the lake. The sky was serene and the silence infinite. It was as though man had returned to his primeval beginnings. She had known then that Erik was right.

In the long and sometimes hopeless months that followed Kirsti thought of the smoke curling from the chimneys of their home in Karelia, of the gentle sounds of the beasts in the byre, of the old man, her widowed father, with his red, wrinkled cheeks and eyes perpetually crinkled in laughter. He had been killed by a stray bullet when fighting had broken out around their home. The winter had been bitter, the soil frozen as hard as the Gulf of Finland, over which the Russians had driven their tanks. It had been an inhuman task to break the soil and bury the old man.

Now they were breaking the soil again and Kirsti knew that this must be so, that only in this way could the fierce, hard root of independence, the sustenance of their beings, come to fruition. So she had camped in the forest, enduring hardship, hunger, discomfort, and danger, while slowly the house had risen and the roof was put on. When they had reached the highest point of the house, the raising of the ridge, they had not forgotten to celebrate. There were three of them, Erik, herself, and old Akseli the Lapp, who had later followed them from Karelia. Kirsti had made coffee and *pulla* for the celebration, and little Kaarlo had run wild with delight, stuffing himself with the sweet bun-loaf which he had not tasted since they had left Karelia.

Long before the house was habitable Kirsti had begun to use the loom and spinning wheel which Erik had made her. She had worked unceasingly, weaving linen and making rugs, using the traditional patterns which had been handed down in her family for generations. With the wool from their two sheep and Kirsti's homemade vegetable dyes, the rugs were woven in traditional colors, like the rugs of long ago. Kirsti had liked to feel that music had somehow been woven into them also, for while she worked she could hear old Akseli splitting logs and singing the ancient runes. He was a great rune singer and carried hundreds of lines in his head. They had lured him into Porvesi to sing his runes at a wedding or a christening. He had bartered his runes for flax, so, Kirsti thought, the sound of singing had been woven into the homespun sheets which were washed in spring water and dried in the sun, and between which she and Erik lay.

They had thought of old Akseli as a father and, indeed, he became to them a father, Kirsti thought. Little Kaarlo loved him. From old Akseli the child was learning how life had been lived many years ago in the vast solitudes, learning how close to the spirit of all things is man, learning from the old Lapp how earthy and hard and tough is the life of man, filled with gaiety, cunning, and danger—a whirlpool. But at the heart of the whirlpool lies a dark core of silence, and this is man's soul. And to know his soul, said old Akseli, a man must listen to the silence.

Akseli was a true Lapp from the farthest north. Erik's family were Finnish Laplanders, Finns who had moved northwards and been held there by the spell, the Lapland sickness, from which they had never recovered. When he had wandered south, little more than a stripling, Erik had been drawn by a sense of adventure, a longing to see what lay beyond the sparse forests, the swamps, and blue rivers, beyond the purple moorland and the wild, galloping reindeer, the crystal air of winter and its darkness, and the long unearthly vigil of the midnight sun.

The hawk-eyed old Lapp with his gentle voice had wandered south with Erik, filled, like Erik, with the desire to build something new. The Vainens were foresters and old Akseli had worked for them. He had lived with them, eaten at their board, watched Erik grow, and it had seemed natural, when Erik had felt the urge to wander, to strike out on his own, that old Akseli should accompany him. In Karelia, Erik had found a bride and a home, and a place, Erik had thought, for Akseli to come to rest.

But Akseli had followed them, after the war, nevertheless. There were places, he had said, not so gentle, nor so gay as Karelia, where the forests were deeper and denser and where there was silence. He had known, he said, that Erik would find such a place, for it was Erik's need also.

The place had no name. It was not in Porvesi, twenty-five miles away, nor part of Vituri, which lay in the opposite direction, fifty miles distant. It was a place unknown, uninhabited, part of a forest knowing only wild birds and the elk and the lynx.

All men of the north have a need for solitude and independence. Erik's need was greater than most. The place he chose was nameless and insofar as it now had a name, it was called by the people of Porvesi simply Vainen. Where Erik's

few fields stopped and the forest began, there the region was
nameless until one came to Porvesi.

Yet between Vainen and Porvesi, in that hitherto nameless
region, others had once been. Half hidden in the forest was
what had once been a church of ancient medieval times,
massively built. The forest had grown up around it, encroaching on the path once worn by pilgrims to its door. It was
strange to come upon this church in the forest. Part of its
roof was open to the sky and tendrils twined and birds nested
on what was left of the altar and what must have been the
decaying confessional, so that there was still a sweet choir.
Around the walls could be seen sacred murals and for the
most part the colors were still soft and true. There were
saints, with long, slim-fingered hands pressed palm to palm,
wearing robes of purest blue. There were beasts of the field,
lambs with gentle, triangular faces, and pilgrims, accompanied
by a devil, mounting a green hill. Erik and Kirsti, with the
child, had spent their first night in the ruined church.

The church had drawn him back often in the years that
followed. His feet had often taken him there almost without
his volition. Inside the church was a living stillness, unlike
that of the forest. The forest watched and listened and it had
strange voices of its own to which a man must listen. In the
ruined church he might listen to his own soul. In it was the
echo of all the prayers which had once ascended like incense
to the great rafters through which the sky was seen.

The people of Porvesi knew of the church. "But," they
said evasively, "nobody goes there now. One day the forest
will devour it completely."

While they revered its antiquity they felt for it a faint,
superstitious fear, something drawn from their deepest in-
stincts. Elsewhere in the land were shops, factories, great
power stations, renowned sculptors, architects who had in-
fluenced the world, artists in glass and ceramics, and these,
too, were theirs. But here were lakes and forests where no
footfall was heard, where nature held dominion, and all the

spirits of nature, and the ruined church was part of this other world that a man had left behind with his childhood. The church was stubborn. It had defied wind and weather, time and decay, persisting like a voice out of the unrecorded past.

Porvesi had its own church and in this it was better off than many villages. The church was small, built of wood, with a separate bell tower. It was simple and plain, in contrast with the Eastern magnificence of some of the few Greek Orthodox churches still remaining, for the people of Porvesi were Lutherans.

When Akseli had found Erik and Kirsti and the child in the place they had chosen he knew that they had done well. "This is a good place," he had said at once. "People have trod a path somewhere hereabouts to pray to their God." Erik had told him then about the church, but without surprise. It was well known that Lapps, and many Finns, had second sight. Akseli said that there had been a community of people here too, surely monks, he told them, but it must have been hundreds of years ago. They had died out through hardship or sickness, he supposed, and all that the forest had left to mark their passing was the ruined church.

The forest was tenacious, with a strong secret life, always encroaching stealthily on the acres man wrested for himself. But forests were the riches of the country. Erik's family had been foresters for generations, and the sight of the tall trees and their resinous, aromatic smell were as necessary to him as the sight and smell of the sea to a seafarer. Here, too, he lived by his own endeavors, as did his neighbors, in a country which had never known a feudal system and where every man was his own master.

He stood now, a man in his early forties, in the full prime of his manhood. He was above average height, strongly built. Years of hard physical labor had toughened and hardened a resilient body. His eyes, very blue, were the deep-set eyes

of the northerner, eyes used to great distances, to the dazzle of
sun on snow or the mercurial shimmer of a summer lake. His
thick, fair hair was streaked with gray, hair which had the
thickness and vibrance of an animal's pelt. His body, and
the carriage of his head, gave out this sense of vibrant vitality,
but the face belied it. It was the face of a man with a strong,
inner life, a man for whom experience had turned inward, to
be consumed. The body was the body of a man of action. The
face was the face of a hermit, a contemplative.

He wore a fleece-lined jacket and boots to the knee. His
fur cap had earflaps drawn close. His breath was visible on
the frosty air. He glanced back at the barn, from which he
had just returned from feeding his animals—a few cows, a
sheep, a cluster of hens, pigs, and a horse. Their winter
quarters were under the one roof, divided by partitions. The
horse was a roan, small, hard, and wiry, a horse formerly
used for timber hauling which he had bought cheaply in the
spring. It was a tough little animal and earlier in the day
had nosed for anything edible and kicked up its heels in the
snow-covered paddock. It had the milky mane and long eyelashes of the Finnish horse, eyelashes which are a protection
against the continuous hours of sunlght. The cows had them
also, ringing their large, deceptively pensive eyes. On the
horse these long eyelashes looked incongruous, almost thea-
trical, lending an air of false glamor to a hard, stubborn
little animal capable of great strength and endurance.

Smoke eddied from the chimney of the *sauna,* where earlier
in the day Erik had stoked the furnace with wood from the
woodpile laid in during the summer. It was Saturday and the
night on which he took his bath, a bath which had its symbolic overtones of ritual purification as well as cleansing. The
sauna, which he had built of strong, massive logs, stood a
few hundred yards from the house. The lake was near enough
to dive into after the bath.

In the old days the women in labor had gone to the bath-
house to deliver their children in its soft, enveloping warmth.

Erik stood a moment watching the smoke spiraling upward. The agony which had once arisen within him like the spiraling smoke, to dissolve in the recesses of his being, transmuted into memory, as smoke into air, could still stir and rise from the banked-down fire. Like her forebears, Kirsti had gone to deliver her second son in the *sauna,* where it was warm and dry, and had died in childbirth and the child with her. She had never lived to see the full fruit of their labors after the wandering, the toil, and hardship, after the laughter and the promise.

Again he remembered that day. He had perforce acted as midwife but the child had been badly placed and Kirsti had struggled in vain. Suddenly like an apparition, it had seemed to Erik, out of another world, Akseli had entered the *sauna.* Before Erik could speak Akseli had spoken softly.

"The boy is in danger."

"The boy?" Erik had raised his eyes to the old man's and a swift, wordless communication had passed between them.

"Come outside," Erik had said. Kirsti lay on an improvised bed, absorbed in the grim struggle.

"Kaarlo?" Erik said swiftly. "Kaarlo? Not the child to be born?"

"Kaarlo. He is five miles away, on the shores of the lake. He is in danger, Erik. I must go."

With scarcely another word, a glance, the old man had gone. Erik had known that Akseli's strange gift of prescience had pierced a veil. The child had been playing near the woodpile, gathering the sawdust and shavings into a little barrow, wheeling it away, and making a miniature woodpile of his own. Absently Erik had noticed his absorption, the sturdiness of his body as he trotted to and fro, while the anguished minutes—or perhaps they were hours—dragged by in the *sauna.* Akseli had set off previously for Porvesi, to get help. "Hurry!" Erik had said. "There must be a midwife there or an experienced woman you can bring back in the cart with you. Hurry, Akseli, hurry. It is life and death."

But Akseli had scarcely started on the road before turning back, and with his swift words to Erik, set off in another direction. But the lake was deep and did not yield up its secrets easily. No one would ever know whether Akseli had found the boy before both sank to the bottom of the lake, on which the summer sun shone so serenely on an afternoon of clear light. Certain it was that Akseli would have dived and dived again till his lungs burst and his heart ceased to beat, sooner than give up his search. Nothing was left of Akseli, and nothing of Kaarlo, save his little barrow upturned by the woodpile and his small footprints in the dust.

Days passed, and weeks, while the people of Porvesi tried to show their sympathy and give help to the stricken man who in one day had lost wife, family, and lifelong friend. It seemed to them that Erik Vainen could not now continue to build but would leave and wander elsewhere and find a new place to build, a place without bitter memories. Or perhaps he would go to a town where a man could bury his past and in time find the courage to start again.

But it was clear that Erik would do none of these things. Slowly he withdrew from them, not in bitterness or rancor, but like a man who is sufficient to himself, a man who is pitted against a force stronger than himself but who will wrestle with it the long night through, as Jacob wrestled with the angel.

The sound of his ax still rang through the forest. His hammer strokes were heard through the long summer nights. He came to Porvesi to barter and sell, a powerful, quiet man, a man without bitterness but a man drawing his strength from something fierce and hard and unyielding in his own nature. He spoke little. With their deep-rooted acknowledgment of a man's right to be himself, to eschew the herd if need be, they left him to himself. None would cross the invisible barrier that Erik himself had raised. They knew from afar when he had cleared a field, levering out the tree roots, they knew the progress of the birch plantation made for his

son, the "curly" birch that did not grow wild and would one
day yield a rich harvest for furniture. They knew when a
horse was bought and a cow calved. They knew that what
Erik Vainen had set himself to do for a son and a future he
was now doing for himself, not for gain or for money, but
for a debt he owed to himself, an iron, unflinching determi-
nation to tread the road he had marked out for himself in
spite of the hammer blows of destiny.

They called the place he had marked out for himself, this
home, this habitation, simply Vainen. But the word was more
than a man's name. The word was a man's life, a man's
destiny. As the years went by the knowledge of why this was
so dulled a little. They neither loved nor feared Erik. For the
most part they were indifferent to him. But the word Vainen
retained an unconquerable ring, like an echo of martial glory
in which the participators are dead or forgotten.

Erik Vainen himself, as he stood watching the smoke eddy
from the chimney of the *sauna*, knew that he had finally
come to his place, the place he had sought and striven for.
Now he had come to it and it was his, possessed. But he knew
that it was more than a place. It was a region of the mind,
the heart of the whirlpool, the dark core of silence which
Akseli had said was a man's soul.

Beasts must be fed and land tilled, and in the long winter
nights he would continue to carve skillfully in wood and
create things that were strange or beautiful as he had done
for many winters past. All these things must be. But as he
watched the lingering spiral of smoke, Erik knew that for a
long time now he had finished with the world and its ways.
He had reached the heart of the whirlpool.

As he turned away, Erik heard the little horse snort and
stamp in the barn, and then whinny. There was nothing in
sight except his swift, exuberant Lapp dog, reddish brown
against the snow as it came bounding to meet him. The first
rays of sunset slanted across the birches. They suffused the sky
and touched the snowy landscape with a serene, unearthly

light. The forest breathed and listened. Sound and silence
were one. Water and light merged into one pure element that
might vanish at a breath.

The dog leapt up at him, and suddenly water and light,
sound and silence were splintered by his shrill bark.

"Quiet," said Erik softly. "Down, Penna!" The panting,
foxlike body subsided at his feet. Still the horse whinnied
and stamped. Erik walked to the house. The snowfall was still
comparatively light. The wooden house was in darkness, its
outlines further blurred and softened by the fresh snow.

Erik's boots crunched the snow as he made his way to the
house, Penna leaping beside him and giving short, agitated
barks. Something had disturbed the dog. As Erik pushed open
the door he heard another sound, an unfamiliar neigh and
whinny. It came from the other side of the house. A strange
horse must have wandered there.

The narrow wooden passage was in darkness, as was the
living room. There was still, partly from choice, partly from
necessity, no electric light in the house. Erik paused, the dog
silent beside him. His senses were those of a man accustomed
to the silence of the forest, the greater silence of the lake,
where the ear could catch the faintest ripple or the remotest
cry of a distant bird. Someone was breathing in the room, a
stealthy, uneven breathing, and now whoever it was had
stopped and was holding his breath.

Erik crossed to the table, every inch of this kitchen-living
room familiar to him, and reached for the matches which lay
where he had left them, and slowly and methodically lighted
the lamp. He turned in the soft glow to face the bench beside
the door from which the sound came. A man was seated there,
young, handsome, dark, and wild-looking. His clothes were
nondescript, but his long, slender legs and feet were encased
in good boots of supple leather. Erik ordered Penna to his
corner by the hearth.

He saw that the man was one of the nomad gypsies, mis-
trusted by all. His face darkened. Then he noticed that the

gypsy, either by accident or intention, had taken the bench
by old custom reserved for beggars, and the fact touched a
chord of compassion in him. He, too, had once been homeless. But hostility filled him again at the gypsy's expression.
It was alert, wary, full of calculated charm.

"What are you doing here?" Erik asked.

"I came to sell you a horse. A fine animal. I tethered it
near the birches."

"I have a horse. Where did you steal this one?"

"I came by it honestly," the gypsy said.

Erik stood looking down at him. From time immemorial the
gypsies had wandered through the country in summer and in
winter, following the occupations of gypsies all the world
over. They were horse-dealers, tinkers, and fortunetellers, when
they could find a gullible woman or a romantic girl. They
pilfered anything on which they could lay their hands. A few
of them settled down, bought farms, even became rich. This
one, he saw, had been running hard, and only now was he
breathing evenly again.

"I have a horse," Erik repeated.

"I need food," the gypsy said, ingratiatingly. He rose from
the bench quickly, as tall as Erik but seeming taller because of
the slenderness of his body. He was as supple as a young birch.
Erik remembered gypsies he had seen one summer day in
Viipuri, particularly the women, lithe as panthers, wearing
gay blouses and long, full skirts of black velvet. He remembered now, clearly, how one had tossed up her skirt to reach
a purse hidden somewhere amongst its heavy folds. Beneath
the wide, velvet skirt her body had been naked, the legs and
thighs slender, supple, with a suggestion of steely strength
beneath the silky brown skin. He had been young then,
scarcely more than a boy. Nakedness had meant, hitherto,
nothing to him, except that it was a fine thing to plunge
with others, free and untrammeled, into a clear lake or roll
in the crisp snow fresh from the deep cleansing of the *sauna*.
But the slim, naked body swaying like a flower beneath the

swirling black velvet had sent the hot blood rushing under
the skin. This youth before him now had the same quality of
grace and abandonment.

Erik turned away. The room had sprung into relief in the
mellow light of the lamp. Kirsti's copper kettle, the hub of
the home, which she had brought from Karelia, reminded
him, if he had needed to be reminded, that the duty of
hospitality was a sacred one. As in medieval England, the
benighted traveler here must be fed and housed and no
questions asked about his condition or degree. Erik was sure
that the gypsy was fleeing, perhaps from the wrath of a housewife in Porvesi who had found him stealing at her door,
perhaps from some graver sin. Time would tell.

He set about making coffee in Kirsti's copper kettle and
stirred the fire, for the man was cold. Coffee was his most
precious luxury and necessity. Like most Finns he could drink
twenty cups a day. The young gypsy's eyes shone as the ex-
quisite aroma filled the room. He looked about him with
quick, darting gaze, like a wild creature, long lashes veiling
his eyes suddenly as though to hide the thoughts which might
be visible there. He was quick, watchful, alive. He brought a
hint of savagery into the room.

Erik handed him a steaming cup of coffee.

"The horse must be fed," he said.

"I have watered and fed him," the gypsy said with charming
insolence. He would know, Erik realized, where both water
and fodder could be found. He made no reply. "He is sheltered also," the gypsy added, as though to forestall further
unnecessary questions.

They drank their coffee in silence. The silence engendered
a sense of kinship and communion.

The time for further questioning, Erik knew, was not yet.
The laws of hospitality forbade it.

As they drank Erik glanced around the room as though
seeing it through the stranger's eyes.

It was warm, enfolding. To the gypsy, fresh from the rigors

of the forest, it must have seemed as close and safe a world as the womb.

It was dominated by the deep fireplace with its hooded chimney, in which the great fire of logs was now burning. The walls and floor were gay with the bright rug Kirsti had made, on which the firelight flickered softly. The huge wooden rocking chair in which Erik sat creaked every now and then as he moved. A pine-wood table stood on one side of the room. It was bigger than Erik required but he had hewn it, in the beginning, to serve the needs of a growing family. Now he sat alone at the head of it and no longer, with a mixture of stubborn unyieldingness and aching bereavement, laid plates for Kirsti, Kaarlo, and old Akseli. Along the wall opposite the fireplace was the bookcase he had made during the first long, lonely evenings. It was filled now with the books for which he had sent to Helsinki. Most of them were in Swedish, which Erik had learned at school. There were classics and modern books and Kirsti's great family Bible printed in the Finnish language, which she had wrapped in a linen cloth like the body of Christ and which little Kaarlo had helped to carry from Karelia. In one corner of the bookcase was a pile of seed catalogues and farmer's magazines. Above it was a photograph of Kirsti's father, who had been, in his younger days, a captain on a lake steamer. He was wearing his uniform and a luxuriant beard. His small, laughing eyes looked out from beneath the traditional top hat. Kirsti had brought the photograph in the family Bible and Erik had carved the frame for it and hung it in the place of honor. Of his own family he had nothing. He had never been back to the north and now his parents were dead and their home sold.

Everything in the room had been made by Erik—the loom, the spinning wheel, which he now used himself, the chairs with their painted flower motifs, the dresser, Kirsti's footstool, the wooden cradle, the heads of Kirsti, Kaarlo, and Akseli which he had carved from wood. He had caught Kirsti's expression so that the wood seemed to listen, as she had seemed

always to listen, as though she were listening for the approaching footfall of her destiny. In the firelight her braided crown
of hair glistened as though it were alive.

Erik raised his eyes from his cup and looked at the gypsy,
a wild creature for whom life was freedom. The gypsy gazed at
the room, his glance resting greedily and fleetingly on every
object. He rose swiftly and his slender brown fingers caressed
Kirsti's braided hair.

"There are people who would give you money for this,"
he said.

"I don't need money."

"This is no longer wood. It is a woman."

Erik made no reply. He put down his empty cup.

"You will not sell?" the gypsy asked tentatively.

"No." Erik took the man's cup. "I will give you food and a
bed. You can have a bath too, if you like. The *sauna* is ready."

The gypsy nodded. He watched while Erik put out plates
and knives and forks and put a pan of potatoes to boil on the
fire. He had taken them from his potato pit earlier in the
day and had scrubbed them ready to boil in their skins. With
them he had salt herring, rye bread, and a dish of gruel to
follow. There would be nothing to drink except coffee. It
was not lack of hospitality which prevented Erik from offering
his meager reserve of schnapps, which he drank only in the
bitterest weather, but fear of its effect upon the gypsy.

As Erik worked, the gypsy padded swiftly about the room,
like a confined panther. Presently he plucked at the strings of
the ancient *kantele* which had belonged to Akseli and which
was placed near Erik's chair, and as the melody arose from his
plucking fingers he began to sing. The words were in his own
dialect. In speech he had used many Swedish words and Erik
had immediately understood. The song, however, was haunting
and unintelligible. Presently he put the small Finnish harp
aside abruptly after drawing his fingers wildly and impatiently
across the strings. They gave out a sound like a woman

weeping. The gypsy tensed suddenly, like one poised for flight. Erik summoned him to his place on the bench to eat.

He paused gracefully, arrested in the act of tearing the bread, by Erik bowing his head in a short grace. Then he ate as though he had not eaten since dawn, after a violent and exhausting day, which in fact was the case. The potatoes were good, enriched with butter, and the salt herring gave them the savor that appetite needed in Erik's somewhat monotonous diet. They ate in silence broken only by the crackling logs and the sound of the wind in the forest. The night was closing in with light though steadily falling snow.

When the gypsy had eaten and drunk his fill Erik cleared away plates and dishes and washed them at the sink in a small outer room in the passage. There was a simple bed in the room, no more than a plank, with a thick, bright rug spread on it. Here Akseli had slept.

"After the bath," Erik said to the gypsy, "you can sleep here." He lifted the lid of a wooden coffer and pulled out a sheepskin, for the room was cold, and offered it to the gypsy, who thrust it back in the box, laughing.

"The rug is enough. I am not a woman. I sleep well in the forest."

"As you please," Erik said.

"But tonight, after the bath, I will sleep here." He measured the bunk with his hands close together.

"Narrow, like a grave," he laughed. "Tomorrow I sleep in the forest."

2

THE TWO MEN went together across the snow to the *sauna,* which stood near the lake among the trees. The stars were full and clear, the snow no longer falling. The gypsy paused on the way, to whisper to his horse. The small animal was younger than Erik's horse, with a blaze like a star on its forehead. It stood blinking beneath the rough shelter of branches which the gypsy had made silently while Erik was in the byre. It was tethered to a sawed-off tree trunk with sufficient rope to lie down if it chose. The gypsy's eyes glittered in the starlight as he whispered to the horse. It pricked its ears and then lay down with an air of great submissiveness.

"It must rest," the gypsy said. "It will sell better. It understands."

It was known that gypsies could commune with their horses in a way unknown to other men. Erik glanced curiously at the animal and spoke softly. It laid its ears back and showed the whites of its eyes.

"Come," whispered the gypsy, and put a hand on Erik's wrist in a conspiratorial manner. Erik shivered. Akseli would have said that the spirits of the night were not benign.

Within the *sauna* all was warmth and comfort. They undressed in the small, outer room. The gypsy flung off his

26

strangely assorted garments, secured by a belt with a silver buckle, as though sloughing a skin, and scrubbed and washed himself. He stood, tall and slender, his waist as small as a girl's, his flanks lean. When he stretched Erik could sense the whipcord strength of his body. His round, dark head was set on a neck which now was long and seemed delicate but which in maturity would have the solidity and strength of a bull's. His teeth were strong and white, his eyes dark and slanting. His dark hair curled closely over his head and temples. For the first time Erik noticed the tiny gold rings glinting in the small ears almost covered by the close-curling hair.

In contrast Erik's body was that of a man in full maturity, deep-chested, close-knit, with powerful flanks, and legs planted as solidly as tree trunks. There was no fat on him; all was muscle and bone and sinew, covered by unblemished skin. In years the two men might have been father and son. In appearance they were men of differing race, a differing clime. Erik looked at the beauty of the young man's body with the satisfaction with which he looked at anything that was perfectly made. Suddenly he yearned for the wood and the chisel, the stubborn wood which could be made to yield up this form, this shape of beauty.

They went into the inner room, the *sauna* itself. Erik had stoked the furnace soon after midday. Now the great stones were red-hot and the heat of the *sauna* was like a blast of air from the Sahara. Erik motioned the gypsy to lie down on one of the slatted wooden benches. That nearest the roof was hottest and the gypsy chose a lower one. Erik seized a wooden pail and flung water onto the red-hot stones. A cloud of steam rose, choking the lungs, so that for the moment only a gasping cry was possible. Gradually the enveloping warmth stole over body and mind like a benediction.

The gypsy lay relaxed, watching while Erik rose from his bench under the roof to throw water from time to time upon the stones. Sweat poured from Erik's body. He seized two bundles of birch twigs and dipped them in water to free their

scent. Handing one to the gypsy he used the other upon
himself, beating his body till the flesh stung and the blood
coursed through the veins. The gypsy did likewise, laughing
now, his eyes glittering in the dimly lit log hut. Suddenly he
had come to life again, like a wild creature startled from
its lair.

Presently they rose to a sitting posture and the gypsy, growing used to the heat, climbed to Erik's platform. They sat side
by side, alternately resting and using the birch twigs upon
their backs and chests and limbs and on each other.

"Why did you come to my house?" Erik asked.

"For shelter. I came suddenly upon your house at the edge
of the woods."

"What have you done? Have you stolen? Murdered?"

"Neither," said the gypsy. He smiled voluptuously.

"But you have committed some crime."

"No. I have committed no crime," the gypsy said thoughtfully.

"Tell me, then, whatever it is. You have received my hospitality. Repay it with your confidence."

The gypsy plied his birch twigs idly, reflectively, for some
moments. Then he began to speak, partly in his own dialect,
but the few words he uttered in it were negligible. Chiefly he
spoke in a mixture of Finnish and Swedish, with expressive
gestures.

"My grandmother is the matriarch of our tribe. I am the
youngest of her grandsons, the best loved. And I am unmarried. Two days ago she chose a wife for me. She was a girl
I have known since we were children. We met from time to
time in our wanderings." The gypsy paused. His dark hair
was damp, his eyelashes glistened.

"She was good? She was beautiful? You liked her?"

"She was good. She was beautiful. But I did not like her."

The warm, somnolent air relaxed the body but quickened
the mind. The gypsy spoke swiftly now.

"Looking at her was like looking at a sunrise when the belly is empty. And I knew it would always be so. Yet this was the woman decreed must be my wife. When my grandmother had spoken there was nothing to do but obey."

"You could not refuse?"

"To refuse was to insult the girl with a deadly insult. An insult that could only be wiped out by mutilation—" Here the gypsy made a quick gesture as of one slitting the nostrils. "By mutilation, or death, or marriage. I wanted to stay as I am. I did not want to die. And more than all I did not want to marry. The way was not easy."

"But the matriarch was your grandmother. And you were her best-loved grandson," Erik said in his even, measured tones. "Surely a way out could have been found for you?"

"That is possible," the gypsy said. "But a young man must not think of things which are possible. That way lies danger. He must think of things which are certain. To hope for help from my grandmother was a great risk. I could not take it. So I fled, on my brother's horse. A stolen horse, you understand. We made good speed from dawn . . ." The gypsy paused sullenly.

"You haven't finished," Erik said.

"From dawn, then, to dusk," the gypsy said reluctantly. "We came many, many miles through the forest. And then the snow began to fall and I saw your house. All day I had not eaten or drunk and neither had the horse. So I stole food for it from your store and water from your well. I saw you go to the byre. I was afraid that the neighing of your horse would betray mine. And the dog barked. But luckily there was a greater noise in the byre."

Erik sat, silent, studying the gypsy. He had a feeling that not all had been told.

"What do you plan to do now?" he asked. "Where do you intend to go?"

"I would like to hide somewhere around here till the

spring. My tribe will not come this way till spring, or perhaps
late summer. But by then I shall be gone."

"By then they may have forgotten. The girl will have
found another bridegroom, your brother another horse."

"It will not be forgotten that I have defied the matriarch,
insulted a woman, and stolen a horse, and these are my crimes.
The girl's family and my family had an understanding with
the matriarch. The pact had been made in blood not yet shed.
If I am found I must marry the girl."

"Is she so unpleasant to you?"

"A man has only one life. And he must live it as he chooses."

It was a cry to reach the heart of a man of Erik's proud
and independent race. This cry—the right of a man to choose
his own destiny, the right of a man to be free, the right of a
man to be himself. It was a cry he understood.

"You may stay here if you wish," Erik said. "You have
chosen a good place. Because of certain matters—which are
neither evil nor strange—the people hereabouts do not know
me nor I them. Nobody will seek me out here and for what
is needful I go to them. Except for shopping in Porvesi and
some errand here or there perhaps, I do not go abroad. If you
need sanctuary you have been led to a good place. What is
your name?"

"You can call me the gypsy," the man muttered.

"As you please. As for me, my name is Erik Vainen and it
is a matter of some pride to me that all the people hereabouts,
in Porvesi and in Vituri, call my home Vainen and the place
it is in Vainen. I have given my name to this part of the
forest."

"But I see no sons in your home. Your sons will not know
it."

"No," Erik said. "My sons will not know it."

He got up from the bench and told the gypsy to do likewise
and showed him the pail of warm water and the scrubbing
brushes so that again he might scrub himself clean.

As they scrubbed Erik felt a great tenderness well up in

him for the young man, a tenderness which was close to love. The man was young, hard, cunning, and proud, thrusting himself already against the harshness of destiny as a young ram thrusts its sprouting horns against a tree.

"You shall be my son," he said.

This slow thawing back to life is painless, he thought with surprise. It was long since he had felt an impulse of warmth to any human creature. Life had existed for him in his brain and his eyes and his hands. Nothing had quickened the beat of his heart. But to this young man, with his ruthlessness, his stealth, his graceless charm, he felt the impulse of tenderness, the awakening of paternity. For the youth had sought shelter under his roof as a child comes in out of the storm.

"Until the spring, then," the gypsy said. "If I am safe here I will eat your bread and work for you until the spring."

Now as he scrubbed himself Erik felt the blood tingle through his veins as he had not felt it for many years. He saw the swift color stain the gypsy's brown cheeks. His lips were the color of rowanberries. Erik thought of the wild tribe which could split such proud nostrils flared like a Pharaoh's. Again his fingers flexed for the chisel and the wood. He would carve a statue of the youth before he left in the spring.

Erik put his hand down on the wooden bench as a hand might be placed on an altar.

"Give me your hand. It is a bargain," he said. "Now—the snow waits. We will finish the bath." He flung open the outer door and the white night rushed in like a devouring beast. With a gasp that was half pleasure, half pain, Erik flung himself into the snow. The gypsy followed, gasping and shouting with delight as extremes of temperature met and every cell in the body sprang to life. In the forest the trees were silent save for the creak of a bough or the sudden snapping of a twig heavy with snow. The forest was there, benign, white, unseeing, but in its secret fastnesses mysterious and terrible as a god. The sense of its presence was with Erik always and now the gypsy stood up in the white night and pointed toward it.

"Many would have lost their way in the forest," he said. "But a gypsy sees tracks no other man sees. Besides, I was born in the forest. The cuckoo called when I was born."

"A bird of good omen," Erik said.

When they had dressed again they sat awhile by the flickering fire while Erik played Akseli's ancient harp and sang some of the runes which Akseli had taught him. It was good to see another opposite him at the fire, good to hear the voice of another. From time to time Penna thumped his tail vigorously on the floor and at other times he would howl and come to lay his head on Erik's knee.

"He's jealous," Erik said, "that's what it is. For a long time now he's heard no other voice but mine."

"He is afraid," the gypsy said. His face darkened and he got up. "I shall go and sleep."

Erik went to a stout wooden box and took out a candle and fixed it in a candlestick. It was one of the few remaining, hoarded carefully, of those which Kirsti had made so long ago. There was something symbolic, Erik knew, in giving it to the gypsy. It was as though he were giving something of himself.

"Here are the matches. Be careful with the flame. Wooden walls burn easily."

"Women make candles like these. But I have seen better in the market," the gypsy said critically.

"My wife made this."

"Where is she. Has she run away?"

"She is dead."

"And the child?" the gypsy asked, looking at the cradle.

"That was for the child that was coming. But my wife died in childbed. I had another son. He was drowned."

"There was ill luck in your stars. So that is why you live alone?"

Erik nodded. The gypsy looked thoughtfully at the candle and at the rugs on the walls, and the floor, and at the carved face of Kirsti which seemd to be smiling in the candlelight.

"It is not good to live alone," he said.

"I have wanted nothing," Erik said, "except to be left alone."

"To want nothing is to be dead." The gypsy smiled. "You are not alone now."

"I shall not be alone till the spring."

It was true. They had made their bargain. Perhaps tomorrow he would regret it. But he could not regret the feeling of fatherhood, the tenderness, and when the spring was over he could return to his solitude unsought, and seeking none. The deeper roots of his being had perished with Kirsti and his sons and Akseli.

The gypsy took the lighted candle away, shielding the guttering flame with his hand and singing his strange song. It was not long before he had flung himself on his bed and the sound of his deep, even breathing seemed to fill the house.

There was work to be done, in spite of the snow, and the gypsy seemed eager to spend his exuberant vitality. He had slept and eaten well and as soon as breakfast was over Erik led him to the shed where his farm implements were stored waiting for days such as this for the oiling and greasing and repair work which had accumulated during the summer. There were axes to be sharpened, the plow mended, newly turned wheels waiting to be fixed to the cart. There would be outdoor work also. There was compost to be spread. Together they would thin out the spruce and pine near the house. For the first time in years Erik would wield an ax in company and adapt his rhythmic strokes to those of another.

The gypsy surveyed the farm in the crystalline morning light. His keen eye was trained to the gap in the fence, to the overgrown ditch which would conceal him and his booty. But here all was in order, as far as he could see, under its thin blanket of snow.

"Who is to have all this," he asked, "when you are gone? None of your tribe are left."

"I have some cousins in the north, children of my mother's brother. But I haven't seen them for many years."

"Yet when a man dies the tribe gathers from the north and the south." The gypsy shrugged and smiled disarmingly. "You would do well to remember that I am your son."

"A son takes his father's name, settles down. You will do neither."

"You do not trust me," the gypsy said, his darting glance going from left to right.

"Men trust one another," Erik said, "as far as they can. Today I am going into the forest. If you wish to leave, take your horse and leave. If you wish to stay, stay. Eat your fill and work, or don't work. You have said that a man has only one life and he must live it as he chooses."

"In giving me so much choice, you have taken choice from me," the gypsy said sullenly.

Erik made no reply. He went to the byre and brought out the horse and harnessed it to the sled to bring back the logs he had sawed previously. The gypsy watched him, his manner indecisive. If he is going to go he will go now, Erik thought, but if he is here when I return then he will stay. The bells on the sled jingled as he set off, leaving the gypsy standing, etched sharply against the light. The faint sound of the bells and of the runners sliding over the snow died away on the still air.

Erik drew in deep breaths of the frosty air. Already he needed solitude as though the weight of another personality were beginning to press too close. Yet, at the same time, he was conscious of frail tendrils reaching out to unite him with the gypsy, tendrils frail as gossamer which yet had taken root. He was conscious for the first time, after years of inner silence and rigid calm, of tensions stirring beneath the surface. Movement and growth were painful. He let the memory of the gypsy subside and gave himself up to the forest.

It seemed to him that he had absorbed forever its silence, its intensity. The unchanging nature of its landscape outran time into eternity. He had known the forest in winter and in summer since he had been conscious of life, of himself. He had wandered among the trees, climbed them, slept beneath them, played in their great aisles, white and cloistered or green and arabesqued with golden light. When he had come to manhood he had pitted his strength against theirs, bringing them down in their strength and beauty. Yet even in this there had been a sense of rightness, of completion. He knew that he was more at one in the forest than anywhere in the world that he might come to rest.

The horse trotted easily over the fine, powdery snow, snuffing the air with enjoyment. The icy breeze whipped against Erik's face, found its way through his clothing to seek out the hardness of his body which felt clean, lithe, and resilient after the *sauna*. His keen eyes marked the condition of the trees, the weight of snow in the sky, sensed the leaden gray which would descend before the day was over.

In a little clearing among the trees he found the huge logs already half embedded in snow. The horse worked patiently, an old, worn sheepskin thrown over his back, while the logs were hauled and levered onto the sled. Erik rejoiced in the hard physical effort it entailed. The sale of timber from time to time had brought him money for grain and the necessities of food and clothing which he could not grow or make.

Now, however, he required wood to replenish and maintain his winter store. Together he and the gypsy would split the logs. He would set aside pieces for his carving. Often his eye discerned the form already there in the undisciplined wood. He carved for his own pleasure. His touch had grown more and more skillful with the years. There was more than good craftsmanship, however, in his carvings. His human figures had a memorable quality of grace and vitality, and in moments of inspiration, as in the head of Kirsti, the wood had seemed to yield, to become pliable, so that the inner essence of the subject had emerged, the quality of personality caught and held. Only two people knew his work. One was the gypsy.

The other was Jussi Erfelt, who kept the village store in Porvesi and who had driven out in his sleigh one winter day when Erik had failed to make his regular visit either to the market or to his shop. Curiosity as much as neighborly consideration had prompted Jussi's visit to Vainen. He had found Erik suffering from a toothache so violent that he had attempted, without success, to draw the tooth himself. Jussi had completed the task with more zeal than skill, an operation which Erik had endured stoically. Afterwards he had made coffee for his guest. Jussi was slender, with bright eyes and dark hair, his expression lively and his speech quick.

"You are hiding your light under a bushel," he had said when he had seen the head of Kirsti. "Don't you want something out of life, Erik? Money? Or fame, perhaps?"

Erik had given a slow smile at the word fame.

"A man who sculpts and carves like this could become famous," Jussi had said stoutly.

"And I have enough money," Erik had said.

They had drunk four cups of coffee while Jussi had argued and Erik had listened.

"But there it is," Jussi had finished, "men have a right to live as they please."

"I will make a head of you in return for pulling my tooth," Erik had promised, and at Jussi's look of quickened interest he had added, "There'll be no need for you to come here, Jussi. I'll carve you from memory. I'll bring the carving to you one day."

He had been as good as his word. But since then no man from Porvesi had set foot in Vainen.

As he worked Erik thought of the gypsy. Was he still busy in the work shed? Or had his restlessness overcome him and made him depart? The house was open to him. Anything he wished to steal was there for the taking, but not, Erik thought with sudden fear, the head of Kirsti. Erik found that he was clenching his hands instinctively at the thought. For a long time now conflicting emotions, or indeed strong emotions of any sort, had been foreign to him. They weakened him now as the hard physical labor could not have done. He sat down suddenly on a log and listened to the silence of the forest. He struggled against the desire to leave the rest of the logs and return home. He glanced at the horse and sled. The little animal, half drowsing, seemed telepathically aware of his glance. He opened his eyes and tossed his head, and the bells on his high yoke trembled and rang.

Erik rose to his feet. He must get back to the enclosed world that was his home. Now he knew that he was torn between his longing for the gypsy to be gone and his longing to find him there. Painful emotions gripped his heart. The boy would be there. He, Erik, would feed him for many days yet, teach him to read and write a little, learn from him the strange rune that he sang, teach him others. Here was a human being, wild, untutored in any law save the law of the forest, of the herd, and of self-preservation. The youth was his charge. Now, clearly, Erik saw that this was the knowledge which had stirred painfully beneath the surface of his mind. This was the knowledge that, in the heart of the forest, he had tried to lose in silence. He was committed to another human being. The painful processes of love had begun. Already he had surrendered something of himself. He had known it last night when the gypsy had taken from his hands the lighted candle.

From now on, through the long weeks ahead, from a winter scarcely begun, until the spring, another being would make inroads into his life. He would create links which could not be broken. For a moment Erik felt as though a hand had plunged into his body and twisted his entrails.

The horse whinnied. The load, he seemed to say, is already enough. It was time to return.

Half willingly, half reluctantly, Erik found himself releasing the horse from the sled. The impulse had come to him to put a little time between the old life and the new.

It was long since he had visited the ruined church. He would go there now, before the heavy snows of winter, and listen to the silence and possess his own soul.

His hermitlike existence was over. It might never be resumed again. Some deeply rooted instinct warned him that he had reached a crisis in his life.

Erik mounted the horse, the sheepskin his saddle. He turned the horse's head in the direction in which he wanted to go and the sure little hoofs sought out the invisible path. The loaded sled was left behind them, to be picked up on their return.

Free of the sled the horse walked briskly. If the gypsy had come this way the previous day all tracks had been obliterated. But the horse sniffed and snorted and whinnied occasionally as though it sensed the proximity of one of its own kind. Nothing stirred in the forest. The powdery snow fanned into mist around the horse's fetlocks. Erik sat, his gaze withdrawn, his body yielding to the motion of the horse.

The eternal whiteness had a hypnotic quality. When the horse's hoofs hit a stone it was as though a fine goblet had been struck, or as though the air itself were the goblet, ringing into silence on a crystalline note, high and clear. With heightened sensitivity a distant bird caught the sound and repeated it. But there was no bird in sight, no sound of wings. There was only the whiteness, the pure cold, the silence.

As the horse walked or trotted, according to the ease of the rutted path, here visible, there already obliterated, Erik's thoughts went back to his childhood. He thought of his father, a God-fearing man with a quiet voice. In the long hours of the dark winter they had all slept a great deal, saving their energies for the swift, delirious hours of summer. In the winter his father would read aloud, often from the Bible. Now, like a refrain, Erik heard that quiet voice intoning the seven corporal Works of Mercy: *to feed the hungry . . . to give drink to the thirsty . . . to harbor the harborless. . . .* Out of the past his father was speaking to him. It was long since

Erik had been to the little wooden church in Porvesi, long since he had followed the simple service with its own austere beauty. His vague, earliest memories had been of another faith in which color and sound, chant and ritual magnificence, had mingled, felt but not understood, with his father's voice. Since Kirsti's death he had not read aloud from her Finnish Bible as had been his habit in the evenings before they went to bed. Kirsti had begun to make the linen cloth in which the Bible had been wrapped, into a little gown for the child which had been stillborn. Now the unfinished gown lay in a cupboard amongst the linen, like a little shroud.

Lost in his reverie Erik was scarcely aware of the patient plodding of the horse as they continued deeper into the forest. Now, however, it began to prick up its ears and increase its pace as though sensing that the object of the journey had been reached.

Through the snow-laden trees Erik saw the white bulk of the ruined church held fast in the forest's grip like an ice-bound ship. He shivered a little at the thought as though indeed in that icy fastness the souls of men were imprisoned. But as soon as he had dismounted and secured the horse, which would not in any case have strayed, Erik felt the old sense of tranquillity and peace which the vicinity of the church always gave him. His feet found the ancient path which wound through the trunks of trees that had sprung into being since the church had been built. Erik himself had cleared the deep-rooted, matted undergrowth to clear the path. Perhaps the original path had been somewhere else, but this was his path, he had made it, and he alone kept the forest at bay.

His feet crunched the snow as he walked toward the great opening where once a door had been, its wood long since fallen away and rotted, to nourish the trees which now towered above it. The heavy nails were buried so deeply in the ground that only pick and shovel or plowshare would reveal them.

Erik paused in the doorless opening. The sky above was

pure and glacial with unfallen snow. There was a faint twittering inside the church and nothing to be seen from where
he stood but a white nave and white columns and a broken,
heavy-raftered roof, to which the snow clung.

Above the faint rustlings and twitterings there was another
sound, which stopped his breath as the grip of icy cold might
stop it. For a moment Erik stood without movement while all
fears that were dark and secret in the recesses of his soul
rose to the surface like a flight of bats.

The sound was a woman sobbing, a thin, faint, unearthly
sound such as a disembodied being might make. The sound
was muffled by the snow, by this cloistered silence which itself
seemed to possess a voice. It was no mortal woman who sobbed
here, Erik thought, while the hair on his neck seemed to rise
and his skin to shiver. They were not false, the old tales of
magic, of enchantresses, of the spirits of lake and forest. In
this white silence, when man must keep to hearth and home,
the elemental spirits claimed their own habitation. But their
habitation was not this church, sanctified! Yet were they not
spirits older than this sanctity?

The sobbing died away. Erik entered the nave, his footfall
soundless. From the distant altar there was a faint stir. A
large bird rose, wide-winged, and soared between the broken
rafters and was lost in the glacial sky. There was silence. Erik
glanced at the confessional, covered with snow. It was from
this that the sound of sobbing had come.

Now he knew that whatever might await him there he must
not draw back. Without sound, with the spare, light footfall
of the hunter, Erik walked to the confessional and entered it.
The strong wood had defied the years, its sheltered position
had protected it from the elements. In front of him the small,
rough bench on which the priest had sat was still intact. In
the confined space Erik felt the bulk and strength of his body.
This space had served for smaller men.

Instinctively he crossed himself as he had seen his father
cross himself, an action foreign to him, and sat upon the

bench and waited, his senses alert. In front of him the iron grille which had separated priest and penitent was clogged with the dust of centuries. An iron crucifix was still attached to the grille. Before it Erik bowed his head. Through the jagged holes in what remained of the bars of the grille, through which neither penitent nor priest would see each other, Erik strained with keen eyes. He discerned the form of a woman kneeling before the grille.

He drew back. The spirit had taken human form. It was silent, matching its presence, its power, against his.

A wave of superstitious fear flooded Erik, and then as suddenly receded and common sense took its place. This *was* a woman, a woman needing, perhaps, succor. He half rose and then was arrested in movement as the woman began to speak.

"Where can I go? What can I do?"

She spoke in Finnish. Her voice was soft, low, distraught. Erik waited. His lips moved to speak, but no words came. He groped at the back of his mind for the words which he knew were there, words which lay like dark stones in the heart of a pool. But he could not find them.

"It is true that I answered his glance. He looked at me and smiled. And at his smile something rose in me . . . I suppose there was sin in my heart. I shouldn't have smiled back."

She began to sob again, exhaustedly, sobs welling from deep within her. Erik remained silent, held in the grip of an emotion that was a mingling of pity, and the desire to help one who sought solace in an empty church, and something else that he could not yet define: a stirring in his mind, a premonition, the instinct that warns of hidden danger.

"Oh God . . . I am lost. Tell me what to do. Have pity on me."

The words came.

"God is your protector."

He could feel her tense into watchfulness, into stillness, as though she were listening to these words which must come from her own soul, or from the church, or from God himself.

Half fearfully she whispered, *"Tell me what to do."*

Erik buried his face in his hands.

This was a mortal creature. Her dilemma was mortal. Here, in this ruined church, she had put her trust in him. She had put her trust in a voice which spoke out of the silence. She had no fear. Who was it whose innocence could believe that the silence could answer her? Who was it who knew that God fashioned counsel and consolation out of the empty air?

"You must recite a decade of the rosary."

The pool of his mind had stirred. Now the words rose, an echo of the distant past.

There was a cry of anguish from the other side of the grille.

"But I am not . . . I haven't a rosary. And if I had how could it help me?"

"God is good, my child."

He was himself, yet not himself. Eternity seemed to have entered the cold, small room. Now he was a youth again and had never known sorrow and his sins had been the little sins of those who had yet to learn sin. He heard a voice out of the past, a tongue which informed his tongue.

He began to whisper, *"Indulgentiam, absolutionem et remissionem peccatorem . . ."*

He discerned a faint movement behind the grille as though —could it be so?—the penitent were making the sign of the cross.

Slowly, heavily, as though he were returning from a great distance, he said in Finnish,

"God bless you. Go in peace."

He waited. If, after all, this had been the work of an evil spirit, the woman would vanish into thin air. In the icy cold of the confessional he felt drops of sweat on his forehead. He gazed steadily at the jagged, dark spaces in the debris of the grille. He saw the woman rise slowly, her face averted, his vision of her body blurred by the leaves and cobwebs which hung across the grille. But this was no spirit. It was a woman who rose painfully to her feet and left the ruined box.

3

SHE STOOD, seeming tall and slender, in the nave, swaying a little, and then groped toward a snow-covered pillar and leaned against it. He came toward her softly, fearful of alarming her.

"Who are you?" She gazed at him incredulously, whether because he was clothed as other men or whether because he was there at all Erik could not say. She was young, not more, he judged, than eighteen years. Her neck was white above her sheepskin coat, her body young and supple. But her face was ravaged, with deep discoloration beneath the eyes and with a look of extreme exhaustion.

"I am not a priest—if that is what you think."

"But you were there . . . you were there . . ." She gazed back fearfully toward the confessional. "You were there, in the church."

"This isn't a church any longer."

"It is a church," she said. Her eyes were blue and as widely spaced as Kirsti's had been. For a moment, when she had looked full at him, he had seen Kirsti. His throat constricted at the thought of Kirsti in the place of this battered child.

"Who are you?" he asked. "What is your name? What are you doing here in this ruined church?"

She looked at him a moment longer and then her body shook with sobs. "You gave me absolution," she said bitterly, "as if that would help." And she repeated the words accusingly. "You gave me absolution. I know that is what they call it."

"I think God moved me to do it. At first I thought you were an evil spirit who had found sanctuary in this church."

"Are there such things? Evil spirits? Now?"

"People said there were—in olden times. And perhaps still."

"I have heard of them. But surely . . . things are different now?"

They were speaking, words were passing between them, but they meant nothing. The gulf between them yawned deep. Erik had a feeling of unreality as the girl gazed back at him with those wide blue eyes above the soft discolored pads of their sockets.

"What has happened to you? Tell me, child. You can't be alone here in this ruined church forever. Where do you come from? Where are you going? Who has injured you?"

The insistent questions were slowly bridging the gulf. The girl gazed up at Erik, who seemed to tower above her, and after a while the look of fear and resentment vanished. Erik waited.

When she did not speak he said gently, "You are hungry. And thirsty."

"Yes. I have been here all night. I hid in that box—the confessional, I suppose it is—where it was dry. But it was very cold and I could not sleep."

She pulled her coat and the thick woolen scarf beneath it more closely around her.

"How old are you?"

"I am seventeen. Nearly eighteen."

"Where do you come from?"

"Porvesi," she said reluctantly.

"Who are your parents?"

"I have none. I come from Turku. Jussi Erfelt, who has

the store, was my mother's cousin. I came from Turku two months ago, when my mother died, to live with Jussi and his wife Maia. To help in the house and have a home."

"Turku is a long way off."

"Yes."

"I have a horse outside. I will take you home with me. You shall ride on the sled, which is not far away. When we reach home I will rest the horse and then take you back to Porvesi."

"No!" the girl cried. "No! I will never go back to Porvesi." She began to run from him and then stopped and moaned, clutching her body and her thighs as though the seat of her pain was there.

"I have food outside. And something to drink. Wait," Erik said.

The horse was standing patiently outside but turned a reproachful glance on Erik as he removed the saddlebag and carried it into the church. In it was a hunk of cheese with some rye bread. There was also a small flask of schnapps. It was Erik's habit to take a little food and drink with him to the forest. Sometimes, on a day like this, he would be away for hours, returning only in time to feed the animals and perform necessary tasks before nightfall.

The girl fell on the food hungrily and drank a little of the schnapps, which burned her throat and brought the color into her cheeks. Erik waited silently while she ate. His silence seemed to give her confidence.

"Why did you give me absolution when you are not a priest?" she asked.

"I have told you. God moved me to do it."

"Then I am absolved from my sin? And . . . it will be all right?"

He said gravely, considering his words, "You are absolved from your sin."

"But can those words undo what has happened?" she asked.

Beneath the heavy homespun skirt which showed beneath

her coat she wore thick white woolen stockings. Erik saw that
one of the white stockings was stained with blood.

"You have hurt your leg," he said.

"No," she whispered, her face turned from him. "The man
forced me."

"Tell me," Erik said, "so that I can help you." His voice
was so quiet that the girl could not guess at the violent rage
which had stabbed him suddenly. The violence of the emotion
ravaged him. It had been as rending as a physical pain. Yet
he looked gravely at the girl, who seemed to him no more
than a child, and spoke softly.

"The man came to the paddock at the back of the house,"
she said. "Yussi bought the paddock from the farmer Vasola,
but everybody knows when Jussi bought the paddock. He had
wanted it for a long time. You know all this too, I suppose."

"I am a stranger in Porvesi."

"The man came to the paddock. I was there with Yussi's dog.
He wanted water for his horse and food for himself. It was
natural. He had come a long way."

"The horse had a star on its forehead," Erik said.

She looked at him, startled. "You *are* a priest . . . or a wise
man. There is a woman in Turku who tells your future from
your hand."

"No. I am not wise or a priest. Eat your fill and tell me
what you have to tell."

"I gave the horse water, but I did not give the man food.
Suddenly he did not seem to want it. He smiled at me."

She paused.

"And you answered his smile with yours."

"Yes. He smiled in a way I had never seen a man smile. It
was like . . ." She closed her eyes. "I cannot tell you what it
was like. He shouted fiercely at the dog and it ran away. But
I—I stayed."

"Why did you stay?"

"For no reason. And every reason. Soon he would mount
his horse and ride away, but I wanted to remember his smile.

He was handsome and dark. Yussi is dark but he is old. This man's darkness was a different darkness and he was young."

The girl broke off a little piece of rye bread and crumbled it between her fingers thoughtfully. "I offered him food but he refused," she said. "He asked me the way to Vituri. That is many miles away, through the forest. He asked me to walk a little way beside him, to set him on his way. This I agreed to do."

"That was foolish."

"There was nothing bad in his face or his voice. I said I could go no further than the beginning of the forest, where the village ends. It was sufficient, he said."

"You have said enough," Erik cried. His voice was anguished. It was the gypsy. He remembered suddenly his own words. *"Have you stolen? Murdered?"*

"Neither," the gypsy had replied; and he had smiled voluptuously.

Erik saw the young body in the gypsy's cruel embrace, the young body which might have been Kirsti's body, the wide eyes which might have been hers. It was to this man that he had surrendered something of himself, this man who had kindled in him, as life returns to a frozen limb, the painful processes of love. It was to this man that he was committed.

"You have said enough," Erik cried again.

"No," the girl said, "I must finish because it is true and you will see that it is true, that my sin was only the sin of returning his glance. I could have gone away and let him go but he was a stranger and he had asked my help. He would not stay for food, not even for a hunk of bread, though it was midday, because he said he must reach Vituri before night. So he mounted his horse and set off and I walked beside them."

"Did nobody see you go?"

"There was nobody in the paddock or on the road." Now the girl's face hardened. It was just and right, Erik thought, to let her finish.

"When we came to the edge of the forest I pointed to the

path he must take. The snow had begun to fall again but
only lightly and if there was no path he could find his direction from the sun. While I told him all this he laughed at me.
I was about to return when he put his arm quickly across my
body and pinioned me and swung me to the saddle over the
horse and galloped into the forest. The horse went like the
wind. I tore at the man's hand but it was like trying to move
a tree. I have never known strength like his. Though I fought
and struggled and screamed I had no more power against him
than a child. In his grasp I might have been no more than a
feather."

The girl fastened the straps of the saddlebag neatly, as
though she were used to housewifely tasks and liked to see
them done well. She said in a toneless voice, "He leapt from
the horse and swung me with him, down on the ground in
the snow. I remember the horse shivering and neighing but
the gypsy called out to him once and he was quiet. There,
among the wet cold branches and the snow he did as he liked
with me. Not once, but more than once, and there was not an
inch of my body that did not feel bruised or any of my flesh
that did not seem torn. Now I will never trust a man again,"
she said, and her voice was as hard as her face.

"You trusted me in the confessional," Erik said.

"That is true. But this is a church and suddenly it seemed
natural . . . to ask for help. The voice of a man here could
only have been the voice of a priest. I am a fool. I thought
that there would be a priest even in a ruined church."

"There was a priest. It was God who ordained me for those
few moments. How did you find the church?"

"I just came upon it. I had walked many miles. I didn't
know where I was going. I only knew that I could never go
back to Porvesi. *Voi! Voi!*" she cried suddenly, like a child
unable to express its sorrow, and clung to his arm.

Erik put his hand over hers as he had put it over the
gypsy's.

"What is your name?" he asked.

"Annikki Berling. What is yours?"

"I am Erik Vainen and my home is Vainen."

"I have heard of you," she said and studied his face closely. "People say you are a strange man. But they respect you. Jussi respects you. I have seen the head you carved of him."

"I will take you to Jussi and tell him what has happened to you. He and Maia will understand and forgive—if forgiveness is needed."

"No!" She shuddered. "No! No! I can never go back to Porvesi. I'm not the same and never can be and no man there will marry me. And what is there for me, if not marriage?"

"Then I will marry you," Erik said calmly.

"You? *You* will marry me?" She stared at him, bewildered, yet catching at this straw of hope.

"If there is no one else?" he said compassionately.

"Who else could there be?" the girl cried. "In Porvesi there are less than a hundred people, all told. Turku is big but I can't go back there. And if I did, and found work, the day would come, perhaps, when a man would want to marry me . . . and he would have to know . . . and no man wants . . ." She began to sob and shudder. "This is something that can never be undone! It was so little for him and so much for me."

"Then there are two men who could marry you," Erik said gravely. "I am one. The gypsy is the other. It was a gypsy who waylaid you."

The girl clenched her hands. "He will never be found! And even if he were found I would kill myself first."

"Then, if it is necessary, you can marry me and be protected by me. But first I must tell you this. The gypsy is at Vainen. He had fled from his tribe and came to my house and asked for my protection and I gave it to him. I pledged my word that he should have it till the spring."

The girl's face blanched. "Then I cannot go to your house."

"Then you must return to Porvesi. There Jussi and Maia

will surely protect you. But if you will not go to Porvesi you must come with me to Vainen, where I will give you my protection and we will think of some explanation for it. That is the choice."

"I have no choice," the girl said.

"I will treat you with kindness. You will need kindness, and a home, and warmth and protection . . . if your time should come on you."

The girl looked up at him. Her eyes darkened. Her eyelashes were long and honey-brown and curling a little. She closed her eyes suddenly. "I have thought of that all night long."

"It is something we must think of."

"We?" She opened her eyes again. "I work," she said, "for Jussi and Maia and they give me a home. Why can't I work for you at Vainen? It would be a good place to hide . . . until . . . at least until I *know*."

"It would not be seemly. There is no other woman there. If you come to Vainen I must marry you."

"I never thought to marry without love. I have thought of marriage—all girls think of it—but I did not expect it would be like this."

"Life is never as we expect it. If it were I would not be alone now. Do you wish to trust yourself to me? I am like other men. I have had wife and children."

"But they say in Porvesi that you have chosen to be alone."

"Now the choice has been taken from me also." As Erik spoke he knew that with every word he was forging his destiny. He accepted it with fatalism.

They were silent a moment while the cold air that filled the church blew softly about them, and the girl shivered. In the silence the bird which had flown from the altar entered silently and skimmed the nave and alighted on the altar with a faint rustle of folding wings. It was a gull which had flown across the lake and the forest and found this place good. The girl opened her clenched hand. It held the crumbs of rye bread. Carefully and slowly she walked toward the altar and

put the crumbs there. The gull watched her, its eye unflinching, and then came cautiously to the crumbs and pecked at
them swiftly.

"It is almost tame," she whispered.

"It hasn't learned to fear men. It lives in lonely places,"
Erik said.

"Like Vainen," the girl said thoughtfully. She came back
to Erik and put her hand on his arm.

"I am the gull that will take your bread," she said softly.

"So you haven't learned to fear men," Erik said. He picked
up the saddlebag. "Tonight you will sleep in my wife's bed.
You need rest. You will sit on the horse now and I will walk.
I will make a place on the sled for you for the rest of the
journey."

"Jussi and Maia!" the girl cried. "I have been away a night
and a day. They will be searching everywhere for me. The
whole village will be searching and gossiping."

"I have thought of that," Erik said. "I will send the gypsy
to tell them."

"Not the gypsy! Not the gypsy!" she cried in horror.

"Yes. The gypsy. He will go because it will be his safeguard.
When you return with me he will know that his crime is discovered. I will put the words in his mouth which will save
him and ease Jussi and Maia."

"Why should you save him!" she gasped.

"Unless his guilt is covered Jussi and Maia will know everything. And so will Porvesi."

"You are good," she whispered. "What will you tell the
gypsy to say?"

"He will tell them that he was passing Vainen and saw you
here with me. A gypsy hears everything that happens in any
place he passes through. His ears and eyes are sharp. Jussi
will reward him. An old cockerel perhaps, for his pot, or a
little money."

The girl trembled. "They will think I am shameless . . . at
Vainen, with you."

"We must run with the wind," Erik said, "if you are to find the right path. I will think of a story."

"Will the gypsy come back?" she asked fearfully.

"If he returns both of you will eat my bread until the spring. Then he will be gone. That is the way it must be."

When they reached the house the sound of hammering could be heard coming from the work shed. The girl on the sled trembled again.

"I am not afraid," she said, "but I couldn't look at him."

"There is no help for it, child. Your choice was a cruel one but it is made and done with." As the girl buried her face in her hands Erik added gently, "And each step afterward will be a little easier. In time you will look at him and not see him. I have promised him sanctuary till the spring. I must keep my promise. I am pledged."

"You are a just man. What name can I call you?"

"You can call me Vainen."

"You know my name. It is Annikki."

"Stay here on the sled." Erik flung the reins over the fence and walked toward the work shed. The gypsy heard him approach and came to the door of the shed as Erik reached it.

"You have been gone a long time," he said resentfully. "Look." He pointed proudly to his handiwork. Farm implements shone, the wheels were fixed to the cart, and out of a pile of odd pieces of wood the gypsy had whittled a store of clothes pegs and strange mannikins. His expression had the absorption of a child, the cupidity of a miser. "These are for you to sell," he said, "when you go to Porvesi. Each week I will make something that women and children like. Then when I leave you in the spring I shall take money with me. I shall not take your money. I do not rob because I am a gypsy."

"You have taken my wood," said Erik evenly.

"You are a hard man. When the gypsies pass, it is people like you they run from."

"You have not run from me."

"The bed was warm and the supper filled my belly."

"Now I have other work for you to do," Erik said. Once he had looked at this youth with tenderness. Now that hard, supple body told another tale. That whipcord strength had held and pinioned the helpless. "Come." Erik motioned him outside curtly.

The afternoon sun was red-gold in the sky. It touched the house and outbuildings, the trees, the snow, the sled on which the girl sat huddled in her sheepskin coat. Erik put a hand like a vise on the gypsy's shoulder. He felt it strain and harden beneath his hand but the grip held.

"You have seen this girl before. This is the girl you ravished in the forest."

The gypsy's eyes were wide, dilated. "What are you going to do? Do they hang a gypsy for that in this part of the world?"

"It has been known. There is no lack of trees to hang a man from."

"The girl offered herself to me. She ran after me and caught my bridle and begged me to take her with me." He smiled. "Women are all alike when they see a man like me."

Erik struck him hard across the mouth and the gypsy tensed into stillness.

"What do you want me to do?" he asked wearily.

"You will take your horse and ride to Porvesi to the house where you found the girl."

"She was in the paddock," the the gypsy muttered, "waiting for me."

While he spoke the girl's eyes had not left his face. Her gaze was steady. "That is a lie, gypsy," she said slowly. "You came to the paddock for food."

"You will go to the house," Erik continued, as though she had not spoken, "and find Jussi Erfelt, the master of the house. Tell him and his wife that you were passing through Vainen and that I stopped you to give you a message."

The gypsy's bold eyes flickered. He said cunningly, "What is the message?"

"That the girl is here."

"How did she come here?"

"She came, that is all. The girl is at Vainen and no harm has befallen her and she will return to Porvesi tomorrow."

"No harm has befallen her, you say?"

"I said that is the message. Go at once and put their minds at rest. Soon, if there are search parties, they will find their way here. Look at the girl. Will Jussi Erfelt say that no harm has befallen her? If they find her here you will be hunted by two tribes—yours and mine." Erik removed his iron grip from the man's shoulder. "Get your horse and go. And come back so that I know you have given the message."

"Why don't you take the girl back and tell them yourself that no harm has come to her? There is nothing to stop me from going off now and leaving you."

"To your tribe you are a marked man. Vainen is the one place you might hide without being discovered. That is why you will give the message and why you will return."

"Why are you helping me?" he asked suspiciously.

"It is not you I am helping but the girl."

The gypsy shrugged. "Very well, I will give the message. And I will come back and tell you that I have given it. But tomorrow, when my horse is rested, I shall go. There are worse things than having your nose slit. One of them is staying in one place all winter."

"You are free to choose."

The gypsy gave Erik a sly glance. "So you mean to send her back tomorrow?"

"That is what I said." He turned and went back to the sled. The girl gazed straight ahead as the gypsy untied his horse and leapt onto its back and disappeared into the forest. The dog came rushing out and barked angrily.

"Now," Erik said, "go into the house and rest. The stones are still hot in the *sauna*. I will stoke the fire so that you can

cleanse yourself and you will sleep well afterward. First I
will show you my wife's room. Her name was Kirsti and she
is dead."

The girl walked with him into the house. The door of the
bedroom was closed and Erik paused outside it. "This is where
I slept when my wife was alive but now I sleep in the little
room at the other end of the house which belonged to my son.
You will sleep here alone." He lifted the latch and pushed
open the door. There was a clean smell of wood, still faintly
resinous, as the door opened. Along one wall of the room
stood a large wooden four-poster bed covered with a woven
rug in black and scarlet, and a black and scarlet rug made a
gay oblong of color on the pale wooden boards of the floor.
Dominating the room was a porcelain stove which reached
almost to the ceiling, its tiles depicting bright, clear, country
scenes.

"In winter this stove warms the whole house," Erik said.
"There is no better stove in Porvesi or Vituri. I laid the tiles
myself. It is like one I remember in the north. There was
little comfort here when we first came but as soon as it was
possible Kirsti had the stove I promised her."

"This room hasn't been used for a long time," the girl
said. "There is no dust, and it is fresh and sweet. But I can
tell that it hasn't been used."

"It has been waiting, perhaps," Erik said wearily. He felt
drained suddenly, and exhausted. Even the mere effort of
talking seemed too great. For so long he had been accustomed
to saying little, speech had been reduced to the least necessity. The future rose before him in this girl's face, pale,
diminished, yet alive, now, with interest. She had given herself trustingly into his hands. There was nothing to fear here
save the burden, the immense charge. Yet, in the ruined
church, he had felt the stirring in the mind, the premonition,
the instinct that warns of hidden danger.

"Why," she asked him suddenly, "did you tell the gypsy to
say that I would go back tomorrow?"

"Because tomorrow we must go to Porvesi together. When tomorrow comes you may feel differently about staying here."

"You don't truly understand. I *cannot* go back to Porvesi. If you were a woman you would know. Also, I am afraid. Each day I will wonder . . . and fear . . . and Maia's eyes are very sharp." She looked around the quiet, gay room. "Keep me here," she said. "Keep me here. You are good. And I will do . . . whatever you wish."

"I shall ask nothing of you."

"What shall we say to Jussi and Maia?"

Erik looked at the last rays of the sun glinting on the porcelain tiles and closed his mind against a thousand memories. "I will say that I have been courting you secretly. I will tell them that you are young and foolish, little more than a child, and that you ran heedlessly to me here. I will tell them that I want to marry you."

"We must marry, quickly," she said practically. She says it, Erik thought, like a child arranging a doll's house. "We must marry quickly, then I shall be safe. And I will keep house for you, and cook. Both of us are alone in the world."

"I will get the *sauna* ready. Make some coffee if you are not too tired. You will find clothes in the cupboard that will fit you. I think you are about the same height as Kirsti."

He went to the doorway and then turned and looked at her a moment. Her glance was trusting, the drawn contours of her face already relaxing. How easy it is, Erik thought, to forge a destiny. How simple are the gestures by which men and women embrace their fate.

"You haven't once spoken my name," she said. "It is Annikki."

"I will remember," Erik said.

While Erik stoked the *sauna* and fed and watered the horse Annikki stripped off her clothes. She huddled herself into her coat and ran across to the *sauna,* which was visible, standing among the silver birches, from the window of Kirsti's room.

Once in the *sauna,* enclosed in its warmth, she began to feel the coldness of her body thaw, and her mind with it. The long hours of loneliness, of darkness, which lay behind her, came to life. During the long night in the ruined church she had forced her mind back to that moment in the paddock when the man had smiled at her and had tried to believe that the events which had followed had been a hideous dream from which she would awaken. When the voice had spoken in the ruined church, the dream had taken on another quality. The answering voice which had absolved her had given to the disorder of her mind and body the quality of inevitability. Instinctively, almost without volition, she had accepted the inevitable. The voice embodied relief, succor, the transference of responsibility, the promise of escape. Whatever power it was in the ruined church which had absolved her from her grief would somehow ease the burden. The voice had been calm, strong, authoritative, the voice of a priest. She was no longer alone.

But it had not been a priest who had confronted her, but a man like other men, and her confidence had ebbed away to be replaced by confusion and fear. But confidence had returned. She had heard of Erik Vainen. All Porvesi had heard of him. Many things had been said of him but none of them had been bad. In its own way Porvesi was proud of him as a man who had of his own free will chosen his own lonely path, had chosen to come to terms with destiny in his own way, asking nothing of any man. With a trust that was half that of a child, half that of a woman, she had accepted him. "I am the gull," she had said, "who will eat your bread."

Just as she had accepted the protection of Jussi and Maia since it had been inevitable, so, now, she accepted Vainen's. After the long cold hours of desperation, during which her frantic thoughts had subsided finally into numbed shock, into

a cessation of thought and action, the necessity for thought
and action had been removed. Vainen would think and act
for her. It was for this that she had been guided to the ruined
church. With the same fatality with which Erik had accepted
his destiny Annikki now accepted hers.

When she had dressed again in Kirsti's clothes Annikki went
to the living room to make the coffee. With the resilience of
youth nothing now seemed as terrible to her as she had feared.
The quiet strength, the calm, the authority of the man whose
protection was now hers were a barrier between her and the
past. Even the dread fear that she might bear a child began
to lose some of its power. Safe here in this homestead there
would be none to know who had fathered it. That secret
would be hers and Vainen's alone. She was still young enough
to believe that in life everything remedied itself, still un-
prepared to accept the final responsibility for herself which
comes with maturity. She had not yet learned that every human being stands alone.

As the aroma of coffee filled the room, with all its pleasant
associations of warmth and comfort, Annikki found herself
humming a little song. The atmosphere of Vainen was tranquil, secure. She preferred it to the house of Jussi and Maia
even though they were her kin. Events had moved too quickly
for her to have put down roots. Suddenly she felt that it would
be a fine thing to be Vainen's wife, mistress of Vainen, a
woman in her own right. Beyond the present moment she
refused to think.

When Erik returned to the house with a hare he had shot
night had already fallen. The uncurtained windows showed
him the living room and Annikki in a pool of lamplight,
wearing Kirsti's blue woolen dress belted tightly at the waist.
The light fell on the snow beneath the house, leaving the forest beyond to its own darkness. Erik stood a moment feeling
the weight of another existence already upon his shoulders.
His very bones seemed to ache with the need for solitude.
The need was physical, like the need for water, light, air.

Something had drawn from him the words he had uttered, the promise of marriage, protection, something stronger than himself, something caught out of the dark past, and enclosed in the shell of the ruined church. A voice, not his own, had spoken, he thought; a command, unresisted, laid upon him.

He entered the room. Annikki was laying the table for supper, all her movements sure as though she had always known this house and where things were to be found in it. She had put the potatoes on to boil and found the tub of salted herring, eggs and cheese and bread. She turned as he entered the room.

"Maia taught me how to make this cheese," she said. Her voice was matter-of-fact, with a touch of housewifely pride. "I have put three places. The third," she said, "is for the gypsy."

"Perhaps he will not return tonight. He might rest his horse and sleep in the forest."

"Are you sure? Do you think that he has been to Porvesi at all?"

"He will have given the message. Not to have given it would be foolish and he is not a fool."

"The supper is ready," Annikki said, and paused. "The supper is ready . . . Vainen." She spoke his name as though its utterance must seal the bond between them.

Erik glanced round the room. "Already you seem to belong here. Are all women the same?"

"No," said Annikki, "they are not. If I seem to belong here it is because I belong nowhere. And you have been good to me."

"So have Jussi and Maia."

"With them my need was not so great."

"What was your need?" Erik asked. He took the head of the table and began to break the bread. He remembered the girl in the church walking painfully to the altar to place the crumbs for the gull. Annikki was watching the movement of his strong hands as she spoke.

"My mother died, as I told you. She had tuberculosis and she died in a hospital in Turku. . . . You needn't fear for me. I am healthy and strong." She paused for a moment watching Erik's quiet movements as he filled a plate and passed it to her. "My father died when I was a little girl. He worked in a paper mill. There was an accident. He was killed." She spoke with a certain fatality. "There is nothing to be done about such things, is there?" she asked.

There was a pattering in the passage and Penna nosed open the door and came to his seat by the hearth, where he settled himself and looked up anxiously at Erik.

"He will have to get used to the three of us," Annikki said.

"Then Jussi sent for you?" Erik prompted her.

"Yes, of course, Jussi sent for me. He was my mother's cousin and he had given her his word that he would care for me if anything happened. He and Maia have been good to me. But the house is quiet. I would have liked to work in the store but Jussi does that. Often I spent all day alone with Maia, and she taught me to milk cows and to cook, but sometimes the days seemed long." She leaned toward Erik suddenly, her wide eyes full of entreaty. "They must never know what has happened. Jussi is a good man and Maia, though I do not like her very much, is a good woman. I was foolish to go one step on the road with the gypsy . . . but Jussi would feel that he had broken his word . . . about looking after me . . . after what has happened."

"They shall not know," Erik promised her.

"Because," Annikki said, eating with the sharp appetite of youth, "it breaks a man to know that he has broken his word."

Erik looked at her without speaking, seeing the face still round with the soft curves of youth, hearing the words which fell softly, each one a link in the chain which would bind him.

4

THE GIRL WAS SLEEPING in Kirsti's room. She had washed the dishes and mended a hole in Erik's thick woolen stockings. Penna had padded softly after her till the door of Kirsti's room had closed behind her and then he had gone to his own place by the hearth. The homestead was silent. Erik sat in his rocking chair, his hands idle, looking at Kirsti's carved head in the lamplight. The girl had looked at it without curiosity.

"She was beautiful," she had said, and then her eyes had gone to the carving of little Kaarlo. Into the room then, both of them silent, the consciousness of other lives had entered. The girl had looked at Erik uncertainly as though groping for those strong cords which bound him to the past. She had taken her candle from his hand as the gypsy had done. In the soft candlelight Erik had seen faint shadows beneath her eyes, shadows which even youth and warmth and rest had failed to remove.

Now, through the door, in the silence, he could hear the faint sound of her even breathing.

The gypsy had not returned nor, Erik thought, would he. Either he had gone on his way or he had found shelter in the forest. But he had given the message, of that Erik was certain. He had not attempted to deny his attack on the girl—indeed he had admitted it—and the story he would tell to Jussi and Maia would exonerate him. Erik looked around the room as though he were seeing it for the last time. He reflected on the strange chance by which he had given sanctuary first to the gypsy and now, through him, to the girl. The strangeness of it was still mirrored in Penna's perplexed and troubled gaze.

"We have grown used to our solitude, you and I," Erik said to the dog. Penna answered him with a faint whine and then his head sank onto his paws. The dog was uneasy. There was uneasiness in the room. Erik sat alert, watchful, scarcely breathing, as though he were in the heart of the forest, sensing, but not seeing, danger.

Penna whined again. Erik got up and went softly for his boots, drawing them on with difficulty, for the leather had stiffened a little in the warmth of the room. He put on his fleece-lined leather jacket and fur cap. His ear had detected a faint sound in the darkness outside. He motioned the dog back to its place when it showed signs of joining him, and crossing the room silently, he opened the door and entered the dark passage. The girl still slept. The little room off the passage with its narrow bed—"as narrow as a grave," the gypsy had said—was empty. Erik let himself silently out of the house and walked toward the *sauna,* from which the sound had come.

The night air was piercingly cold and sweet. There was a soft, muffled murmur in the snow-laden branches. Beyond, in the star-pricked darkness, the lake glimmered, only its faint rippling surface distinguishing it from the snow-covered earth. Erik breathed deeply of the sweet, icy air which caught at his throat, his lungs. Here, in the silence, conscious of the forest beyond, he was in his own element. He felt strength flow through his limbs, charging him with vibrant energy, yet he walked as silently as a cat.

His instinctive knowledge of the gypsy told him that the

man was in the *sauna*. He had not wanted to come to the house. Fear, perhaps, or the instinct to burrow in forbidden warmth, dislike of sleeping under a roof, all these would combine to make him seek the obvious shelter of the bath-house. A soft sigh, which was unlike that of the breeze in the trees, told Erik that he was right. The gypsy's horse was somewhere near, the little sinewy animal with the white star on its forehead.

Again Erik was gripped by emotions difficult to reconcile. The gypsy had come to him first, hunted, wild, like a creature of the woods. It was the gypsy who had stirred in him the first slow awakening to life and living. It was the gypsy who had come close to the heart of the whirlpool and stirred the still waters.

The little horse sighed again. Erik thought of the girl sleeping in the house, the innocent victim of the gypsy's lust, yet hatred against the man would not rise in him. We are all victims of our own natures, he thought. This man ravishes, I embrace solitude, and who is to say which necessity was the greater. None of us must suffer, not the helpless girl, not the gypsy, not myself. We shall live, the three together, in peace and amity till the spring.

Had not the girl herself said, *"The third place is for the gypsy."*

Erik went silently to the door of the hut and pushed it open. At once the gypsy sprang to his feet with wild, startled grace.

"It's Vainen."

Erik reached for the ledge on which he knew he would find candles and matches and lighted a candle. In its light the gypsy stood facing him in his habitual attitude, as though poised for flight, his eyes glittering. On the floor beside him was his hoard: a loaf of rye bread, a hen whose feathers shone gold-brown, flecked with red, in the candlelight. Its glazed eye gazed up at them, one yellow claw held up as if in supplication.

"You have given the message, gypsy," Erik said.

The gypsy smiled.

"They were in a fine state, those two. They feared the girl was dead, that she had wandered off and was frozen in the woods. She comes from a town and is not used to country ways." The gypsy picked up the hen and swung it gracelessly by one claw. "If they had known what I know . . . if they had seen me . . . and her . . . together . . . I should have swung like this hen. I saw it in the man's eyes."

"But now all is well."

"When I spoke your name then all was well. They did not suspect me. It was a good lie," he said admiringly. "Why did you lie to cover me?"

About them the night was soft, enfolding. The frail candlelight held back the watchful forest, flickering in the room, bringing a fitful light into the darkness. Erik watched the gypsy steadily, without replying. The youth's gaze was bold, full of sly conjecture. He drew himself up to his full height and measured Erik with his gaze. Erik looked at the man's hand, held behind his back. The gypsy brought it forward, empty. He dropped the hen and it fell to the ground in a heap of huddled feathers.

"I shall sleep here tonight," he said, "in the bathhouse."

"You are welcome."

"But you—you will sleep in the house."

"That is where I belong."

"And the girl?"

"She sleeps there also. She is sheltered as you were sheltered."

"It is a fine house. And there is a good living to be made from a farm."

"You are welcome to share both. That is our pact—till the spring."

The gypsy laughed softly. The candlelight accentuated the bold, beautiful planes of his face, the grace, the wildness, the strength of his body. It is fitting, Erik thought, that such beauty should come out of the forest. The gypsy's soft laugh vibrated along his nerves; his muscles tensed, like the hunter's, or the hunted, he did not know which. Into the resinous, smoky warmth of the *sauna,* through which the candlelight filtered, another element had entered—not wind, not fire; a vibration, unheard, unseen, unclean. It had entered with the gypsy's laugh. The gypsy's soft laugh was the uncleanness.

"I gave you tonight alone," the gypsy said softly, "to enjoy the girl."

Erik's gaze did not waver.

"After that"—and the youth smiled voluptuously—"after that we will enjoy her together. You are not young but you are a strong man and lusty," the gypsy said judicially. "That is why you brought her here, isn't it? You wanted her for yourself. But you must find some excuse to keep her here, since they listen to your words in the village. Then we will enjoy her together, sharing her, according to our pact. By the spring I shall have tired of her. I am young. Women are easy for me."

Still Erik did not speak, holding the gypsy with his steady gaze.

"Tonight she is yours," the gypsy urged. He smiled and closed his eyes so that his long, dark lashes lay on his cheeks. "Her body," he said, "is very white and soft and firm. She is slender, like our women, and supple, and her breasts are round and set high and quiver in the hand." He opened his eyes. "She is ripe for the taking."

Something snapped in Erik. Control snapped like the crack of a whip.

A light of dazzling crystal, clear as the light of morning, seemed to fill and blind his brain. Like the land which had bred him, dangerous forces slept deep within the man, forces which could strike, destroy, annihilate, in one harsh paroxysm. The inner tension snapped.

In one movement Erik's hands were around the gypsy's throat. He held the man in the clamping grip of iron. The

gypsy's body undulated in anguish like a snake's, his strong,
slender fingers caught at Erik's hands, clawed them, gouged
them with prehensile thumbs, left them suddenly and clawed
the air and then, somehow, in the final extremity, found the
knife in his belt and lunged it at Erik's face. His frantic aim
failed. Erik continued to throttle, the sweat starting on his
face, his breathing heavy. The gypsy's body sank, his eyes
staring, the knife clattering to the floor.

How easy it is, Erik thought with horror, to snuff out the
life in a man. The candle flame flickered on the gypsy's dis-
torted features, on the glossy, sun-gold feathers of the hen.
In the darkness outside, the gypsy's horse gave a loud, terrified whinny which was answered from the byre.

The sounds died on the air. Erik looked down at the man
on the floor. Here, he thought, is where we cleansed ourselves
as brothers, here I put my hand on his and offered him my
home and protection. It has not gone as we thought. Now the
gypsy lies dead and the girl, unthought of then, sleeps in my
house.

What had to be done was done.

Erik stood a moment breathing deeply. His thick fair hair
was drenched with sweat beneath his fur cap. The candlelight
marked hollows beneath his deep-set blue eyes. He stood very
still for a few moments, then bent down, and turning the
gypsy over, felt in his pockets. There was little there of value,
a few coins, some sort of talisman, a handful of red whortleberries from a precious winter store, Maia's perhaps, the knife
on the floor.

Calmly Erik replaced everything in the gypsy's pockets, and
lifting the dead youth with the ease of muscles trained to
heavier tasks than this, hoisted him onto his shoulder. Some
of the red berries rolled from his pocket to the floor. Erik
contemplated them a moment. The pain he felt now was not
new; there was, in this, the same anguish with which he had
thought of the body of his son, deep within the lake. To the
lake, also, he would commit this body. His mind was clear,

his thoughts ordered, his decision made. The lake must close over the gypsy. He, Vainen, must live. His life was already in forfeit to the girl.

Snow was falling when Erik went outside. It fell lightly on the gypsy's dark head, his body, Erik's shoulders. There was no sound except the soft crunch of Erik's feet, his tread heavier with the weight of the gypsy. There was no sound from the lake, no faint swish of water against the sandy, reedy shore, where his boat was moored, blanketed in light snow. The lake was still. Tomorrow, perhaps, there would be a thin film of ice which would grow in breadth and thickness.

Erik knelt down beside the lake with his burden and weighted the body with a heavy stone he found there covered in the snow against the water's edge. He took off his cap and bared his head to the icy air. He wanted to pray but now there was nothing in his mind but darkness. He could remember no words of prayer or else his stiff tongue refused to utter them. He tried to recall old Akseli's runes, words born of wind and water, of magic and death and fire, of the beauty of life and its harshness. But these words would not come either. The body of the gypsy was dark against the snow. Erik remembered with anguish and pity the red berries in the youth's pockets, the red berries and the talisman for his journey into the unknown. The berries were as red as blood. Now, out of the past, he heard his mother's singing voice. He prayed softly, blindly, to the cold lake, to the icy air, to the dark body of the youth on the fresh snow.

> And you shall see the soldier's lance
> That cuts the deadly hole,
> And you shall see the red red blood
> That down My sides does roll.
> And you shall see four cherubim
> That catch it in a bowl.

The gypsy stared, unseeing, into the dark sky.

Erik raised the body of the gypsy and put it in the boat and rowed a little way across the lake. Then he lowered the youth's body into the lake and let it sink, dragged down by the weight of the stone. There was a faint splash and the ripples closed around it.

He rowed back and pulled his boat up onto the narrow, snow-covered shore. He was exhausted as though he had come many miles through the forest.

He remembered the hen, a huddled heap of feathers on the floor. He went back to the *sauna* and picked it up and carried it to the forest, where he buried it lightly. A hungry lynx would find it before morning and the glossy brown feathers would be blown to the four winds.

The gypsy was gone as though he had never been.

But there was the horse. It whinnied among the trees on the other side of the *sauna*. Erik went to the shivering animal and spoke gently. It reared up on its hind legs and struck out at the man with sharp, shining hoofs. Its white mane flew in the wind. Its nostrils quivered and reddened and its teeth were bared. It reared and lashed with fury, and screamed, a sound to rend the nerves. Yet all was still in the homestead. There was no answering cry from the byre, no sound from Penna. All creatures were asleep, as in primeval peace. Only the white fury of the little horse stood between the man and silence.

"Hunger will tame you," Erik said. Tomorrow it would take food from his hand. He would care for it, subdue it by kindness, work it with his own horse. He shrank from telling some lie that must be told—*The gypsy left his horse and took a pair of skis. He is cunning. I must feed his horse while snow is on the ground, then, in the spring, he will return for it.*

The horse strained against its rough halter, its ears set back, its eye-balls glittering. It reared again suddenly and pawed the air then tore itself free, wrenching undone the rope with which the gypsy had tethered it. Rearing and wheeling in one movement it was gone like a wraith, a rider-less horse, its pale mane streaming, into the white forest.

Silence closed over it like water. Erik leaned against the birch tree, trembling, and then with a deep sigh walked slowly back to the house.

In the morning the lake was lightly frozen over. The girl rose early and stoked up the fire in the living room. She could hear Erik already abroad. He had made and drunk his coffee and its heart-warming aroma filled the room. The girl held out to the fire the thick woolen stockings which she had washed the previous night, to air them. She was wearing her own homespun skirt which she had sponged and brushed and now hurriedly she drew on her stockings as she saw Erik approach from the direction of the bathhouse. When he entered the living room she was standing motionless in the room. They looked at one another.

As though no time had elapsed since their last conversation the girl said, "I want to stay here, Vainen. This house has grown up around you and holds you and now it is holding me." She looked about her as the gypsy had done. But the girl's glance was not covetous. It was the face of one seeking an anchorage.

"We will eat first and then we must go to Porvesi. You must listen to Jussi's advice."

"Jussi will want what is best for me. He will be angry that I seem to have acted deceitfully, but that is all."

"And Maia?"

"Maia will look sharply at me to see if there is anything amiss. Women see things about each other at once, things which a man would never see." She came closer to him. "Look at me, Vainen. Will Maia's eyes tell her what has happened?"

Erik looked down at the girl. She appeared to him, after her night's rest, as fresh and unblemished as a child. He stepped back unconsciously as the gypsy's voice echoed in his brain. *"Her body is white and supple . . ."* The voice defiled her . . . them both.

"What is it?" the girl asked. "You look exhausted, as though
you had not slept. Eat your breakfast. I know that we must go
to Porvesi—and the sooner the better."

Erik took his place at the head of the table and watched
the girl busy herself. He served the rice porridge and watched
her eat as heartily as the night before. She has changed, he
thought, but the change would not alarm Maia. There was
a subtle difference in the girl. She had a faint suggestion of
authority in her manner, no more than the bloom on a grape.
He waited painfully for the question he must answer.

"The gypsy has not returned," the girl said. Erik was not
sure whether it was a question or a statement.

"No."

"I thought I heard his horse whinny in the night. I know
the sound of his horse." She tensed suddenly. "It whinnied and
snorted when the gypsy galloped it into the forest." She broke
off a piece of bread and looked at it thoughtfully as she had
looked at the crumbs in the church. "I thought I heard it
whinny . . . and scream . . . but my dreams," she said, "were
full of the gypsy and his horse, and when I woke later there
was nothing but peace. I knew then that I had been dreaming."

"You must not think of the gypsy."

"I shall never think of him. He will not come back, I am
sure of that."

"Why are you sure?"

"Because, if he gave your message he has cleared himself of
his crime and he has ridden away."

"But last night you laid three places. One was for the
gypsy."

The girl continued to look downward at the bread in her
hand. "When I woke this morning I remembered the gypsy's
words. He said, 'There are worse things than having your
nose slit. One of them is staying in one place all winter.'"

"You have a good memory."

"I remembered that because I wanted to remember it. Gypsies are like that, they are wanderers. We will never see him again." She looked up suddenly. Her eyes, wide and blue with their honey-brown lashes, met his levelly. "You spoke from your heart when you offered," she said, "to marry me. And I think that is how it will be. We will be married and I will keep your house and the gypsy will never return. But I was right to lay the third place. Because I think I shall have a child."

"That is something you cannot know yet."

"Already there is a heaviness in my body. A tiredness. As though it is getting ready." Her steady gaze did not waver. "You are right, Vainen. I must not think of the gypsy because it is done and forgotten and he will never return."

Erik found no words to answer her. They finished their meal in silence.

As soon as the animals were fed, and the necessary work about the farmhouse completed, they set off. "We will take the track through the forest," Erik said. "It is shorter than by road." He harnessed the horse to the sleigh. The animal was restive, eager to be gone. That morning he had had a rare feed of oats and his thick mane was glossy in the clear light. The girl settled herself in the sleigh. Her face was filled with pleasurable anticipation of the journey ahead. One moment she is a woman, Erik thought, the next she is a child. He took his place beside her and gathered up the reins. The runners slid over the snow behind the horse and soon the only sound to be heard was the ringing of the sleigh bells as they penetrated the cold, hypnotic silence of the forest.

Erik looked about him keenly. There was no sign of the gypsy's horse. It had gone, as the girl had said of it, like the wind. Perhaps it was a Kuopio horse, a district which bred horses reputed to be as fast as the wind, a horse stolen or bartered for by the gypsies at a fair.

All night long, or what had remained of it, Erik had thought of the gypsy, had seen his body sink into the icy water of the lake. Yet what was done was done. He, Erik, had been power-

less to control the blinding rage which had swept over him
at the man's second defilement of the girl, a defilement which
had been greater than the first hot lust of youth, a defilement
of intent, a bartering. *We will share her, according to our pact.*
Every instinct had risen in Erik to destroy the foulness; out
of the depths his deepest nature had stirred and erupted like
a volcano. The gypsy had been his destiny. There was nothing
for a man to do about his destiny but to accept it.

Erik's quiet face, his silence, betrayed nothing of his
thoughts. The girl sat beside him, silent also. In one short
hour she had crossed the barriers of experience. Was she bewildered? Resentful? Bitter? Her face revealed nothing either.
They sat side by side as strangers yet united by a bond which
grew stronger every moment.

There were words which Erik wanted to say to her but his
tongue, so long accustomed to silence, betrayed him. The
words could not be formed. He touched her hand once, fleetingly, and the girl turned to look at him. It was a deep, searching look, but she did not speak.

Erik gazed straight ahead to where the wraithlike trees
waited in silence to sentinel their passing. He said slowly,
"Everything is forgotten in time. Pain is forgotten, betrayal,
death."

"Have you forgotten pain and death? Your son in the lake?
The empty cradle, the carved head that is all that is left of
your wife?"

She speaks with strange maturity, Erik thought, and looked
again at the round, still childish curve of her cheek.

"I am not young. These things are behind me and with me.
They are my past, my present, and my future. But you are
young. Nothing, yet, has really begun for you."

"It *has* begun, and nothing," the girl said, "will stop it now.
You are my present and my future."

The track wound on. The sleigh slid smoothly or bumped
over ruts or hillocks. The little horse was tireless, its eager
breath steaming on the dazzling air. Soon the heavy snows

which would keep it in the byre would descend. Now it was rejoicing in its freedom, in the wiry strength of its body, and every now and then gave a snort of pleasure.

The girl dozed, lulled by the rhythm of the bells, the changeless scene. Once they stopped to rest but the girl urged Erik on as though there were no time to be lost.

"Everyone in Porvesi will know now that I am with you," she said. "*Voi! Voi!* The women will gossip." She looked frightened, her eyes darkening. "You have lived alone so long, you don't know what it is like in the world."

"Porvesi is not the world."

"It is my world," she said.

They left the forest and turned into the road which ran beside it. There were glimpses of the lake, and fields standing under light snow. Soon the first of the scattered houses on the outskirts of Porvesi came into view.

It was a farmhouse, with a few outbuildings, standing in the middle of a field. Near the barn the food store, a natural refrigerator, showed its white roof close to the ground as though housing troglodytes. It was a well, sunk deep into the ground, lined with snow, where animal fodder could be kept all winter.

"That is Eino Salonen's farm. His wife Margit, is a friend of Maia's. She comes once a week to use Maia's loom but they only speak once an hour," the girl said mischievously, "because they are both Tavasts."

Erik smiled. The Tavasts, from the center of Finland, were reputed to be dour and impassive. Stories were told at their expense which they enjoyed as much as the listener.

"Their son, Arvo, has gone to sea and their daughter, Meri, is in Helsinki. She has passed her examinations and is going to be a teacher."

Suddenly, with the girl's words, a new world opened for Erik. They were, indeed, entering a new world with every yard that the smooth sleigh runners covered. Here, in Porvesi, a hamlet of some ten farms and a few houses, the girl was bringing the world close, close to the dark forests, the lonely lakes, the granite outcrops, where man, it seemed, could surely not find sustenance. The echoes of another life struck suddenly against this timelessness of man, horse, and sleigh gliding across the changeless distances.

Porvesi is my world, the girl had said.

"You are young. Surely you want to go to Helsinki also? It is a fine place I am told, though I have never been there."

The girl said with certainty, "No, those things are not meant for me. My world is Vainen."

They drove in silence. Presently she said, "That is the pastor's house. Soon we will see the church. Where have you seen me . . . in Porvesi . . . Vainen?"

She is shrewd and practical, Erik thought. She knows what must be done and will do it.

"I have seen you in the store," Erik said impassively. "But it is not yet too late to draw back if you want to."

"It is too late. I know it," the girl said. She sat silently as the sleigh drew up outside the store set in the straggling, rutted street with its scattered wooden dwellings. Almost immediately Jussi and Maia appeared from the house. It was Maia who spoke first. "Come into the house, Vainen," she said. "Jussi will attend to the horse."

5

THE LIVING ROOM was on the right, the store on the left. Maia led the way. She was approaching middle age, her gray hair drawn back, her cheekbones strongly marked, her eyes shrewd and penetrating, deeply set. Her face, but for the penetrating glance of her eyes, would have been expressionless. With her stocky figure she was shorter than the girl and came no higher than Vainen's shoulder. She motioned him to sit and turned to the girl.

"You have turned out badly," she said coldly. "Jussi and I searched for you the whole of a night. We thought you had run away to bring shame on us."

Maia stood with her arms folded and looked up at the girl impassively.

"I have deceived you," the girl said submissively. "I know it. But I was in love and I wanted to see Vainen. I didn't know how far it was to his place. I thought I could walk there."

"The girl is young and heedless," Vainen said. "I am to blame. I courted her secretly."

Jussi entered the room and looked incredulously at Erik, who rose to his feet.

"You, of all people, Vainen!" Jussi exploded. "I tell you, when the gypsy brought the message I could hardly believe it. Annikki . . . with you! The girl hasn't been further than Porvesi since she came here."

"That is where I saw her. I fell in love with her and I am a man of few words. We exchanged glances. The girl knew what was in my heart."

"And that was enough for her to go rushing off to find you? Are you mad, Annikki? How have you been brought up that you know no better than to go chasing the first man who smiles at you? There has been enough gossip, I can tell you. A girl has her good name to think of, and ours too. You have slept the nights at Vainen, alone, and Vainen will have to marry you and I wash my hands of it."

"I was coming to that," Erik said.

"It's something you should have come to sooner," Jussi cried angrily. "You have lived alone too long and that's unnatural. The girl is not much more than a child. Oh, she'll soon be eighteen, but she's lived alone with her mother and seen nothing of the world." Jussi sat down suddenly, his bright dark eyes darting over Vainen and the girl. "I've nothing against you, Vainen, no man has, but this is something I didn't ex-pect. Why, the girl has hardly been out of our sight." He slapped his thigh and began to laugh. "You're deep, Vainen, deep as the lake. Not a word out of you, coming or going, and the girl flies to you, my cousin's child flies to you, at a glance. Weren't you happy here, Annikki? Weren't we good to you? Couldn't you wait for a man of your own age? Couldn't you have waited for Arvo Salonen to get back from sea? Maia had her eye on him for you and I saw your eye on him before he went, don't deny it." Jussi drew a quick, indignant breath.

"Enough of questions," Maia said shortly. She looked up at the girl with a close scrutiny. Annikki blushed and hung her head and covered her face with her hands.

"I know I was wrong to deceive you, Maia," she said and began to cry a little. "I should have told you that I had seen

Vainen. It was because the winter is coming . . . and the days
are short . . . and perhaps Vainen would not come to Porvesi
in the winter . . . and I was lonely. And I love him." She
looked through her fingers at Jussi.

"Lonely?" Jussi cried. "You didn't give us a chance, girl.
There'll be company for you all winter. There's the play to be
acted in the parish hall. And the last months went quickly,
with you busy and settling. And there's the young people's
dance every month in the old barn, and dancing in midsummer as well. Wait, girl, wait, I'll think of some story to tell
Porvesi, so that they won't think of you as a girl who runs
to the first man who—"

"She wants to marry Vainen," Maia said dourly. "She has
her reasons."

"I love him," Annikki said, and cried a little more.

Erik stood silent, marveling at the girl. She was acting, he
knew. She was playing the heedless child that he had pictured
her, running to him without thought, a heedless child, foolish
with love.

"I want to marry her," Erik said, and he felt the sweat
break out on his forehead. "I want to marry her. I have years
enough and wisdom enough, for her foolishness."

He sensed rather than heard the girl's deep breath of relief.

"You are lucky, Vainen," Jussi said, "to have found a
bride so easily. Truly there aren't many suitors here now but
there's plenty of time and Arvo Salonen spoke of her before
he left for sea. A fine, handsome lad he is too, Annikki . . ."

"So is Vainen," Maia said. "Not a lad, but a handsome man
of years." She pulled the girl's hands away from her face.
"This girl's head will never lead her astray," she said grimly.

"It's already done that, Maia," Jussi pointed out.

"This is a girl who wants a man of substance. Arvo still has
to make his way. But Vainen has made his—a man with a bit
of farm and forest and a well-built house who lacks for
nothing that I can see." Maia turned on her heel. "Annikki
is no child and no fool," she said, "and neither am I."

Jussi threw up his hands. "I am ruled by women, it seems. Maia has said her say." He held out his hand to Erik. "The thing is settled, Vainen. Maia, make the coffee."

Without another glance at the girl Maia did as she was bid. Annikki stood where she was. Maia will rebuff her if she tries to help, Erik thought. He studied the older woman. She was no fool, he judged. The girl had been right to hide her face from those sharp eyes, eyes which missed nothing. She might have read what he had read in the clear blue eyes of the girl, something hidden deep, no more than a shadow, the shadow, not of love, but of fear.

When the coffee was made it was Jussi and Erik who took their places, according to custom, at the table on which Maia had placed a snowy cloth of her own weaving.

"It is, after all, an occasion," she said in her dour way and brought out her best china cups and some *pulla* and filled the cups for the men with good, strong coffee. She and Annikki took their places at the great fireplace and ate and drank there. Annikki was silent but Maia joined in the conversation every now and then with a few words.

The room was not unlike the room at Vainen, Annikki reflected. There was a fine hand-carved table in it, and Maia's woven rugs, but hers were in harder, yet duller colors, whereas those at Vainen were bright and gay. The spinning wheel beside the fire, the Bible on its own carved stool, the spotless cleanliness of the boards, were not matters for astonishment, they were everyday things. Yet, in some mysterious way, they evoked only Maia, spoke only of her, the white boards witnesses to her energy, the spinning wheel to her untiring hands, the Bible an hourly reminder of the precepts by which man must live. Annikki knew that she had fallen short of Maia's standards.

"The girl will bring you little, Vainen," Maia said. "She has little craft in her hands, either."

"I can make cheese," Annikki said. "I can cook all that is needful. Vainen will teach me to spin. In Turku we did not

spin and weave and even if we had, my mother was too ill to
teach me."

"That is true," Jussi agreed. "My cousin was never strong
and lost her husband when the girl was small."

"She has already told me," Erik said.

"Where did the girl sleep last night?" Maia asked from her
seat by the fire.

"In Kirsti's bed," Erik said. "The bed that was hers and
mine."

"And you?"

"I slept in my son's bed. In the room I built for him when
my second son came."

Maia turned to the girl. "Kirsti was Vainen's wife and well
I remember her. There was nothing she could not do in the
house or out of it. You'll be a poor second."

"The girl will learn. You have said yourself that she is no
child and no fool," Erik said shortly.

"True enough. Well, you want to take her off our hands,
Vainen, so the sooner the wedding is over the better. Yet . . .
if the wedding is quick the gossips will have their say."

"And if it is not quick they will have more time," Jussi
laughed, "to say it in."

"I am a man of few words," Erik reminded him. "I have
asked for the girl and you have given your consent. Let the
pastor marry us as quickly as such things may be done. No
man has anything against me and no woman has anything
against the girl."

"You cannot speak fairer than that," Maia said. She got up
to refill their cups. Annikki sat with her head lowered and
now and again looked up at Erik. His shoulders above the
table were broad and strong, his face composed, while Jussi's
bright eyes darted from one face to another, his slender body
overshadowed by Erik's. A tremor of fear ran through the
girl's body. She remembered the forest and the wild usages of
men. But this man was quiet and calm, still, like the lake
under its frail coat of ice. There was nothing to fear from

such a man. He had said he would ask nothing of her and he
was a man of his word.

When four cups of coffee had been drunk Erik rose to go.

"The arrangements will be made," Maia said. "I will see the
pastor tomorrow. Annikki will bring such things as she has,
her clothes and trinkets and her mother's wedding ring."

"It is in the box in the pine-wood press," Annikki said.

"I know where it is. Now it will serve for you. And what
better could you have?"

There was a sudden wild sound. A horse whinnied on a
drawn-out high-pitched note.

Annikki's glance went swiftly to Erik's face. He remained
where he stood but the fingers of his right hand closed slowly
into his palm.

"That is the gypsy's horse," he said evenly. "It whinnies
like no other animal I have ever heard."

Jussi sprang up. "I had almost forgotten it! The horse came
galloping out of the forest this morning, it came down the
road like the wind and across the paddock to the house. There
was no one on its back, its halter hung loose and there was
foam on its neck. For a moment," Jussi laughed, "I thought it
was an apparition, a horse with such a long white mane galloping out of the forest alone. And giving that strange cry!
Listen! There it goes again. You're right. There's something
ghostly in it."

Maia snorted. "A tired, thirsty animal, that's all the poor
creature was. I watered and fed it."

"It's that gypsy's horse all right," Jussi said. "He must have
stolen it and turned it loose for reasons best known to himself. You'd better watch out for him, Vainen. He'll be back
looking for what he can find. Maia was so glad to get your
message that she gave the lad a loaf of bread and a cockerel.
He'll be back for more, you'll see, so keep your doors closed,
Vainen, I'm warning you. As handsome a gypsy as I ever saw,
but with a crafty, sly look like the whole pack of them."

"Enough talking," Maia chided. "You make my head spin.

There's nothing to do but keep the horse here till someone
comes looking for it."

"Someone in Vituri has lost a horse I'll wager. We'll hear
soon enough. I'd like to keep it," Jussi said, "it's a beautiful
creature and has a way with it. Come and see for yourself,
Vainen."

"I saw the horse when I gave the gypsy the message."

"So you did. But come and look. It's worth another look.
On second thoughts it can't be from these parts. I'd have
noticed it sooner or later. No, it comes from further off, from
the devil, the way it goes," Jussi laughed.

The two men went outside. As soon as they had gone Maia
turned to the girl.

"Is it true that you slept in Kirsti's bed and Vainen in
the child's?"

"It is true, Maia."

"All the night long?"

"All the night long."

"Then Vainen hasn't touched you?"

"Vainen hasn't touched me."

"I didn't really think so. Vainen is no man's fool, or woman's either, and he is a truthful and honest man. But there's
something about this," Maia pondered, "that I don't understand."

"There's nothing but my foolishness . . . and that I could
deceive you and Jussi after all your goodness."

"Get up, girl," Maia said, not unkindly. She faced Annikki,
her authority no whit diminished by the fact that she had to
look up at the girl.

"Men have ways," she said, "you might not understand.
Ways you might not like—if you did understand them. If you
marry Vainen you'll do more than make rice porridge."

"I know that, Maia." Under the older woman's scrutiny
Annikki felt as though her body were contracting. In that
piercing gaze she saw the gaze of other eyes, the dark, liquid
eyes of the gypsy, the red lips which had come closer, the sud-

den cruel strength which had pinioned and torn at her like
some beautiful, obscene, wild bird. She flushed and trembled
and her face paled.

"Hm . . ." Maia said. "Keep those blushes for Vainen, not
for me. I see well you're not a child. Why should you be?
When I was eighteen my child that died was already born."

"No, I'm not a child, Maia."

"Vainen is a man who knows his own mind and sees clearly.
His mind's been set one way for many years. Now the time
has come to change it. A son . . . that's what he wants."

"I know that."

"See that you give him one—and quickly."

The men came in, bringing the cold air and the feel of the
snow with them.

"Would you believe it!" Jussi cried. "There was the horse
as gentle as a child when I spoke to him. But Vainen here—
I tell you Maia, if I saw hate in a beast's eye it was in the eyes
of that horse. It reared up and would have savaged him and
nothing Vainen could say would stop him. Vainen—who can
tame dog, bull, and horse with that quiet voice of his."

"I wish yours were as quiet," Maia grumbled. "The animal
is nervous, naturally."

Annikki was looking steadfastly at Erik. "You're not hurt?
He didn't hurt you, Vainen?"

"No. I kept out of his way."

"Your horse is rested," Maia told him, "if you want to
start."

"Thank you, Maia. And you, Jussi." Erik looked at Annikki. "Everything is settled. I will come to Porvesi to marry
you. Till then you will stay here."

"Good-by, then, Vainen," Annikki said.

"Good-by." He looked at her a moment longer and went
out with Jussi to where his horse and sleigh waited.

"Well," Maia said, "I am a woman of few words. But there
goes a man with fewer."

The girl went to the window and watched Erik as he got

into the sleigh and drove away. One or two faces appeared at
the windows of wooden houses similar to Jussi's. The sight of
Vainen in Porvesi in midweek would have been unusual if
they had not known the reason for his visit. Now they were
consumed with curiosity. Would he or would he not marry
the girl?

"That's what comes of keeping her like a caged bird," Harri
Vasola said. He was the farmer who had sold Jussi the paddock.

"Maia was teaching her to be a good housewife," Pia, his
wife, explained. "The girl had learned nothing in Turku. Besides, she had to earn her keep. But to look at her—who would
have thought she'd go rushing off to Vainen like that!"

"Has she turned his head or not?" Harri asked. "But it
would be no more than you'd expect. Vainen hasn't looked
at a woman—hardly spoken to one—since Kirsti died. And
the girl"—Harri nodded sagely—"the girl saw a fine, handsome
man and slam went the door of the cage and out she flew.
They were meant for each other, I'd say."

"It took a bit longer than that to slam the door of my
cage," Pia said smugly.

Harri looked at his wife. For all her fifty years her skin was
still unwrinkled over plump cheeks. He gave her a sly nudge.
"I never heard it slam," he said. "As far as I can remember it
was already open when I came courting."

"That's what you'd like to think now, Harri. But I could
tell a different tale. Who was it who slipped off the ladder in
the snow, climbing to knock at my window—"

"That's enough," said Harri, "get on with your spinning.
You're too old to be remembering such things."

He heard Pia laugh as she settled down to her spinning
wheel, to be joined by their daughter-in-law, Inger. The two
women's voices murmured above the wheel and presently
broke into peals of laughter. Harri went off to join his son,
Timo, who was mending the roof of the byre. He felt melancholy suddenly. Here was Vainen, about to marry a young
girl while he, Harri, with less than ten years in hand, had a

daughter-in-law and grandchildren and was beginning to feel the years on his shoulders as heavy sometimes as the wrath of God.

"That was Vainen," Timo called out, "Vainen, going a-wooing. He's been courting the girl for weeks—Maia's just told me—and the girl couldn't wait and ran to him, and now there's to be a wedding." Timo grinned. "If I'd been single I'd have courted her myself, and done all the running. But Vainen hasn't waited long, has he?"

"Perhaps he thought ten years long enough to wait," Harri growled.

"He's a deep one, that Vainen. Even Jussi admitted it. As deep as the lake, Jussi said, and no man will ever get to the bottom of that."

"Unless he finds where the swallows sleep in winter," Harri grunted as he began to climb the ladder.

6

ALL THE INHABITANTS of Porvesi would be invited
to the wedding, seventy-five all told, from ninety-year-old
Heikki to the newest babe in arms. Heikki could mumble,
through toothless gums, of the far-off days when he had been
a novice in a Byzantine monastery and of how he had felt the
call of the world and had left the monastery to become a
droshky driver in old Viipuri. He would tell how he had
taught his wife to read and write before she could receive her
permit to marry him. Heikki's wife was seventy now, as thin
as it was possible to be, her frail bones like those of a bird.
"You could make a quill pen from her legbone," Heikki said,
his mind going back, as it often did, to the monastery and old
parchments and the scratching of quills. Heikki called his wife
Fat Catherine after the Round Tower which stood in the
square in Viipuri, where he had met her selling vegetables
and *viili* in little wooden tubs. The soured milk was still old
Heikki's favorite food. All Porvesi called the old woman Fat
Catherine, ludicrous as it would have appeared to a stranger,
seeing Fat Catherine with her frail, anxious face, her ear
cupped with a little batlike hand so as not to miss a word.
Nobody knew her real name. Heikki said he had forgotten it,

at which Fat Catherine only laughed, a faint, high tinkle of a laugh, a sound almost too faint for mortal ears to hear, like a bat's.

The youngest wedding guest was Eliel Vasola, Harri's latest grandson, who was certain to cry lustily throughout.

The wedding of Vainen was in itself a cause for much conjecture. The years had slipped by and the solitary Vainen had become part of the order of things. No man had pitied him. He was accepted, not in his allotted groove, but in the groove he had chosen for himself.

"But, nature will out," they said, even though it had seemed Vainen's nature to live alone. The girl, also, was regarded with a new interest. Few had talked with her, except for chance moments. A quiet girl, Maia had said, alone in the world and finding her place in Porvesi, not one for book learning, either, the moment her school days were behind her. She had helped in the house and learned to cook a little and milk the cow and clean out the byre side by side with Maia herself. She was good with the animals as every woman should be since she was responsible for their care and cleanliness during the long, roof-bound winter.

The girl, it was considered, was making a good match. As for Vainen, in the natural order of things, any wife was better than no wife and he had lost no time in finding this young one, and pretty into the bargain.

Maia, watching the girl in the days which had followed Vainen's visit, felt a mixture of womanly concern and curiosity. The girl was young and untried, though Maia was quite sure that she lacked nothing of feminine wiles, but surely such youth and inexperience should show itself in a little eagerness, a little excitement, even pleasant apprehension of what lay ahead? But the girl baffled her.

"I would say she is like a novice about to take her vows," Maia told Jussi, "if I knew of such things. But certainly like a woman who does not question but just accepts her fate."

"She has made you talkative, at any rate," Jussi laughed.

"I have watched her," Maia persisted. "She is neither happy nor unhappy, slow nor eager, caring nor uncaring."

"Vainen found time to court her. Perhaps he found time to make her a little like himself. But leave the girl alone. One day she is orphaned, the next here with us, and the next a promised bride. Tell me how she ought to be, if you can."

"I thought in time she'd make a match of it with Arvo Salonen," Maia said stubbornly.

"Arvo is at sea. Vainen is here. There's your answer, woman." Jussi considered a moment. "Does Annikki know what marriage means? She was a quiet girl in Turku, by all accounts, and my poor cousin was too ill to look after her much. Still, the girl is no fool. But marriage—that's another matter. Does she know what it means?"

"She knows it's more than making porridge."

"We know so little of Annikki when you come to think of it. Childless ourselves, we didn't know much about the young ones."

"She knows," Maia said. "You can depend on that. When I spoke to her the color came and went in her face and down went her eyes not to meet mine."

"It's understandable . . . A young girl . . . and we're little more than strangers."

"She's lived under our roof long enough to know us for what we are."

"But your words can bite when you have a mind."

"So it's I who have driven the girl to Vainen?"

"Neither you nor I, nor Vainen did that. A lonely man and a girl ripe for marriage—only a fool would make anything of it."

"I'm a fool then," Maia said stoutly. "For I make something of it. The trouble is, I don't know what."

Jussi roared with laughter. "Nine months from now you'll see what to make of it. Vainen wants a son."

"What troubles me is not what's under my nose," Maia cried. "But no man will ever understand that the things which aren't said are more important than the things which are."

Jussi looked at his short, plump wife in amazement. "This marriage has loosened your tongue. You've talked more in an hour than I've known you talk in a lifetime." He got up quickly from his rocking chair, where he had been rocking lightly, one foot on the floor, the other on the low stretcher. "It's time I got to my work and you to yours."

He went to the door which led to the store. Maia took a can and began thoughtfully to water the green plants which stood in pots on the window ledge and on the floor, tracing an arabesque of soft green leaves and slender branches against the wall. At the doorway Jussi paused.

"There'll be things in plenty to do for the wedding," he said. "It will be here, I suppose?"

Maia snorted. "Where else?" she asked indignantly. "We're not too poor to give the girl a proper wedding in her own home."

"I knew you would do the right thing by the girl."

"Did you think I'd give her a vicarage wedding with half a dozen guests?"

"You've asked everybody here, then?"

"Yes." For a moment Maia's face softened and then she said with pride, "I shall put down the wedding carpet that we were married on, Jussi."

"And your parents before you."

"And theirs before them. And before them if I remember."

"It's the oldest in Porvesi and made by your own ancestress. You've a right to be proud." Jussi stood a moment longer and there was silence in the room, a silence woven of a tissue of memories. In that silence were their own wedding, birth, death, and the flying years.

"It's a good carpet and a beautiful one. It will be put down for more weddings than this," Maia said abruptly. She glanced out of the window. "The snow has stopped falling. Now we shall get no more till Christmas. We'll be alone, after all, Jussi."

Jussi looked at his wife, at the sudden bleakness of her expression. Beneath the chiding, the aloofness, she had felt affection for the girl, Jussi thought.

"We all make our own little cages," he said slowly, answering, not her words, but her thoughts, and was gone before she could be exasperated by his insight.

Annikki, meanwhile, went through the days as Maia had said, like a woman who does not question, but accepts her fate. In this the pastor, Tuomas Palin, saw a sense of rightness. It seemed to him that these two people, Erik Vainen and Annikki Berling, had found each other as two grains of sand find each other. Both of them were alone, both solitary. He had spoken to the girl and seen that she had not yet adjusted herself to the change from Turku to Porvesi, the change from a proud university town, once the capital of Finland, to a small village. The *Kirkkoherra* had himself been born in Turku. When he preached in Porvesi church with its fresh white walls, its pews painted in white and dove-gray, its blue velvet altar rail and billowing pulpit, Annikki's face below his was absorbed, withdrawn. But her mind was filled with memories that he, also, would have found familiar.

While the pastor's words flowed over her head Annikki would be thinking of the river at Turku, softly flowing, with its bridges and moored boats; of the golden rain of the birch trees on the heights beyond in the setting sun of early autumn, each leaf quivering and scintillating till it was surrounded by a visible aura of golden light. She would remember the old wooden houses by the river, the cobbled street where as a child she had walked, holding her mother's hand. Turku had been full of young life, of her school friends, remote—seeming as figures in a dream, as unreal now as the plays they had performed in the open air in summer. It had been a life like any other, with school and play and examinations to pass. Time had flowed as softly as the river, as softly as her mother's life had flowed away. Then, suddenly, all was over.

The withdrawn, absorbed face, the detached mind on which

the pastor's words left no Sunday trace, seemed to be all that
was left, Annikki sometimes thought, of herself. The remoteness of Porvesi, the kindness of Jussi, and the long silences of
Maia had provided a strange climate, a stubborn soil in which
Annikki had not yet taken root.

All this the pastor sensed. Jussi and Maia, he knew, were
the salt of the earth. But Maia did not know how to unbend,
her strong feelings were held in check, her manner was one of
inbred reserve that usually approached coldness. Vainen, too,
was sparing of words, but he and the girl would meet on the
oldest ground of all. Vainen's desert would blossom like a
rose.

As for Annikki herself, Maia was right. She had accepted
her fate. A feeling of security filled her, the security of accepting the inevitable. Of the gypsy she refused to think. He
had become no more than a dark shadow at the back of her
mind and between that dark shadow and herself stood the
figure of Vainen.

For Vainen she felt a deep gratitude. The emotion was true,
strongly rooted, and pervaded her being. If this was not love,
which was something Annikki had not yet experienced, this
emotion, she thought, must be something very near it.

For it was for her sake that Vainen had killed a man.

It was in the moment of knowing this that her attitude
toward Vainen had crystallized.

How still it had been that night! Still, silent, so that the
least sound had reached her, lying awake in Kirsti's four-
poster bed. At first she had fallen into an exhausted sleep in
the warm, enfolding bed, which had cradled her in a private
world. It was an old bed, or made in the style of one, two-
tiered, its roof forming a second bed where, she supposed, the
little boy had slept soundly above his parents. Over both beds
gay rugs had been thrown, and the wooden sides had been
painted a soft green, with a border of flowers.

The moon had risen and perhaps it was the silvery light
which had awakened her, for suddenly she was awake, her

body rigid with a nameless fear. She had not been dreaming of the gypsy nor had she been awakened by the pain of her bruised and scratched body, for the *sauna* had soothed and eased muscles tensed by pain and fear.

It was something else which had awakened her, a consciousness of a menace in the silence, of fear in the moonlit night. She had pushed back the bedclothes and started up, aware now of the faint crushing sound of feet on snow.

Creeping to the window she had parted the shutters silently. The dark form of Vainen with another, darker form over his shoulder, was passing almost soundlessly over the light snow from the *sauna* to the lake.

Shivering, Annikki had watched and waited, her breath suspended, the room and the warm, dark bed behind her seeming now like the safety of a womb to which she would never return. Vainen passed and was lost to view among the snowy trees, threading his way, a dark shadow beneath a shadow darker than his own. There was the soft crunch and slither of a boat pushed out, and then the distant ripple of water as oars parted the lake.

Before the splash came which froze her veins Annikki had known quite surely that the dark shadow on Vainen's shoulder was the gypsy, and the gypsy was dead.

She had gone back to bed, her body icy cold, and pulled the gay rugs high up to her chin, but the ice in her body would not thaw. Afterward, long after it seemed, she had heard the high, ghostly whinny of the gypsy's horse, then a wild, staccato screaming that had died away on the white night, leaving silence behind it and its echoes in her brain.

She had known then that the innocence which the gypsy had taken from her had been but the prelude to this second ravishment. It was as though her primal innocence had been protected by a covering which had now been ripped aside. Stark and clear, knowledge was revealed, the knowledge that now she and Vainen were bound to one another. The pact was sealed. They were bound together by that shadow in the lake.

For Vainen, as the long night wore on, she had felt a welling sense of pity and a bitter self-reproach. He had been caught up in the web which had so suddenly enfolded her. From the moment she had answered the gypsy's smile to this moment when she lay in Vainen's house, in Vainen's bed, there had been no escape for him. It had been like some strange game such as she might have played with her friends in Turku in those long summer days, a game where one step led to the next, each one more dangerous than the other, till finally there was no escape and capture seemed frighteningly real. Her bewildered mind, confronted by experience from which there was no retreat, capitulated suddenly into accept-ance. But now it was a mature acceptance of destiny. Yet, running like a thread through this new pattern was the image of Vainen which from the beginning had been imprinted on her mind—a Vainen calm, strong, authoritative, with an inner sureness and strength. She was not alone. She would never be alone again.

The question of guilt or innocence had not arisen in her mind. Something that had, for whatever reason, to be done, had been done. Nothing now could stop the course of events. She would be Vainen's wife.

The journey back to Jussi and Maia, the explanations that were necessary to secure consent to the marriage were obsta-cles, simply, to be overcome. Vainen would overcome them in his way, she in hers. Only to be feared was Maia, with her sharp eyes, her probing mind which did not accept facts easily.

Yet, in the event, how simple it had been, how few words had proved necessary. Vainen's attitude of calm acceptance of the outcome, her own helplessness had prevailed. Life, now, would begin again for them both, for herself and Vainen. He would be her husband but he would never come to know what she knew.

The pattern wove itself in her mind as simply and cleanly

as the geometrical pattern in Kirsti's rugs, clear and precise in their scarlet and black.

She had fallen asleep and had slept dreamlessly. In the morning she had seen her face reflected in the mirror let into the corner cupboard in the angle of the wall. In the glass, between the carved and painted panels, her face showed smooth and firm, with the soft bloom of girlhood. She had gone to the living room, where the ticking of the china clock on the wall seemed already a sound familiar to her ears. She had seen Vainen coming toward the house as she would see him uncounted times again.

Her real life, she knew, had already begun.

Maia had already called a meeting of her neighbors to help with the wedding preparations.

"The pastor thinks it a good thing for the girl to be married as soon as convenient," she told them. "Annikki is finished with school, she has little heart for the tasks here—but a home of her own will be a different matter, says he."

The women nodded in agreement. Ulla Hassi, a pale woman of forty with high cheekbones and gray eyes that slanted a little, said quietly, "It's time Vainen found a wife." For all her quietness she had a habit of emphasizing each word with a prod in the chest of her listener. Maia drew back now almost mechanically, out of long habit.

"He'll be a good husband," Maia said, "but a bit old for the girl."

"Marriage ages women," Ulla said, with three prods.

"Where did she spend the nights that she was away?" Elisabet Lahti asked. Elisabet was barely thirty. She had brought her youngest child, fat little Lauri, who was playing on the spotless boards by the window. The thought of the young girl lost both repelled and attracted her. She would have liked some such adventure herself, especially one with this particular outcome.

"With Vainen," Maia said simply.

"With Vainen?" Elisabet echoed in shocked tones.

"That's where she went. He took her in and put her in Kirsti's bed."

"While you searched for her?"

"Jussi and I, to tell the truth, thought she had run away. Back to Turku."

"She never settled here," Margit Salonen said. "That I could tell when I came to spin with Maia. The girl's mind was elsewhere."

"It was on Vainen," Maia said.

"And it was a gypsy who told you where she was?" Elisabet persisted.

"Vainen sent the message by him. Manlike, he didn't think to ease our minds till morning. But he's an upright man. The girl was safe with him."

There was nothing more to be said. But Elisabet rushed in with the last word. "She's quick, that girl," she said grudgingly, "for all her quietness."

Maia turned swiftly on Elisabet her piercing gaze. It was known that Elisabet would have liked to marry Vainen and the match would not have been a bad one, all things considered. Elisabet had proved herself a good housewife and was now the mother of three fine sons. But she *was* a housewife and a mother, and would do well to remember it.

"Vainen has made his own choice," Maia said shortly.

"And taken his time about it," Margit added. "For that reason the marriage will prosper."

Under the stern looks of the older women whatever there was of doubt and speculation about the matter was dismissed or else not voiced.

Maia was no longer young. Had there been children of her marriage she would have been preparing for the wedding of her last, rather than her first. But the wedding preparations, Jussi observed, brought color to her cheeks and a sparkle to her eye. Annikki watched the preparations with an inner restlessness concealed beneath a calm exterior. She would have preferred to have been married simply and quietly by the pastor, and gone on her way. But the preparations, once started, were like an avalanche.

"I never thought to marry a girl from my house," Maia said. "All shall be done as it should."

There were scrubbings and scourings and bakings of pies and of bread which filled the house with appetizing smells and the clatter of women. Jussi was driven to the parish hall to discuss village matters with the pastor and Eino Salonen and others. Maia, with Annikki's help and that of the women, baked rye bread and barley bread and the sweet *pulla*. Jussi killed a young bullock. "Three days," Maia said, "three days for the feast, as it was when I was a girl."

"As it was when you and I married," Jussi said, resigned. "Now, if Annikki were being married in Turku, none of this—"

"But she is not," said Maia. "She is being married in our own village, and country ways are best." Maia surveyed her cupboard with a housewifely eye. There were bottles of apple cider and bottles of wine made from ripe juniper berries. There would be meat and good vegetables with mounds of potatoes boiled, as on Sundays, without their skins, white, floury and delicious. Nothing would be lacking, from brandy for the men to the bowls of *viili* flavored with brown sugar or cinnamon which would delight old Heikki's heart. To her own mounds of sweet bread the women guests would add those of their own baking, brought as a gift wrapped in white linen, and decorated with sugar and almonds. "For," said Maia, "in Porvesi, God be thanked, old country ways die hard."

To all this, Annikki was a barely interested spectator. She felt as though all this were happening to someone other than herself. At Vainen, Vainen himself knew of Maia's great preparations for the wedding but he and Anikki barely met in those days so feverish with activity. What was Vainen thinking? Feeling? Annikki wondered. She knew nothing. Yet, when she thought of him, she had a feeling of great calm.

The sudden snow had cleared away altogether and the sun shone palely. The great lake had ripples on its surface which broke the reflections of the reeds on the shore, so that they wavered and trembled in the water. The brooks which had frozen lightly in the forest were released again and there was again the sound of running water if one penetrated deeply into the forest. "There will not be snow till Christmas," Maia said again, "but I wish you could have been married in mid-summer, girl, as I was married."

"I want to be married now," Annikki said evenly, "and be with Vainen."

Within her was a sense of urgent need to hurry, hurry. It was little more than three weeks since that dread day in the forest, but already she had felt, sometimes, a faint nausea. Perhaps it was the pervading smell of food, she told herself, or the exhausting comings and goings. She had dropped her eyes before Maia's glance.

"It isn't seemly to show such eagerness," Maia said abruptly. She added more kindly, "But there it is, you know nothing. Your mother let you grow as you would, like a field of neglected rye. For all that, the grain is good. Vainen will do the rest."

Annikki's silence troubled her. The girl is of Jussi's blood, she thought, and ought to have more lightness in her manner. But, talkative as Jussi was, he would never have revealed his deeper emotions any more than she, Maia, would have done. It was better, as Jussi had said, to let the girl alone.

But there were things which could be discussed.

"You have no dresser to take with you, Annikki, though I suppose Vainen already has a fine one," Maia said.

"Yes, he has a dresser in the living room. All the plates on it are milky white with a milky design."

Now, thought Maia, I am finding the girl's true nature. "Then it will not matter if you can bring no dresser as a dowry. Has Vainen a grandfather clock?"

"Not that I saw. Only the china clock on the wall."

"Whoever heard of a house without a grandfather clock!" Maia exclaimed. "We have two, one of mine and one of Jussi's. Since you are of Jussi's family you shall take his with you when you go."

"But what will Jussi say?"

"You know well, girl, that Jussi would give you whatever you asked, in reason." Maia paused and searched her own heart for a moment. Now she could acknowledge to herself that she had felt a hint of jealousy when the girl had first come, for Jussi had been eager to please her and there had been a touch of willfulness in the girl's manner with him. Perhaps I was too harsh with her, Maia thought, for she does not like me, I know well. She was honest enough to admit to herself that she would not be entirely unwilling to have the house to herself again.

She looked up at the tall young girl. "Yes," she said, "you shall have the grandfather clock."

Annikki's eyes shone, in spite of herself. It would be good to take something of her own to Vainen. The grandfather clock had flowing lines, like a cello, and was painted a misty blue, with a panel showing an elegant young man in fine buckled shoes stepping into a boat. "Yes," Maia repeated, overreaching the bounds of self-abnegation, "you shall have the clock, which was Jussi's grandmother's, and that gives you a right to it also."

"But Jussi might want to keep it," Annikki said doubtfully. Maia shook her head.

"We have no children. As for linen—there are the sheets with the lace border you crocheted—now you will see how right I was to set you to work."

"But the lace is not very good, Maia."

"It won't match Kirsti's. I've already told you, girl, you'll be a poor second. But time will mend that."

"And the cat," Annikki said softly. "I may take the cat Jussi

gave me?" It was the one thing she had come to love in
Porvesi. There was a moment's silence in which both of them
knew that the fact was acknowledged.

"Take the cat," Maia shrugged. "Though I should have
thought that at Vainen there would be a good, working cat.

"I didn't see one. Only the dog, Penna."

"When you are mistress of Vainen I shall come and visit
you, once, at least, whether Vainen welcomes me or not."
Maia's manner held a repressed excitement which brought a
flush to her face, and surprised Annikki. "Do you realize, girl,
that all these years not a woman in Porvesi has set foot in
Vainen? We've wondered about it among ourselves but since
Jussi pulled his tooth Vainen has admitted no man or woman
either. So now I'll see for myself how the house is fixed."

"It's like any other," Annikki said.

But already it was like no other, already it was familiar,
close. It was she who would stoke the fire and listen to the
ticking of the china clock on the wall, and wait, wait to see
which way the path would open in front of her.

Nothing which should have been done was left undone at
the marriage of Vainen and Annikki. The light horse carriage
which was to take them to Vainen was decorated with leaves
and berries in heraldic colors of scarlet and green and gold.
The heirloom wedding carpet was put down, the slender birch
trees were placed on either side of the door and the room
decorated with flowers and fresh young boughs of fir. The
green aromatic branches of spruce were laid on the bottom
steps of the house. All morning the women had worked to
prepare for the wedding, which was held with the midday
sunshine streaming in at the windows on the grave faces of
bride and groom. Annikki wore Maia's wedding dress, altered
and lengthened and a little old-fashioned in cut, and a veil
held in place by twined myrtle leaves. "For faithfulness," Maia
said. "Everything has a meaning, girl, if you look for it."

Vainen wore a dark suit and fresh white shirt. The jacket

strained across his broad shoulders, for it was the one in which he had been married to Kirsti and it had lain for years in a chest. It was as good as new, and Vainen had seen no reason for not wearing it, but Maia thought it had a somewhat out-landish air.

I am being married at this moment, Annikki thought, but the actual fact of the pastor's words seemed less real than her own knowledge, in that stark moment of truth, that she and Vainen were already united. There stood Eino Salonen, spokes-man for the groom, and Ulla Hassi's eldest daughter, sixteen-year-old Iris, who was chief of her three bridesmaids and whom Annikki feared might prod her at any moment, so like her mother was she. Yet even they seemed to have no reality.

When it was over Annikki looked down at her mother's wedding ring on her finger. "What better could she have?" Maia had asked frugally. Moreover, she had been afraid lest Vainen forget to get a ring at all, so long had he lived out of the world and its ways.

"We did our best," Jussi said, when Vainen and Annikki were man and wife. "This has been taken out of our hands."

"But it's what the girl wants," Maia whispered doubtfully. Both of them in that moment were united by a strange emo-tion—doubt, helplessness, the sudden knowledge that they were old and the girl was young and that a world of feeling sepa-rated them both.

But Annikki's face was tranquil, Vainen's wore its habitual expression of grave reserve.

"They look as alike as two peas at this moment," Margit Salonen said. She had known quite well that in all likelihood her son Arvo and Annikki might have made a match of it in time. True, the girl showed little aptitude about the house, but that would have come with experience. She had, which pleased Margit, been born and brought up in a town. Arvo, with his restless, active mind would never have been content with a Porvesi girl, Iris Hassi, for instance, who was ripening fast. But it had not been intended, that was clear, and Margit had a placid faith in and ready acceptance of the workings of destiny. So she said generously now, "Yes, alike as two peas. This is a good marriage, there's no doubt of it. If you leave the young to find their own way, they'll find it, without help from any of us."

Tuomas Palin, the pastor, looked from bride to groom and made a speech, exhorting them to cleave one to the other, to attend church and to bring up children in the love and fear of God. The pastor added, "And bring them up to love and fear you, also, for that is the first step to loving and fearing God." For all his strictness Tuomas Palin was beloved. He was fifty now, unmarried, and lived alone in the vicarage, save for his elderly housekeeper. The vicarage stood close to the church, and around them both his entire life revolved. He kept a tight rein on the parish, his principles were simple and direct—love and fear wholesomely mingled, man's respect for himself begetting respect for his neighbor, and plenty of hard work. As for pleasure, that grew naturally out of such soil, said the pastor. The young people, however, were beginning to find their pleasures further afield. The lure of the towns made itself felt. Off they went, as far as Tampere, to work in one of the beautiful, smokeless factories and live in an apartment provided for them, and some had gone as far as Helsinki with its great granite buildings, its feeling of space and power, its sense of invisible gulls skimming the wind-swept streets. The pastor had been educated at the university in Turku and knew the ways of great cities, and knew that a man's four wooden walls and his own soil were his strength; and knew, also, that the hard core of the country was the men it bred on the small farms, men who worked and tilled and loved the soil, fought it with dogged pride and handed it down from father to son.

The marriage he had just solemnized had pleased the pastor. Vainen, with whom he had exchanged few words, was a man of the soil, rooted in it and in the integrity of his own being. The girl, at the crossroads of her life, had found an anchorage.

When he smiled at them both his stern, deep-set eyes softened, and the furrows which ran from nose to chin were momentarily lost.

He took his place at one of the long tables with Jussi and Maia and the bride and groom to enjoy the feast. The long bench on either side and that opposite was filled from end to end, as were those of the other tables. The children behaved decorously. They had bowed or curtsied to the pastor, their hosts, and the bride and groom, and, indeed, whenever spoken to by their elders. Their small heads bobbed like clover in the wind. Voices were quiet in a land of soft-spoken people. Later, conviviality would break through. Maia surveyed her tables with justifiable pride, each one with its good burden laid upon snowy cloths of her own weaving. She glanced at Annikki. The girl was composed and relaxed, mistress of herself, assured.

7

ERIK ROSE, grave-faced, to lead the dancing. He had not
danced for many years; not, he remembered, since he had
danced with Kirsti at their wedding.

All the events which had led to this wedding had seemed to
him necessary actions to be gone through, rituals in whose
exercise Maia would not be flouted. He had gone about his
days as before, while the echoes of Maia's activities reached
him from Porvesi. But they might have been the ripples left
by a wave breaking on an alien shore. The course of his life
had altered, but as far as he was concerned anything extrane-
ous to the central fact existed merely to be accepted, without
participation. Yet here he was, rising in the suit which
fretted his strong frame, his bride waiting for the embrace of
the dance.

He had never yet touched her. Yet now all Porvesi waited
and watched this first encircling of his arm, for by custom
none would dance until the bride and groom had danced
alone.

Smooth boards had been laid down in the hay barn by Jussi
and his neighbors and a village orchestra mustered. The
village did not exist which could not find its musicians, and

Porvesi could boast a dozen, if need be, who either had his own instrument or could play one. Now, under Jussi's leadership, the fast, gay rhythm of the *Zenka* echoed in the barn, spirited and tantalizing, beckoning and insistent, part waltz, part polka, a rhythm not to be denied.

Annikki went forward as gravely as her husband in the sudden silence of neighbors watching the two strangers among them, strangers united in a world of their own, each one, both man and woman, a little mysterious to the onlookers.

"The girl's a beauty," Jussi said softly. "I hadn't realized it." Elisabet Lahti took fat Lauri on her lap and thought of her youth when she was little older than the bride and had first seen Vainen and felt something stir in her that she had felt for no other man. She watched painfully while Vainen bent his grave glance on the bride.

"It is long since I danced," he said.

"The music will help us," Annikki whispered. She had romped to this music as a child. Now she was a woman, a bride, to dance before all Porvesi. She felt Vainen's arm tighten about her waist.

A tremor ran through Erik as he felt the yielding suppleness of the girl's body. Her breast swelled gently under the close-fitting dress and horror filled him suddenly at the memory of the gypsy's words. The candlelight, the voluptuous smile, the red whortleberries, and the blinding rage seemed to fuse under his hand, to become transmuted into the gentle curve of a breast.

"Come," whispered Annikki, her foot tapping softly. "Now."

The music took control, Erik's tense muscles relaxed, his body yielded to the dance and its imperative rhythm. The pastor watched approvingly, eyes followed the aloof yet committed figures, the insistent melody rose, the rafters rang.

"Vainen has forgotten nothing," Margit Salonen said approvingly. "Loneliness hasn't made a hermit of him."

"A man's world is in his mind," the pastor took the opportunity of reminding her. "And Vainen's world is not empty."

"However you like to put it," Margit said to Maia, "and I'm not one for fine words like the pastor, it's clear that Annikki knew what she was doing. Vainen cuts a fine figure, as strong as a man half his age, and handsome into the bargain. He'll be master of his own house, too, a man that a woman can depend on."

Margit was not alone in her admiration. Many of the women breathed unexpected little sighs of envy as Erik whirled his partner by. Something new had come into the raftered barn, where the music rang and feet tapped the smooth, new boards on the floor—a sense of something beyond the immediate sacrament, a sense of two human beings drawn irresistibly together, two beings dissimilar in age and experience, united by a gravity in which there seemed no hint of doubt and questioning, a sense, perhaps, of destiny.

"Old Heikki is in Byzantium," the pastor smiled, as if to break the spell. Old Heikki had wandered momentarily into his past, as he was wont to do, finding perhaps some sustenance there, gnarled hands folded in the sleeves of a nonexistent gown, eyes cast upon the ground, the rhythm of another chant sounding in his ears.

Ulla Hassi prodded him. "Old Heikki, it's the *Zenka*," she said. "You're not in church now."

"We danced the *Zenka* at our wedding," old Heikki mumbled to Fat Catherine.

"You'll dance it again when the bride and groom have finished," Ulla said. She prodded Fat Catherine. "You're as spry as any of us."

Old Heikki returned smartly to the present. "I need a woman with some flesh on her bones," he grumbled, "a woman I can hold, not a woman like a bird with legs like quills." Fat Catherine laughed contentedly. Old Heikki was himself again.

The dance ended. Jussi came to claim Annikki and now all but the pastor took the floor. The children danced as vigorously as their elders. Outside, the short afternoon was already waning. Erik crossed to Maia, towering over her, and bowed stiffly. He's a man who'll do what comes, Maia thought, like it well or ill. She took the floor with him and to her surprise found his dancing light and easy. She did not speak, neither did he.

"To tell the truth," she confided to Margit afterward, "it's well known that I'm a woman of few words. And he's a man of fewer."

"Annikki doesn't say much either," Margit observed.

"They've said all that's needful," Maia told her, with one of her rare smiles. But beneath the warmth and gaiety, the enjoyment and approval of her neighbors, the contentment of bride and groom, a doubt remained, unvoiced, in the shrewd recesses of Maia's mind. The words she had spoken to Jussi were forgotten, but their echo clung, faint, clear, above the music and the rhythm of the dance.

"I must go," Erik said simply. "There are animals to be fed before dark." The gravity of his expression softened. "You must feast without us, Maia. Now is the time for me to thank you and Jussi for all that you have done."

"Do well by the girl, Vainen," Maia said abruptly.

"I will do well by her," Erik said.

"Annikki, you must go where your husband goes," Jussi said regretfully. "But Maia has set her heart on a three-day celebration and there's food and drink to match it."

"You shall take some with you, Annikki," Maia promised, "when they load up your cart."

"The girl is not going empty-handed," Jussi said.

There were the sheets with their handmade lace. (I will never touch a crochet hook again, Annikki thought, remembering the long evenings and the lace which had seemed to grow so slowly.) There were her clothes, the grandfather clock and the young tortoise-shell cat, Silvi.

The dancing had stopped. This was farewell to the bride. Iris Hassi came out importantly with Silvi in her arms and handed her to Annikki, seated in the garlanded cart. Soon the sun would set but now the sky was filled with a pure, pale light, frail and melancholy above the dark pines. Harri Vasola, with his son Timo, carried out the grandfather clock which ticked and wheezed protestingly, and Timo handed Vainen the great key with which to wind it. Jussi's house beyond them was filled with light and music and voices wishing them good will. "I will come," Maia said hopefully, "to arrange the things in order in your house, Vainen."

"The girl will do it," Erik said.

At Maia's faint look of surprise he added, "My wife will do it."

Later, when the cart had driven away, Maia said to Jussi, "It is strange for a newly wed man not to speak his wife's name."

"Vainen is not like other men," Jussi said. "But you are becoming like other women." He gave her a sidelong smile. "I was proud of your reputation for silence, but now I think there will soon be a clatter-mouth in the house."

Meanwhile, the bustle of departure was in full swing as the villagers called their farewells. It was rare for them to address Vainen since they had respected his wish for silence and only such communication as politeness demanded. But, alone or in a crowd, Vainen was Vainen. His manner was as grave as formerly, his words as few as they had ever been.

The pastor went forward to make a short, farewell speech. Old Heikki came walking, as far as age and decrepitude would allow, like a young novice, his gaze humbly on the ground, but he raised his head to the couple in the cart.

"Beat her," he quavered to Vainen. "That's what I did to Fat Catherine, and neither of us ever regretted it."

It was to the accompaniment of Fat Catherine's high, tinkling laughter that Erik took up the reins and drove away. Annikki, the cat cradled in her arms, looked backwards at the house, the straggling street, the scattered farms, and wooden houses of Porvesi, but it was on the paddock, where Jussi's cows pastured, that her last glance lingered. It lay silent now and empty, a faint mist rising above it as the day waned. The forest was silent and dim beyond it and it was into the silence and dimness of the forest that the cart turned and was lost to view.

The first rays of the sunset fell on the red berries, the green boughs, which made a marriage bower of the cart. As they rode and the cart jolted here and there over a rough patch in the forest road some of the berries rolled to the ground or into Annikki's lap and she picked them up, one arm round the sleeping cat, and held them in her palm.

"They are poisonous berries," Erik said.

"But they are beautiful. You have no flowers in your house, Vainen. I'll put these in the blue bowl on your table."

> *And you shall see the red red blood*
> *That down My sides does roll*
> *And you shall see four cherubim*
> *That catch it in a bowl.*

The words came unbidden to Erik's mind. They were strange prayers, he thought, to have prayed at the burial of a man. His mother had sung them, but not at a burying. She had had a clear voice, a little plaintive. The words were to be sung at Christmas time, they were the words of an old carol, so old that nobody knew who had written them, she had said. Where had she learned them? "From my mother," she had told him.

Erik glanced at the girl. Kirsti had been fond of singing in the house as she went about her work, as his mother had been. But this girl understood silence. Silence had been his most precious possession. Soon, in part, he must surrender it.

The girl's cheek below his shoulder was smooth, with a pure, rounded curve, a flawless line that ran into a white, full throat. His own throat constricted. Was Kirsti looking down at them from some place beyond man's imagining, looking down at the girl so strangely come to take her place beside him at the hearth? Pity for the girl welled up in him. She

seemed to him like a small boat caught in the rapids when
there is no going back and the strong waters sweep it onward,
to toss like a cork or perish.

But the girl's face was tranquil. It is the peace of the ig-
norant, he thought. It is only later when time and experience
have done their work that she will look back at the road she
has trodden. He told himself that he felt no more for her than
for a child who had fallen and whom he had picked up and
comforted. When he remembered the suppleness of her body
beneath his hand it was with an unwilling sense of shame.
Against it he closed his mind and sealed away the memory;
as other memories had been sealed against the inroads of pain,
so this memory was sealed against shame. He would never
think of the girl's body without hearing the gypsy's voice.
It was as though the cruel lasciviousness of the gypsy had
communicated itself to him.

Now the light of the lanterns fixed on either side of the cart
began to illumine the way before them. Night was falling, the
light of the setting sun parting the sky with fingers of molten
gold. A faint breeze stirred the trees, the eyes of a wild creature gleamed in the light as they passed. The horse trotted
eagerly, every step a step toward the warmth and food and
friendly darkness of the byre. The soft pure air blowing over
field and forest smelled faintly of wood smoke, a distant echo
reminding them of the habitations of men. Here all was wild
and silent and free. Only the man and the girl were bound.

A man other than Erik might have broken this strange
silence. He might have asked the girl whether this strangeness
confused or saddened her, whether she would miss the life so
lately left behind. There had been people in that life, people
who, to the girl, were not moving figures on a tapestry as so
often they seemed to him. They were people, alive, differing,
old, young. Of them all he remembered most clearly the girl,
Iris Hassi, with her long, plaited fair hair, her slanting eyes
and high cheekbones like those of her mother, Ulla. But the
girl's face was bold, laughing, the eyes gazed inquisitively upon

the world, seeking experience. Surely Iris and the girl beside
him had laughed, talked, exchanged girlish confidences? But
Erik could ask none of these questions. Nor, strangely, did the
girl appear to expect them. She sat quietly, the berries in her
palm as—how long ago it seemed—she had held the crumbs
of rye bread for the gull. Yet, in that aromatic silence, as they
drove through the darkening night, Erik, his perceptions
heightened by solitude, sensed that the girl's silence was not
the silence of shyness or ignorance or the silence of the weak
depending upon the strong.

She was silent because she had chosen silence. The convic-
tion was borne in on him that the girl was, in her way, as
strong as he himself.

When they reached the farm and turned into the track
which led to the house, the dog came bounding to meet them
and barked frantically. The sound woke the cat, which arched
its back, its eyes glowing fearfully with reflected light from
the lanterns. The dog subsided at a word from Erik, who
dropped the reins and dismounted from the cart. He lifted
the box which contained Annikki's things and carried it toward the house. He did not touch or look at the girl. She
clambered from the cart, still holding the cat, which, safe in
her arms, hissed and spat at the dog leaping soundlessly below.

"You must learn to like Penna," Annikki said to the cat,
"or else you must go." She followed Erik into the house.

He turned in the living room to face her. "I have eaten and
drunk my fill today," he said, "but it may not be so with you.
I will bring in your things and feed the animals and if you
want to eat you can prepare food for yourself."

"There are the pies that Maia sent," Annikki reminded him.
"I will have some for supper."

The room was dim and Annikki took the matches from
their place and lighted the lamp. Her back was toward him
when Erik said, "We are man and wife in the eyes of men,
but whether we are so in the eyes of God is not for me to
answer."

"The pastor married us," Annikki replied, looking down at the ring on her finger. "I suppose God listens when the pastor speaks." There was a faint smile playing around her mouth.

"Be that as it may," Erik said, "you and I know what God knows and the pastor doesn't." He, too, smiled fleetingly. "So we will go on as we began. The big bed is yours and I will sleep as I slept before."

"It is for you to say, Vainen. I am your wife and I will do whatever you want."

"For one so young you are submissive. I remember what a will of her own Kirsti had." Erik paused, conscious all at once of a different quality in the silence between them.

"I will go where I am led," Annikki said evenly. "That is a wife's duty. But there is one thing, Vainen, that I would like to say." She turned and looked full at him. "Do not speak too often to me of Kirsti."

"I will remember," Erik said.

"And besides . . . I have a name, too, Vainen."

"I have not forgotten it," Erik said. He looked at her with grave kindness and then turned and left the room.

Annikki began to unpack the box in which Maia had put her clothes, the brooch and earrings of beaten silver which had belonged to her mother, and her mother's Bible. As Annikki moved her hands her wedding ring shone in the lamplight. Her mother's hands, toward the end, had grown so thin that the ring had slipped off continually and it had been given into Annikki's keeping. At the time she had grieved. Now she was glad to have this strong link between the old life and the new. The ring had long been sanctified. Now, she felt, it would sanctify a marriage whose mainspring had been the impulses of protection and pity. Annikki felt that such emotions were sacred and binding in themselves and she was quite sure that the pastor would have thought so also, had he known. Vainen, she knew, did not love her and perhaps never would. Inexperienced as she was, guileless and free of sophistry, yet her essential being had matured in a night. She knew that the strange ties which bound her to Vainen, the impulses which had brought about their marriage, would perhaps, in the end, prove stronger than love.

On the top of the box Maia had placed her wedding veil with the myrtle leaves, wrapped in soft paper and tied with ribbon. Annikki did not untie the ribbon. She carried the veil, still wrapped, together with her clothes, and put them in the cupboard in her room. She took off Maia's dress, and her expression softened. She had not wanted to wear the dress, fearing the comments of Iris Hassi or her friend Tyyne Savolainen, because of its cut, old-fashioned even by Porvesi standards and unthinkable by those of Turku. Now, as she unbuttoned it, Annikki regretted her own apparent unresponsiveness while Maia had pinned and sewed. This had been Maia's wedding dress. She had worn it first perhaps a quarter of a century ago—and how long ago that seemed! She had danced in it with Jussi at her wedding and thought of the daughter who would one day wear it and of all the happiness ahead. Yet, in the end, it had been worn by a girl who was a stranger to Maia, her husband's second cousin, whom she had not wanted and could not truly like. Maia was frugal, Annikki knew. But this gesture, she was sure, had been a generous one. She put soft paper between the folds of the dress and laid it carefully away.

8

IT SEEMED NOW to Annikki that she had never known another life but this. For a month she had lived the life of Vainen's wife. It was a life of freedom such as she had never known. True, there was work to be done, and work in plenty, and Annikki marveled that a man could keep a house as spotless as a woman could keep it. Erik had lived a life of order and routine, a routine which worked so faultlessly that he had almost forgotten that it existed, detached from, and in a way deadened by, it. The girl, he saw, was willing but inexperienced. As efficiently as, and much more quietly than, Maia would have done, he handed over to Annikki the tasks rightfully performed by a woman, so that Annikki now must scrub and bake, make cheese, clean the byre, sew and spin as other women did. But to Annikki there was no hardship in it. This well-built house was now hers, she had the freedom of it. She was its mistress, and when it shone and sparkled it did so for her. Every feminine instinct in her nature was given full rein. She bloomed and smiled and throve. Even her body filled out a little, she assumed the airs of a woman grown, little airs of authority and contentment which plucked at Erik's heart. Such little airs had Kirsti assumed in the early days of their marriage.

But this was not Kirsti. The memory of a woman's presence about the house had become a memory. Now, like the gypsy, Annikki was stirring within him the painful processes of living, forcing him to recall the soft tones of a woman's voice, the memory of smooth skin, the glint and fragrance of shining hair seen in the light of a doorway or, as now, caught in the midday sun, as Annikki lifted the peaked cover of the well and lowered the long dipper.

Erik, in those early days, would find himself caught by a turn of Annikki's head, the young chin tilted, so that the hand instinctively reached toward it; by the sight of soft lips parted in laughter sending the blood pounding strangely in his temples, strangely, because such feelings had long been strange to him. At the moment of pleasure—in bright hair, a head lifted on a white neck, a laughing mouth—Erik would recoil as though he had been stamped indelibly in the gypsy's wanton mold. It was a recoil which sprang from that deeply rooted trinity: revulsion, violence, death. As though his touch upon the girl must defile her, he pursued his life as though he were alone. Their hands did not meet except by accident. They talked, but it was gentle converse, and neither stepped across the barrier which gradually grew between them as the pattern of their lives together was formed.

It is better as it is, Erik would tell himself. The girl is happy and content. More and more he strove to turn his thoughts inward, to find that region of the mind, the heart of the whirlpool, the dark core of silence which Akseli had said was a man's soul.

If the girl noticed his slow withdrawal she gave no sign. Sometimes, in the evening, while she sat at the spinning wheel, her fingers less agile than Erik's, he would read aloud from the Bible or from one of the timeless stories of Kivi, and the characters would seem to take shape in the room. "They are more real when you read to me than they were at school," Annikki told him.

Occasionally the sound of the wheel would cease, and look-

ing up, Erik would see Annikki's gaze fixed on the listening
head of Kirsti, with the firelight glinting on the carved braids.
Without a word, at Erik's glance, she would return to her spinning. It was the only sign she ever gave of her knowledge that
life had had a past as well as a present. Of the future neither
of them appeared to think.

Unable to restrain her curiosity Maia drove over to visit
them one day. She found Annikki delving into the carved
box in the little room where, unknown to her, the gypsy had
slept.

Maia stepped across the threshold and took in at a glance
the girl's new air of maturity, of well-being. Annikki jumped
to her feet and a slow flush of pleasure tinged her cheeks.

"So you're glad to see me," Maia said, more pleased than
she would admit.

"Yes," Annikki admitted. "I am pleased, Maia."

"A woman needs a woman," Maia said. "We all find it out
in time. What are you doing with that box?"

"Looking, and I've found this." Annikki pointed to the
strange garments lying on the narrow bed.

"They are Lappish," Maia pronounced. "When Vainen and
Kirsti and the child came here they brought a Lapp with
them."

A faint shadow fell on Annikki's face which was not lost
on Maia. "You would have liked to be first here I don't doubt,
girl. To have it all your own. But nothing is our own in
this world."

"It is mine now," Annikki said. In the moment of saying
it Annikki knew that she loved Vainen. But what was love?
She was not sure. Of one thing only was she sure. That her
feeling toward Vainen was compounded of pleasure and pain.
It was the pain, she thought, that was the loving.

"Where is Vainen?" Maia asked.

"He is thinning out the trees on the other side."

"Alone?"

"Yes. He works alone as far as possible, as he has always done."

"Always since Kirsti died," Maia said. The girl is possessive, and possessiveness, she thought, is something to be rooted out of our natures as so much else has to be rooted out. Rooted out here, thinned out there, we poor humans can never be left in peace if we're to have peace hereafter. Aloud she said, "This is The Cap of the Four Winds," and picked up the cap from the bed. "They say that the Lapp, Akseli, had second sight. Vainen will tell you about him. He had strange lore, and a head full of old runes."

"Did you see him?"

"He sang his runes at Inger Vasola's wedding, I remember. They paid him in flax, which Kirsti spun."

Annikki sat back on her heels, listening intently. Vainen, in the evenings, would ask her to tell him of Turku, of the way young people lived nowadays, of the fine schools, the new apartment buildings, the concert hall, and the Chapel of the Resurrection, with its great wall of glass so that the trees and the green grass outside and the altar within seemed to blend one with another. "Like the ruined church," Annikki would say, "where you found me. But there was no glass there. The forest itself came into the church." Vainen would listen as intently as she listened now to this tale of Akseli. There was so much Vainen could tell her of his past. Anyone could go to Turku, perhaps she and Vainen would make the journey together. But only Vainen could take her with him on the journey into his past.

"So Vainen is good to you," Maia said, putting the cap back on the bed by the jacket with its beaded collar. "I can see that," she added. "But you must not let Vainen make you like himself."

"That wouldn't be a bad thing to be."

"It isn't good to be too much alone. There was a time

when Jussi said that Vainen would forget the power of speech."
Maia turned aside, in her impassive way. "You haven't offered
me coffee yet."

"I'm sorry, Maia."

"You're the mistress of the house. Don't forget it. And while
you brew the coffee I'll look around."

Annikki smiled with a touch of complacence as she heard
Maia's footsteps on the boards, the sound of cupboard doors
opening and closing, the lifting of wooden lids in the small
dairy. All was in order, as Maia would find. In the living
room the grandfather clock ticked drowsily, the room was
filled with pale sunshine, and in the distance could be heard
the faint echo of Vainen's ax striking rhythmically. Annikki
paused by the hearth where the kettle shone and looked at
Silvi asleep, her chin on neat paws. A consciousness of happiness filled her, a sense of possessing something complete and
whole in that one moment of time.

When Maia returned, the coffee was ready. "The first snow
came early," Maia said, sipping the coffee critically. "But,
even so, the rain will have brought out the last mushrooms in
the damp places in the woods. The women are making a
morning of it, hoping to find some. Bring your basket and
come with us."

Annikki looked down at her cup. She felt a strange reluctance to cast in her lot with the women, with the wives of
Porvesi. Things were moving too quickly for her. The women
lived a strong community life, mushrooming and berrying in
groups, going from one house to another to spin or help at
a wedding, a birth, or a death. With Maia's words the whole-
ness and completeness of the moment she had just experienced dissolved and was gone. Life was pressing in on her
and she was not yet ready. The fear which had been pushed
to the back of her mind ever since the gypsy had carried her
into the woods sprang sharply into being. The women's eyes
were as sharp as Maia's. If what she, Annikki, believed was
true, and feared to believe, the women would soon know. But

what they would not know was that it was not Vainen's child that she would eventually bear. When the day came they would come into her house, certainly Margit would come, and help with the birth. With a blind, unreasoning instinct Annikki asked for nothing more than to be left alone at Vainen. When she thought of the gypsy, his glittering eyes and predatory smile, it seemed to her impossible that he would not plant his image on her child. The pastor was strict. The women's code was rigid. How would she survive its condemnation?

She saw that Maia was now scrutinizing her. "It's too early to say, girl, but you look to me . . ." Maia leaned forward and lifted Annikki's chin to the light. "Vainen will be pleased. There's a child on the way, or I'm no judge."

"That," Annikki said wildly, in sudden panic, "is why Vainen married me."

"Of course it was," Maia said comfortably. "A man of Vainen's age doesn't fall in love like a boy. You had your reasons. He had his." She got up. "Ask Vainen for the cart and the horse and come to the woods in the morning."

"I must stay here. There is work to do."

"Do as you're bid," said Maia shortly. "You're beginning the wrong way. Women need women, as I've told you."

Maia climbed into her cart and picked up the reins, her duty done. Annikki stood at the gate but there was no sign of her husband, whose ax blows still rang on the still air.

"I will tell Vainen you have been," she said.

"You call him Vainen, like the rest of the world," Maia observed thoughtfully.

"I have only known him as Vainen."

Maia did not reply for a moment. When she spoke it was of other matters. "Next year this road will be on the bus route. I shall not be sorry. This old horse gets more stubborn every day."

"What has happened to the gypsy's horse?" Annikki asked suddenly.

"It's still with us. Nobody has claimed it. Jussi can't turn it loose at this time of year."

"So he'll keep it? I mean, it will be his?"

"Why not? It came to us, didn't it? Jussi has done what he can to find its owner."

"Perhaps, if you turned it into the forest, it would find its way home," Annikki said. The thought of the gypsy's horse so near carried with it a vague menace.

"So you would turn a dumb animal loose in the forest? To starve? Or perish of cold?" Maia's shrewd eyes narrowed. "That was a thoughtless remark," she said slowly. "A thoughtless remark."

"Yes. I didn't think. Only . . . the horse seemed so fierce," Annikki faltered.

"It's as quiet as a lamb and works beside this one. Remember then, tomorrow. Vainen can have mushrooms fried in butter for his supper."

Annikki returned to the house, her feet feeling leaden. Maia had confirmed what she, also, had feared and subconsciously known. Little escaped the women, Annikki knew. Their lives were lived close to the essentials of life, to birth, to death; they sensed alike when the west wind would blow or the imperceptible changes in a woman's face. Tomorrow she would be one of them, a wife gathering mushrooms, and all of them would know that Vainen was hoping for a son.

Tonight she must tell Vainen.

"A son is a son," Vainen said, when she told him. "But are you sure? It's scarcely two months."

"I've been sure for some weeks. And there's no deceiving Maia about such things."

"You are my wife. We married for this," Vainen reminded her.

"But if the child looks like the gypsy?"

"He may also look like you. You are a wife. What have you to fear?"

"I hate this child growing in my body!" Annikki cried.

"That is something I cannot help," Vainen said gently.

Annikki rose suddenly from her seat by the fire and went swiftly to Erik and clung to him. At the contact of her body she felt him stiffen. But Erik's voice was even and kind when he spoke. "Things are as they were. How can you change them now?"

"Things are not as they were."

"They are exactly the same. From the beginning you were sure that you would have a child. It seems you are right. But you are now my wife. All is well. Nothing has changed." He pushed her gently from him.

"I have changed," said Annikki. She walked from him to the uncurtained window and looked out into the night. There was a faint moon and the sky was heavy with stars. Beyond, in the soft darkness, stood the trees, the birches glimmering palely, the jet-dark glitter of the lake visible between their trunks. The *sauna* was in shadow, hidden from her by the angle of the house. Annikki shivered. She had been going to say, I have changed. I have changed because I love you, Vainen. She wanted his arms about her, his words of comfort in her ears. But the soft, mysterious night, the unseen *sauna* hid secrets more potent than her own. For her sake Vainen had violated his inmost being, as she had been violated. He had killed a man. This he had done for her. Could she expect love also?

Penna rose from his seat by Erik's chair and came toward her and looked up into her face. The dog had become Annikki's shadow, as he had been Vainen's. For her sake he had even accepted Silvi who, after the manner of cats, had found the warmest seat by the hearth and gave allegiance to no one.

"How have you changed?" Erik asked.

Annikki turned to face him. He had killed a man for her, but would it avail anything if she told him that she knew it? If she cried, I love you. I love you, Vainen? Instead Annikki said, "Once I thought that to be safe here would be enough.

I am safe. And now, safety isn't enough. I hate what lies ahead.
I want to be free of this burden. I want to be free. I want
freedom," she cried.

"Freedom?"

"I suppose I want the impossible. I want to keep all that
I have—without the price."

"You aren't alone in that," Vainen said. "It is the cry of all
mankind." He smiled. "But you are growing up fast. Those
were the words of a woman."

"Yes," Annikki said. "I am a woman." She came back into
the room and stood opposite him. Vainen put out his hand
and rested it lightly on her shoulder, firm and slim beneath
her woolen blouse. Annikki trembled. In the lamplight her
skin gleamed white where her blouse opened at the throat.
Erik dropped his hand.

"There is no such thing as freedom," he said.

"Men die for it. Our countrymen have fought and died
for it for a thousand years," Annikki said. "That is what I
learned at school."

"I have learned things since I left school," Erik told her.
He walked away from her and picked up the wood he had
been carving when she had told him about the child.

He worked in silence for some moments.

He worked slowly and deliberately at the wood, gouging
cleanly, till his pulses had stopped hammering and his hand
was steady and he no longer saw the white skin beneath the
blouse.

"Freedom," he said, "is emerging from a little prison into
a bigger one."

He had not seen her body. Let the future bring what it
would, he knew he could not look on that ripening body. On
sauna night they took their baths separately, Annikki going
first. One day she had found a feather in the *sauna*, a hen's
feather, golden-brown and flecked with red. It had trembled

in her hands as though it were the scarlet and gold leaf of the aspen tree when the tree is touched by the wind.

"How did it get here?" she had asked, her face pale suddenly.

Erik had looked at her curiously.

"It has blown in from a molting hen. How else?"

Annikki had laughed. "I shall laugh at myself," she had said, "before you laugh at me, Vainen. In the fairy stories I read as a child there was one which frightened me. An evil witch brought a feather to a prince. He had to guess where it came from or be changed into a toad." She had tossed the feather into the air and puffed it away, her young mouth round and red. At the back of her mind she had felt the fluttering of knowledge and fear, remote, soundless, as a feather falling into a gulf.

It is this child in my body, she thought, which is making me fanciful.

While she was in the *sauna* Erik would work at his carving. The figure was taking shape and form, springing into being with a vibrant life of its own. Almost with surprise Erik recognized the figure. It was that of the gypsy.

9

ERIK THOUGHT it was too late for mushrooms but Maia
had said that the recent rainfall would bring out the last
before winter. Mushrooms were a delicacy which the women
prized, especially the small, light brown mushrooms which
were usually plentiful. "It is right for you to join the other
women," Erik told Annikki. "You are a wife now and will be
a mother and you can talk women's talk with them."

Annikki had looked at him steadily. "You speak as though
all is well," she said.

"All is well."

She knew that he was right. To believe that all was well, to
know it, was the only way now in which she could live. But
Erik was not a woman and he did not know how women
thought and felt. Stirrings of an entirely feminine nature,
little, unexpected barbs of jealousy, pricked Annikki. The
carved head of Kirsti drew her eyes more often. The face was
a beautiful face, soft, yet aware. It was true, as Erik had once
said, that the expression was that of one listening. "It was
characteristic of Kirsti," he had told her. In the beginning
Annikki had said, "Do not speak to me too often of Kirsti,"
but now it was she, Annikki, who mentioned Kirsti's name.

Kirsti had died in childbirth, but in her life she had been a woman without fear, a woman fruitful and loved. Why should my life be different? Annikki wondered. Why? Sometimes, when Kirsti's eyes seemed to follow her about the room, Annikki felt that there was urgent life behind the carved face, an awareness of an alien presence in the room. I am the stranger, Annikki would think. I am the interloper.

Annikki's perceptions sharpened, grew more subtle. She found that she was more attuned to Erik's moods as the days went by, sensitive to his reactions, aware that, in him, silence was often more significant than speech. Love made her a willing pupil. She began, unconsciously, to adapt herself to him. The ties which bound them were tightening. Perhaps, Annikki thought, they are another kind of love.

Till the gypsy had touched her, had savaged her mouth with his, she had never known the kiss of a man. A boy's kiss, a swift glance, the shy meeting of hands had been all her experience. I am a stranger to the things women know, she thought, but they will expect me to know everything. It was like setting foot in an unknown part of the forest.

Erik drove her in the cart to the meeting place beyond Porvesi where the women waited in Jussi's cart, to which the gypsy's horse had been harnessed. Annikki climbed down and went toward the women while Erik, with a grave wave of the hand, jerked at the reins and turned his horse in the direction from which he had come.

"A man is no good among a tribe of women." Ulla Hassi smiled. "He grows smaller."

"But put a woman down among a pack of men," said Maia, "and watch her blossom. Have you brought your basket, girl?"

They were all watching her with a curious, yet friendly interest, a crowd of faces among which Annikki saw the familiar ones, Margit's and Ulla's, Elisabet's, Pia Vasola's, her daughter-in-law Inger's, and that of Rauha Savolainen, Tyyne's mother. The rest were faces which had come and gone in those quiet, yet bewildering days when she had first come to Porvesi.

"We'll each make our own way into the forest," Maia said, "and when we've filled our baskets we'll meet here, by the cart!"

"We must go in different directions," Elisabet insisted. "You'll need a full basket, Annikki, or it won't be worth salting them for the winter. That's the best path to take—over there."

The women, in their gay head scarfs, turned to follow Elisabet's pointing finger. Annikki saw ahead of her the dark recesses of the forest and suddenly revulsion filled her.

"No," she said. "I can't."

"You can't?" Maia's voice was sharp.

"I'm afraid of losing my way."

"Keep to the path," Elisabet said. "Mark it and remember it. A fine wife for Vainen, you are. A town girl, afraid of the woods."

Annikki's face had paled. Memory surged over her. It seemed impossible to her that she could not cry out to these friendly, curious, amused faces of the fears which the sight of the dark forest conjured up.

Maia said more sharply, "There's no place for city ways here, girl. She's pregnant, that's clear," she told the women, "but there's no time for fads and fancies in Porvesi. Elisabet is showing you the best place. Take your basket and go."

The fear in the girl's eyes was real, Maia saw. Something stirred again in the back of her mind a question, scarcely formulated, to which there was no answer. Her voice shook with impatience pricked by unease. "You must forget your town ways here," she said again.

"The girl is young," Margit pleaded. "And now you mention it, Maia . . . yes, early as it is, I can see for myself."

"Is Vainen pleased?" Elisabet asked curiously.

"Of course," Annikki said. "Of course my husband is pleased." She turned away from their kind, inquisitive faces and stroked the horse's head. It stood submissively under her hand. The white star on its forehead was perfectly marked and every hair of its mane seemed to glisten separately in the pale morning sunlight.

"How beautiful you are," Annikki said softly and laid her cheek close to the velvety one of the horse. "How beautiful and gentle."

"He eats out of our hands," Maia said proudly. "Jussi will find it a wrench to give him up if ever he is claimed."

"It will be by someone from a long way off," Margit affirmed. "Gypsies wander far and wide and who can say where the horse came from?"

"Jussi thinks he was stolen. That's why the gypsy abandoned him," Maia said.

Annikki stood with the velvet cheek against hers, the horse's sweet breath fanning her forehead. It was a moment of gentleness and peace, and watching her, some of Maia's asperity melted away.

"Come now, Annikki, mushrooming is pleasure, not work. Afterwards we'll have a picnic—the last of the year—and we'll have it in the cart." She looked in at Inger's youngest, sleeping soundly. "Cheer up, girl."

"The young girls nowadays don't know how to enjoy themselves," Margit smiled. "When I was Annikki's age I remember what a day's outing meant. No mushrooms without rain, we'd say, and we'd watch the sky eagerly, and then the rain would come at last and off we'd go. How we gossiped over our picnic! Six months talking done in a day."

"Which is about the size of it now," said Rauha slyly. "But it's true. To come suddenly upon a cluster of mushrooms, and hear the brooks running, and see the birches standing gold and all the colors of the forest—that isn't enough to make young people happy any more."

I was happy, Annikki thought.

"Time to go," said Ulla, prodding Maia, a prod to a word.

Unfocused exasperation and unease found its release now in Maia. "Ulla, do you prod Matti like that?" she cried. "I've often wondered. And if so, does he prod you back?"

"Do I what?" Ulla asked, mystified.

"Prod! Prod! Stab him in the chest with every word you utter!"

"Not that I know of," Ulla said reasonably. She looked from one woman to another and shrugged in bewilderment. "Come, Annikki," she said, and prodded twice.

Elisabet giggled. "We'll go together," she said to Annikki. "I always know where the best mushrooms are."

The short spell of unseasonable warmth and rain after the brief snow had done their work and mushrooms were to be found in scattered clusters. Here, with Elisabet chattering by her side, this was a forest without terror, Annikki felt. Elisabet's eyes shone with curiosity as she cast sidelong glances at Annikki. Elisabet's life, like many of the women's, had been narrowed down by circumstance. She had been a growing girl during the Winter War and the war which followed it and could remember how cruelly hard life had been and how often she had been hungry. There had been many days when bread itself had been a luxury. But she had managed to learn something and grow up and marry Veijo Lahti, who was a good husband, and bear three sons, of whom fat little Lauri was the youngest. But she had never forgotten the day on which she had first seen Vainen, tall and proud and handsome, and from that day he had occupied the sort of place in her mind that a great actor or a singer or a film star might have. Life for Elisabet had been a simple one: enough work, enough food, enough sleep, and good Veijo beside her. But there was a little oasis of her mind which Vainen inhabited. It had not mattered to her that Vainen was married. Kirsti had been a remote figure who had died and soon was lost to memory.

But here, beside her, was the girl whom Vainen now held in his arms.

"What is it like at Vainen?" she asked. What she really meant was: What is it like to lie beside Vainen? An impossible vision took possession of her. She stood with the mushrooms in clusters at her feet, the sunshine filtering through the trees on her face, with its expression of dreamy sensuousness.

"The house is well furnished," Annikki said. "Vainen made everything that is in it. In my bedroom the tiles on the stove are of porcelain, painted with little pictures. There is a bookcase full of books and beautiful carvings." Annikki's face was filled with pride as she recounted her possessions.

"I should think it is as good a house as the pastor's," Elisabet said admiringly. "One of his rooms is filled with books and he has a huge sofa and chairs stuffed with horsehair. If you sit on the chairs they prick your legs, but of course all the furniture is valuable, it belonged to his grandparents."

"Many people don't like such old furniture any more," Annikki said. "They sell things that are much older than the pastor's sofa to people in towns who want them for their country cottages. But I shall never sell my grandfather clock." As she talked Annikki felt all the pride of the housewife, the thrill of her status as a married woman.

"Is it true, what Maia said, that you are going to have a child already?"

"I thought so myself and I feel sure Maia knows about such things."

"She looks right through you with those eyes of hers. But a woman can always tell, I know I could," Elisabet said. "And what's more, I didn't have the doctor for any of my three children. Margit Salonen came to help me. She is the one who helps us all unless anything is wrong and it had better not be, especially with the nearest hospital in Vituri. And the doctor is busy. He expects us to go to him, when it's necessary."

"I'll go to him, then," Annikki said, "but it won't be necessary. I'm healthy and strong." At all costs, she thought, Margit Salonen should not come. Suppose she, Annikki, cried out in her pain, said things which must never be said! She would have the child alone, in the *sauna*, as Kirsti had done. Pain caught at her heart at the thought. Perhaps Vainen would be beside her as he had been beside Kirsti . . . to deliver another man's child.

"But Vainen will be with you," Elisabet said. She saw Annikki's face, white and stricken, below her own, looking up from the damp space between the trees, where the mushrooms grew. "But it's nothing to be frightened of," she cried in surprise. "I'll come and visit you at Vainen every now and then. I'd love to see the house. Besides, you'll need company. I'll bring little Lauri," Elisabet finished eagerly. She would see Vainen's house, touch the things he had made, sit in his chair by the hearth. Elisabet's heart beat faster. She could almost hate the girl who had all these things, who had Vainen's love, Vainen's child, and who seemed unable to rejoice at her good fortune.

They picked in silence for a while, wandering first down one path, then another, their voices echoing through the cathedral-like glades, between the darkness of spruce and pine, the black and silver of naked birches whose leaves had fallen with the first snow. Elisabet thought of Veijo and his goodness, a man like other men, who accepted life as it came, who knew that what must be, must be, as she, Elisabet knew. But sometimes in her dreams, she saw Vainen, a dream Vainen, stronger than other men, more powerful. It had, in a way, seemed right that Vainen should come out of his solitude, silently, to take a wife. "Yes, I will come and see you at Vainen," Elisabet said again, and the thought brought a ripple of pleasure and excitement with it.

They could hear the voices of the other women. They had walked in a circle, Annikki saw, and here they were back on the edge of the woods again. Her basket was full, as was Elisabet's.

Afterwards, they sat in the cart, for the grass was cold and damp, and ate the food to which all the women, except Annikki in her forgetfulness, had contributed. They talked of the activities ahead, the play that was to be produced, the singing at the pastor's house, the dancing for the young ones. "It's

a good life we live here," Maia said, and she glanced at
Annikki reflectively. Perhaps, if the girl had waited . . . had
looked about her a little longer . . . Yet something strong and
real seemed to have brought Anikki and Vainen together,
some emotion out of the ordinary, it was clear to see when
they had danced together. The girl puzzles me, Maia thought,
and always will.

Annikki gave no sign when Margit said, "Arvo will be home
for Christmas. He asked after you, Annikki. I wrote and told
him you had married Vainen. Now nobody can say that
nothing ever happens in Porvesi, I told him."

The women talked quietly, without gestures, of their fami-
lies, of the weaving classes to be started in Margit's kitchen,
where Maia's loom waited to be set up, together with others.
"Iris and Tyyne and the other girls growing up must learn to
weave, as their parents did," Margit said. Between them,
Margit and Maia, who had known how to spin and weave
from childhood, would teach the girls. Of politics, strikes, of
the changing figures on the chessboards of East and West beyond their borders, their men might talk. Here, felt, if un-
spoken, was the knowledge of the true life, rooted, enduring,
for which a man fought in his way, a woman in hers. Their
talk expressed life's strength and continuity as the forests and
the rocks expressed it, as the strong, weather-beaten faces of
their men expressed it.

Annikki sat silent and listened. She knew, now, what Vainen
had meant when he had said, "You are a wife now and will
be a mother and you can talk women's talk with them."
Women's talk was of everyday things but those everyday things
had indomitable roots: they were set deeply into the soil of
the past, they were the roots, also, of the present and the
future.

"You are one of us now, Annikki," Inger Vasola said,
echoing the girl's thoughts. "I married young as you have, and
I have never regretted it." She was nursing her last born, Eliel,
her face filled with contentment. Annikki looked at her face

and at the faces of the other women. What would they say if, suddenly, she asked for their compassion? "The laws by which you live are broken, but I did not break them," she wanted to say. She longed to throw herself on their mercy, to find ease in telling the secret which weighed so heavily on her. But she was afraid to utter the words, lest these rugged, gentle faces harden into censure. Yet Porvesi was not as strict as some villages where they did not even dance; there were dancing, and gaiety, they had said so. But the courage to speak would not come. She smiled at Inger but . . . I am not one of you, Annikki thought.

10

THE DOORS OF VAINEN had opened to admit more than Annikki. They had opened to admit the world, Erik said. The pastor came in his car, one of two in the village, Harri Vasola owning the other, to speak with Vainen.

Tuomas Palin's eyes rested with pleasure on the books on the shelves. "We have wasted time, Vainen," he said. "You and I are men who could have had many a good talk together."

"You have come to talk now," Vainen said.

Annikki was in the tiny dairy scouring out a churn, for Erik sold most of his small supply of milk to the co-operative dairy, keeping enough for household needs and for making the local cheese which Maia had already taught Annikki to make. The sounds of the house were the busy sounds of a normal household. Breakfast was over and Erik had been about to leave for the forest. Between them, he and Anikki had tended the animals, working side by side as he and Kirsti had worked. Time was lapping as gently as the ripples of a quiet lake against their lives, so that day flowed into day and sometimes Erik forgot that it was not Kirsti beside him.

But it was not Kirsti. The two women stood out sharp and clear in his mind. Erik knew this, and because two people

who live together have a heightened perception of one another, he knew that Annikki knew it also.

"Yes," Tuomas Palin said, "I have come to talk now. I
want you and Annikki to take part in the play this winter.
Harri Vasola is producing it. Jussi is painting the scenery.
Eino Salonen and Margit and the rest will be acting. We
have an orchestra, it is the same as always, but this year I want
to see one change. You, Vainen, must join. We need a man
like you—it is a Russian play of the nineteenth century, it was
decided on at the last meeting and," the pastor finished, "all
present said that you were the man for the lead."

"I have never played a part," Vainen said.

"Then it is time to begin. You owe it to your young wife.
All girls love to act and Annikki is the prettiest girl hereabouts. What do you say?"

"I have no knowledge of such things."

"Who has? You have lived quietly, as a man may if he
chooses, but if you had not you would have seen how my
housekeeper played last year. Hilkka can barely read, but she
acted in a play by Ibsen last year like a great tragedienne.
I have never seen gestures more noble or witnessed such
depth of feeling—but she was ready the next morning with
my gruel in one hand and a good clout with the other for
the lad who let the pigs into my clover field. We can all act,
man, given the chance."

"The girl shall decide," Erik said.

"As for old Heikki," the pastor continued, "get him in the
mood and the part, and he can pull a longer face than I can
and sing through his nose as holy as holy."

"Let the girl decide."

"From the sound of it she's in the dairy."

"Call her. Let her decide," Erik repeated. He felt his own
separateness being drawn out of his vitals like the tenuous
thread of silk from a spider's body, a fragile thread which
could not hang in mid-air but would attach itself to the world
which was Porvesi. He felt the tug already, as though it were

physical, and recoiled inwardly. But his face remained calm.

"Annikki," the pastor called.

Annikki came out of the dairy, wiping her hands, and curtsied to the pastor.

"I tell your husband that you should both act in the play this winter. He says it is for you to decide."

"Act in the play? But I'm not good at those things, or at books and remembering. I only finished middle school and got my fifth year certificate."

"And what has all that to do with acting in a play? The words will almost come of themselves, and you can dress up and laugh and cry to your heart's content." The pastor thought that it was not without reason that his quiet country-men, whose emotions lay deep, had a passion for strong, dramatic roles which, perhaps, expressed knowledge of a depth of violence or pity or grief which their tongues would never have uttered.

Annikki had barely left school. To obey those in authority was natural to her, though Vainen, she was sure, was against this project. The pastor waited. His face, Annikki thought, looked as though it had been hewn out of rock and his deep-set eyes were the color of rock pools. Vainen had asked her to decide but the pastor already knew what her answer would be.

"I will if . . . if my husband will."

"You see, Vainen? There's the answer. Harri Vasola has called a meeting for Saturday afternoon in the parish hall. He will decide who shall play the parts and he knows how to produce. Two or three years ago a professional producer visited Porvesi and gave a short course in producing. You heard about that, I expect?"

"No," Erik said. "I have heard little of what went on in Porvesi."

"Why, the state pays such men—and they are very few—who can travel the country and help those who want to learn. The Salonens' daughter, Meri, took the course before she went to Helsinki. And there were others, too."

"That is settled then," Erik said, "and I must go about my work."

The pastor reached for his hat, not at all put out by Erik's forthrightness. He would have used the same himself. "I will tell Harri Vasola," he said.

"I am sorry, Vainen," Annikki said when the pastor had gone, "but I didn't like to disobey him."

"It is your life," Erik said, "that must be lived. And I told you once—we must run with the wind if you are to find the right path." He turned to leave the house when there was the sound of brakes outside and the pastor appeared once more on the path.

"I forgot to tell you, Vainen," he cried, "about the church in the forest. They say it was you who kept a path clear to it?"

"That is true."

"It seems that young Arvo Salonen found the church by accident before he went to sea and told others and now someone is coming from Helsinki, from the National Museum, to look at the murals. They are real treasures—I've been to see them myself—they're obviously of great historic value and will be taken back to the Museum. We've been neglectful here of such riches but to tell the truth I always thought the stories of the old church were exaggerated. I thought that there was nothing more than broken walls and a rotting pillar or so."

"There was more," Erik asid quietly and he felt as though he were falling through a void. So much of himself seemed to have been left in the ruined church. He did not look at Annikki nor she at him.

"The experts say it was once a Byzantine monastery."

"Old Akseli said there had once been a community of monks there."

"Old Akseli? The Lapp? He'd heard some tale, some story handed down, I don't doubt," the pastor said shortly. Tuomas Palin believed that what was decreed by God that a man should see would be put there by Him straight in front of his two eyes. "However, I thought you'd like to know about the church, Vainen," he continued. "People say that if it hadn't been for you the place would have been in ruins long ago. That you cut down trees which threatened it, spent months clearing out the rotting undergrowth of years. You're a dogged man, Vainen."

"So is one sheep like another. I have no more than my share of doggedness."

"We take for granted what lies under our noses here. But you can be sure that the experts in Helsinki will be interested in what you have to say."

"Then you must say it for me. The church belongs to the forest and what's left of it will go to Helsinki. Good day."

"Good day to you, Vainen. Come to my house one night for coffee and bring Annikki with you."

As though emboldened by the pastor's visit—for nothing which occurred in Porvesi went unremarked—Elisabet Lahti set off for Vainen with Lauri in the cart beside her. She would stop on the way back at a point where Veijo waited to load the cart with wood for the return journey. Even the shorter forest road seemed to Elisabet interminable and Lauri was sound asleep long before the outbuildings of Vainen came in sight and the house itself, looking as though it had always been part of the landscape. A tremor of excitement filled Elisabet as Annikki came out of the house to greet her. Something of the silence which seemed to surround the house had touched Annikki's face.

Elisabet was used to silence, the silence of forest and lake, the silence of great expanses where nothing seemed to stir and the eye might rest in peace on a landscape in which the distant roar of a rapid or the sound of a running brook made silence more profound. But this house and Annikki's face alike seemed to possess a strange, inner quality of silence.

"You've come a long way." Annikki smiled, lifting the sleeping Lauri from the cart. "There is coffee ready and I have baked a pie." Silvi came sedately out of the house to gaze at the newcomers. The cat's eyes shone pale-gold as she turned her head and walked purposefully to the workshed, where good hunting was to be found. Lauri, awake now, struggled from Annikki's arms till she set him down and he went off in pursuit of the cat, disappearing after her into the workshed.

"There are saws and knives in there," Annikki said. "Lauri might cut himself." She hurried after the child and presently, after securing the horse, Elisabet followed her.

Inside the shed Lauri had forgotten Silvi, who was seated gazing at a small hole in the corner with the immobility of gaze which suggested that there was all eternity in which to wait. Lauri had found a little pile of wooden pegs and manikins and was holding one of the small figures in a clenched fist.

"Come, Lauri," Annikki invited, and the child left the toys and came toward her on legs so fat that they bulged over his little laced boots.

"Why!" Elisabet cried. "Did you ever see such a pile of toys! And the pegs are strong and well made." She looked at Annikki eagerly. "The gypsy must have made these, the gypsy who passed by Vainen and gave Jussi and Maia the message. Did he, Annikki? Did the gypsy make these pegs and toys? I've often bought such things at a fair. Is Vainen going to sell them? Or did the gypsy just forget them and leave them behind?"

Annikki shrugged. "Vainen must have bought them. It's hard to refuse a gypsy anything."

"It's better not to. Though I don't believe in such nonsense I've heard that if they take a dislike to you they'll steal something or put the evil eye on your cattle. Still, fancy. Vainen buying such a pile of toys. Aren't they funny little things! Look, here's one exactly like old Heikki, and here's a young one with a knowing eye. Look, Lauri, yours has a little cap on his head and a beard."

Elisabet pushed her son ahead of her as she talked, even

so small an incident filling her with pleasurable excitement. With Veijo out most of the day and without much to say when he was not, Elisabet reveled in a listener like Annikki. For Annikki seemed to Elisabet to be giving her whole attention to what was said, fixing her with her wide blue eyes, whose gravity reminded Elisabet a little of Vainen's.

When they reached the house Lauri still clutched his toy, nor would he be parted from it when the time came to leave.

When Erik came in later he saw the two women at the hearth and the child playing at their feet and the years were wiped out suddenly. It was Kirsti whom he saw busy with her needle while she gossiped and the child played, and pain touched him with a sense of irreparable loss. Yet even as he stood there, anguished, another emotion clutched at him with Judas fingers. His eyes followed the young curve of Annikki's throat and breast, and her sudden laughter sent the hot blood rushing through his body. He knew that he wanted her and the knowledge shamed him, it made him one with the gypsy whose seed Annikki was certain she bore. Even as desire and revulsion fought within him Erik glanced at the child on the floor and at the manikin in his hand.

Annikki turned her head to the silent figure in the doorway.

"Here's Elisabet come to see me, Vainen."

Erik made a stiff little bow to Elisabet.

"The boy grows well," he said, his unwilling gaze on the toy in Lauri's hand.

"He'll be three this Christmas," Elisabet said proudly. Her gaze drank in greedily Vainen's broad shoulders, the strong and handsome lines of his face. Lauri scrambled to his feet and ran to Erik and held the toy out to him.

"He found it in the workshed," Elisabet said, and laughed when Lauri drew back and ran away, clutching the toy when Erik would have taken it from him.

"Let him keep it," Erik said as he went to the dairy, leaving the two women to their chatter.

When Elisabet had gone, Annikki went to the shed and gathered up the little pile of manikins. She put them into an old box made of birch bark which she had found in her room. When Erik went into the workshed later to fetch a saw he saw that the toys were gone as though they had never been. He said nothing and neither did Annikki.

The days grew colder, and shortened rapidly toward Christmas, while Porvesi hummed with activity. In Margit's kitchen, which was bigger than Maia's, women and girls congregated, not to chatter but to learn. Together Margit and Maia began their weaving classes, stoutly keeping alive the arts to which they had been born, using looms which had been used by their grandmothers. Katri Niemi, who lived on the most outlying small farm, had risen at dawn, performed her many chores about the farm, and walked through the forest to the Salonen kitchen. Her rosy cheeks were firm and round, her gaze intent, as she followed the intricacies of the loom under Maia's guidance. Maia, watching the girl, could not rid herself of a faint unease. Katri was the same age as Annikki, and thoughts of Annikki were vaguely disturbing. Maia, whose thoughts were usually ordered, whose decisions were clear-cut, found herself a prey to imaginings, to wanderings of the mind which, if she had observed them in Annikki, would have brought down a sharp reproof.

Now, watching Katri's eager but awkward fingers, Maia found her thoughts wandering again. The previous day she had visited Elisabet Lahti and noticed little Lauri's absorption in his new toy. "It came from Vainen," Elisabet had said, aware that to have visited Vainen was in itself something of an achievement. "There was a whole pile of them there which Vainen bought from the gypsy." Elisabet had laughed. "Imagine Vainen buying them! He must have been thinking of his marriage, and children, when he bought the gypsy's store."

Why not? Maia had thought. It was simple enough, surely.

But somewhere there was something which was not simple.
There was still some question undefined, unformulated, at the
back of her mind. Above the hum in Margit's kitchen, Maia
wrestled with the sense of unease foreign to her nature. There
was some memory connected with the gypsy which she could
not grasp, an emotion which eluded her, so transiently had it
touched her at the time.

"Good. That's better, Katri," Maia said abruptly, and suddenly the nature of that elusive emotion was crystal clear. It
had been fear that she had felt, a creeping fear stifled as soon
as recognized.

She could see the gypsy now as he had stood before her and
Jussi, swinging the hen by one claw. Their eyes had met, hers
and the gypsy's, and for an instant Maia had seen fear in his
eyes, a sudden fear which had leapt out and in the same
instant been veiled by a sly smile. But that stark fear had
communicated itself to Maia. The girl. What had happened
to the girl? The gypsy knew more than he would tell. But, almost immediately, the relief which she had longed to feel
overrode her fear. "The girl is safe with Vainen," the gypsy
had said. "His message is that no harm has befallen her."

Vainen's word was the word of a true man, Maia knew.
That moment of fear had touched her and was gone. But,
irrationally, it had sprung to life again at the sight of little
Lauri's toy.

Jussi would laugh at her if he knew, Maia thought, for
Jussi had said that she, Maia, had changed since the girl had
come. Well, thought Maia, now she has gone and she is Vain-
en's business, not mine.

It was easy enough to dismiss something which one understood. Even the worst fears, the starkest hardships, could be
accepted when they were known. How many times in a lifetime had one said: *We know what will happen. What is the
good of worrying? It will happen. We say nothing.* Acceptance
of hard fact was simple. It was a way of life. But the uncer-

tainty which nagged at Maia's mind now was not simple because it was nebulous, a fear not understood, a premonition without foundation, a foreboding without basis in fact.

Small wonder was it that Jussi, troubled by Maia's changing moods, cried, "God preserve us from a wedding every year! Getting the girl off your hands was worse than uprooting the great granite boulder in the garden! You had many a twinge of rheumatism over that, woman, but better any day to my mind than twinges of temper."

11

THE HEAVY WINTER SNOW had come and in places
lay so thick that Erik feared for his young trees, which bent
and swayed under their load. Christmas was close, and under
Annikki's gentle but persistent pressure Erik had agreed to
revive the customs he had shared with Kirsti and which his
neighbors had never relinquished. Together, he and Annikki
rose early and went to the forest to cut their tree, carrying
it home through the snow together. On Christmas morning the
pastor preached his sermon in the cold early morning light
when all his flock could gather. For the first time in many
years Erik sat in the church, Annikki beside him, with their
candle burning softly at the end of the pew with a steady and
unwavering flame. The candle flames shone like little tongues
of fire down the cold aisles. It was a moment of deep, corporate
life and Annikki reached unconsciously toward it. With every
day that passed she had a sense, urgent and increasing, of the
need to fuse herself into the whole and stable life which the
village represented. The blind, unreasoning instinct which had
first prompted her wish to be left alone at Vainen had given
way to the necessity of knowing that she was at one with the
life around her. Even Maia's rough tongue was preferable to

her own doubts and fears. Sitting beside Vainen, the prayers and the singing filling the church with warmth, Annikki's doubts and fears were lulled.

Vainen had no doubts or fears, Annikki felt, or if he had, he did not voice them. He was as calm, as grave, as invulnerable as ever. But sometimes, in the night, lying in Kirsti's bed, Annikki would dream of a cold, white, moonlit night and two dark shadows on the snow. She wanted, then, to run to Vainen's room, to Vainen's bed, to the shelter of his arms. Fear kept her wakeful in the night. She would press her hands to her breasts, already painful and fuller, and lie motionless in the silence of the night, her mind filled with unnamed fears. In the morning, with the gentle sounds of activity around her, the soft, selfish, milky purr of Silvi, the joyous barking of Penna, and Vainen's quiet, unchanging face, Annikki would brush away her forebodings. Nothing dark or secret, nothing menacing and undefined could touch, she felt, this strange serenity which was Vainen. Yet, like someone who looks over his shoulder on a dark night, touches an amulet or crosses himself, so Annikki looked to human warmth for reassurance.

The candles with their tongues of fire gave reassurance, placed there by people seeking it. Outside, in the churchyard, white candles under their glass domes were indistinguishable from the snow-covered graves on which they had been placed, to burn softly through the night, banners in the darkness, living fire to remind the living of the dead who were not dead. Annikki's mind groped in the candlelit church for sustenance, for reassurance, for hope. If the gypsy was dead, did not his child live? Surely, she felt dimly, there must in this be continuity, justification? Her mind was confused, troubled. Yet Vainen himself, quiet, grave, unmovable as granite in his fixity of purpose, was still the background of her days. Her love for him grew.

With Maia, Annikki went to the churchyard to tend the family graves. This was a labor of love which the women performed regularly so that there were always fresh flowers or small rosebushes blooming beneath the splendor of the trees. Beneath this splendor the churchyard had an austere beauty that made it one with the landscape. Here were gravestones that were simply great rough-hewn pieces of granite, black and gray, rising from the green mounds, the green grass, with a harsh yet noble simplicity.

There were other women in the churchyard on this morning of light, a light pure and clear which fell upon the snow-covered graves with glacial radiance. Annikki nodded to the women, most of whom she knew. There, among others, was Margit Salonen and, by Margit's side, a broad-shouldered young man.

"Arvo is back," said Maia. She raised herself from her task. Annikki glanced down the neatly tended paths between the graves and saw the man by Margit's side.

His glance and Annikki's met. Arvo smiled and came quietly down the path toward her.

"Why," he said, "it is Annikki Berling. Annikki Vainen now. Do you remember me?"

"Of course the girl remembers you," Maia grunted, bent double as she was.

"But we only met twice. Isn't that so, Annikki?"

"Twice, that's all," Annikki agreed. She watched Maia move away with her basket of dead flowers and leaves, soaked by the snow, and made a move to follow her.

"No," Arvo said. "Don't go. It was here, in the churchyard that we met before, Annikki."

"Yes. It was toward the end of summer. I had just come to Porvesi."

"And the squirrel. Do you remember the squirrel?" Arvo asked.

He was tall, but not as tall as Vainen, his hair dun-colored, his eyes gray with thick, dark lashes. He had his mother Margit's square chin, his father Eino's big, well-cut mouth. His skin was tanned from wind and sun. His manner, when he spoke, gave the impression that only the listener mattered.

For the moment, Annikki felt, Arvo and herself might have been alone in the churchyard.

"Yes, I remember the squirrel," Annikki said, and laughed softly.

It had been a day of late summer radiance, the birch trees in full leaf, the scent of the pines warm and sharp and pungent, and it was then that Arvo had breathed it in deeply and had told her that he was off to sea. He had looked searchingly at Annikki.

"Do you like it here in Porvesi?" he had asked. "Are you happy here after a big city?"

She had not replied, not knowing what to say, liking neither Porvesi, nor Maia, nor her loneliness. Suddenly a gray squirrel had darted across the path and clambered onto her shoe and clung to it, bushy tail erect, little paws upraised, eyes bright, and tiny voice scolding furiously.

"Go away! Off! Go!" Annikki had cried between alarm and amusement, but the squirrel had only chattered and scolded, and seemed to menace her with tiny paws till Arvo had frightened it away.

"They are so tame," he had said. "Especially here, where there is silence and no one troubles them." He had watched the color run up under Annikki's delicate skin and the sudden darkening of her eyes and had thought what a pretty sight it was to see a girl frightened by a squirrel. "I've heard of them jumping on a man's shoulder," Arvo had said, "and searching his pocket for nuts. And my mother swears that they have come tapping at her window and holding out their paws like little humans."

"I can believe it," Annikki had said and laughed softly again and, with Arvo's eyes upon her, had felt the first little promise of pure delight since she had come to Porvesi.

Arvo had joined the navy, he had told her, not without pride. From Maia, Annikki had heard already of the examinations he had passed. "He will be a captain one day," Maia had said. "Both the Salonens, boy and girl, have heads stuffed with brains." To Annikki it had seemed like a reproof. No one, and certainly not Maia, could say of her that she had a head stuffed with brains.

But Arvo had not seemed to mind that she was a girl who would never go to a university, that she was just a girl who was frightened of a squirrel. He had looked at her then as he was looking now.

"There are no squirrels here today," he said.

"No. They're sleeping, I suppose. Or cracking their little nuts in a warm hollow." The thought of a warm, secret hiding place was pleasant. It brought a dreamy look to her face, and made her smile at her own foolishness.

"Annikki," Arvo said, "why didn't you wait for me?"

Annikki looked at him, startled. "Don't say such things. We . . . we only met twice. And Maia will be back soon. Don't let *her* hear you saying such things."

"Why didn't you wait, Annikki? When we met in the churchyard that day I think you liked me. I promised myself that when I came home again I would get to know you better."

"Don't," Annikki said. "This isn't the way you should talk to me."

"I had the feeling that you would have liked to know me better, Annikki."

"But it wasn't possible."

"But you would have liked it."

"No. No. We were strangers. You mustn't say such things."

"You and Vainen were strangers once."

Strangers, thought Annikki. Yes, that is true. We were strangers, and now we are man and wife and in a way we are still strangers. "Maia will be coming back," Annikki said.

"Maia knew that I liked you, Annikki. That I hoped for something more, in time."

"I am Vainen's wife."

"It was all so quick. It was all so very quick," Arvo said. "Why *didn't* you wait, Annikki?"

He had made her look at him again whether she wanted to

or not. In that look she realized that Arvo was not a boy, but a man, and against her will her breathing quickened as though he had touched her, secretly.

"I love Vainen," she said.

It was true. She loved Vainen. She looked away from Arvo across the black and gray granite beneath the cold white sky.

"When I was at sea," Arvo said, "I read a poem which reminded me of you. I read it many many times because it was beautiful and because of its associations for me."

"Maia is coming back," Annikki said evenly.

Arvo glanced from Annikki to Maia coming toward them. He spoke softly.

> *Enclosed within the birch trees' shade,*
> *A silent bird, a man, a maid.*

"Those are the lines I carried in my mind. Then I heard that you had married Vainen."

"Yes," Maia said, approaching, "and a fine wedding it was, too. I thought we should have the pastor himself dancing before the end of it." She looked sharply at Annikki. "You look pale and cold, girl. You might as well know, Arvo, since everybody else knows, that Annikki is going to have a child and shouldn't be standing about in the snow talking and freezing. Get me some of that wire over there, girl, to support these sprays. Then we'll go back and drink coffee."

Annikki did as she was bid. Arvo watched her go.

"You're too late," Maia told him. "The girl knew her mind and wasted no time. You'll have to wait for Iris Hassi."

"Do you think there are no girls except in Porvesi?" Arvo asked good-humoredly.

"There'll be girls in plenty with the life you're leading. A man who takes to the sea has his pick over the wide world." Maia handed Arvo her basket. "Carry this for me and remember, the next time, to say your say before another man says his."

"Annikki was strange here and a little bewildered. I thought there'd be enough time when I came back again."

"There's never enough time, never enough time. Don't wait till you get to my age to find that out. And take your mind off Annikki."

Arvo smiled. "I can talk to the girl, surely?"

"There's talk and talk and there's silence that says more than talk. I'm no fool, Arvo. The girl chose Vainen and she won't find a better man. What you or I think has nothing to do with it."

"That's what my mother says."

"Oh, so you've talked to her too?"

"I've said nothing. But you women are all alike. If a man speaks you chide him and if he doesn't speak then you read his thoughts, or think you read them. Annikki's married, and that's that. And already, you say, she's going to have a child. But if I'd had more time it might have been my child and Annikki my wife. She was halfway to liking me."

"Stop talking, Arvo. The thing is done."

"I know it. But if I want to speak to little Annikki I shall do it, so don't go reading into every word something that isn't there, and never can be."

Annikki came back, bending the wire this way and that in her cold fingers. Maia arranged such a winter nosegay on the little grave as could be fashioned. Snow fell lightly from the branches of a pine tree which stood near and the voices of the women could be heard murmuring softly as they finished their tasks. Beyond the churchyard the tree-line of the forest could be seen, the branches heavily laden with snow, and against the skyline the curling smoke of a wood fire.

Arvo moved to Annikki and took her hands in his. "The girl's hands are frozen, Maia. Where is the coffee you promised us?"

It seemed to Erik to require as much discipline and concentration to merge himself into the life of the village as it would have required to learn a new language. The dramatic group, the moving spirit of which was Harri Wasola, welcomed him and Annikki. "What you can do," he said, "we shall soon discover, Vainen, but it isn't beyond you to play a younger man, you with a young wife and, the women say, a handsome face into the bargain." Jussi, who was painting scenery, had, in previous years, with the help of Margit and Maia and some of the women, made costumes and properties. They were kept in a chest in the parish hall and Annikki's interest was quickened when the chest was turned out and filled the cold room with glitter and make-believe.

"Last year," Margit said, "it was my Meri who played, and now she has gone you must take her place. It will keep your mind nimble by the fire at nights, going over your part. It isn't a long part, as you'll see, Annikki."

"Vainen has the biggest part," Maia said.

"Vainen," Elisabet said softly. "Who would believe that Vainen would stand on a stage for all to see and make long speeches! How you have changed him, Annikki."

"And about time," said Maia, with a sharp glance at Elisabet.

On Saturday afternoons and sometimes on Sunday evenings they met in the parish hall or at Margit's house, or Harri Vasola's, to rehearse. The days were crisp and white with thick snow. Erik took out his skis and shaped and shortened a pair of his own for Annikki. "We'll ski through the forest whenever we can," he told her. "It won't harm you yet. I remember that Kirsti went on her skis in the winter before Kaarlo was born."

When Erik spoke of Kirsti now it was with something approaching matter-of-factness, Annikki thought. In a way it was almost as though the mention of Kirsti brought them closer, was an acknowledgment that she, Annikki, was a wife as Kirsti had been. With Erik ahead and Annikki following they would move swiftly through the clear, cold silence of the forest. The sky seemed always the same, a glacial sky stained with limpid blue. Their heads and faces muffled, their hands heavily gloved, they moved with rhythmic grace, the blood coursing through their veins. Annikki's eyes would sparkle, her cheeks glow, her young body bend and turn with the suppleness of a bow. Soon it was too cold even for Annikki and she sat muffled in the sleigh beside Erik in silent companionship. Their relationship had acquired closeness, a form and pattern—a strange relationship in which no word was spoken which did not deal with everyday matters.

Annikki looked forward to the rehearsals with as much eagerness as the others. She knew that both the dresses she would wear suited her, one a dress of cotton, the other of brocade. They had tight bodices and tiny waists, the brocade cut lower than any dress she had ever worn. Annikki took an innocent pleasure in the admiring glances of the men. What she wanted, however, was some sign from Vainen that he, too, saw her as a woman, as the other men saw her, but if he did so he gave no sign.

Annikki had as yet no very clear idea of what the play was about, but it gave opportunity to them all for scenes of strong feeling. There was laughter, death, betrayal in it and one scene for her with Vainen, a love scene between husband and wife.

"These are people like ourselves," Erik told her, anxious that she should hold her own, "people who plow poor soil and know what happiness and hardship can be and know, like us, how to drink and hate and love. These things happen to all of us in the play. Forget that you are Annikki. You are Olga and I am Stepan and you are saying good-by to me."

"You are going to Moscow and you may never come back," Annikki said, intent on her part.

"You know it and I know it but the other characters in the play don't."

"That's what makes it so tragic," Annikki said. "All the Russian writers seem to have written tragic plays. It must be because of the long winters."

Into the cold parish hall on those nights a colder wind blew from across the icy steppes. Margit seemed to draw from her placid soul strange depths of unsuspected bitterness, Jussi's merry, darting eyes could snap with cruelty while Maia pleaded in anguish. All saw Vainen take his young wife in his arms with sudden, unexpected fire. When Annikki gave her mouth to his she trembled and returned his kisses with passion. This man who held her so fiercely was not Stepan. It was Vainen. Her last anguished cry of farewell rang through the room with its flickering gaslight and drafty corners like the ancient cry of a keening woman.

"Acting," Tuomas Palin had said, "is as good a catharsis as confession."

But Harri, now warming himself, after a rehearsal, with schnapps, merely nodded approvingly. "I thought you had it in you, girl," he said, "and you too, Vainen."

Maia looked at Annikki's figure and took the girl aside. "Nothing shows yet," she said, "nor should it for some time. You're young and supple and the dresses have full skirts. But later I'll ease the waist a bit."

Erik, drinking with the men, looked across at Annikki. Her face had lost the immature look of girlhood; it was the face of a woman, soft, tender, and sensuous. He remembered the feel of her lips under his, the passion in her kiss which had aroused in him the old conflict of desire and revulsion. Every impulse of a body hardened and disciplined by abstinence had sprung to life when he had held her in his arms. He did not love her; memory of Kirsti held him too closely in its grip. He did not love her but he wanted her. The gypsy's voice echoed in his brain with obscene sibilance. Erik drained his glass and refused another. He felt again the defilement of that voice. He felt one with the gypsy, scourged by lust. Was it for this that he had fought the soil and the elements, the bitterness of bereavement and the harsh dictates of his own nature?

When Annikki moved beside him later in the sleigh he

felt desire leap treacherously, and as suddenly as flame leaps
to a struck match. He sat, grave-faced, his profile etched
against the light. The moon shone with a chill radiance.

"Harri was pleased," Anikki said. "Were you, Vainen?"

"You acted well, you brought to life all that the part called
for."

"I think the part is well written. When I said the words
I knew they were the right ones."

"You played the scene well. Not only Harri and Jussi but
Arvo Salonen remarked on it afterward."

"I thought I saw him at the back, watching."

"Arvo? Well, he has traveled and been to the big theatres in
Helsinki. You acted well, he said, and he should know how
to judge."

Annikki looked at Erik sitting gravely beside her while the
snow-covered road slid away beneath them to the sound of
bells.

"Maia will have to alter my dresses at the waist when the
time comes for me to wear them. Nothing will show, she says."

"I think it will. But what matter?"

"After all, we are man and wife as we are in the play. Sometimes, Vainen, I forget that the child is not yours."

"It is better that way than to think of the gypsy."

"I don't think of him often. He seems to me now like a
shadow." Annikki moved closer to Erik, remembering his arms
about her, his mouth pressed on hers. Such things, surely, did
not lie? Could this be a moment for another kind of truth?

She said softly, "Yes, like a shadow, nothing more—shadow
on the snow."

Had Vainen stiffened beside her? Or had she imagined it?
He must speak now, he must know that she knew, and afterward there would be nothing to come between them.

"He was a shadow, nothing more. Think of him like that.
It is best," Erik said. He jerked at the reins. The sleigh gathered speed and soon the long low line of the house came into
view illumined by the moonlight. Penna heard them and

barked twice. The sleigh drew up at the house and Annikki got out. As on the day of their wedding, when they had returned to the house, Erik did not look at her as she went inside. She heard him busy in the byre as she undressed and prepared for bed, heard him come in later and the door of his room close. After the heightened tension of the evening a sense of unreality gripped Annikki as though none of this concerned her, none of it was happening to her. It was like a dream from which she struggled to awaken.

So strong was the feeling that she sprang from bed and flung off her nightgown and looked at her body, running her hands over her breasts. Even her body was strange to her now, it showed the subtle, perceptible difference made by the ripening seed.

12

ANNIKKI WAS CARRYING two pails of water to the *sauna* in readiness for the evening bath. The short afternoon had already waned. Darkness fell softly on her mouth and eyelids, the snow-cold air was sweet with the smell of pine and wood smoke. The full pails in either hand seemed effortless to carry. Annikki opened the door of the *sauna*. Through the trees the lake glimmered coldly. Silence and night enveloped her with the texture of dark velvet. Behind her the light shining through the uncurtained windows of the house was reflected, a warm glow on the snow.

Annikki paused a moment before picking up the pails. Suddenly the radiance of the northern lights filled the sky and wavered across the snow. Annikki gazed upward at the great fan of light with its quivering streamers merging from pale-gold to blood-red in which, people had once said, the souls of the dead danced, giving a promise of hope to the living. Hope for the spring, for renewal, for the sun, and continuing life. As she gazed Annikki realized fully, for the first time, that life would go on when the child was born. The birth would not be a completion, but a beginning. There would be other winters, other springs. Her feet were set upon a road from which there was no turning back. It was as though her future were illumined suddenly in this ghostly radiance which cast upon the clarity of unmarked snow the gold of morning, the blood-red of sunset, fusing time past, time to come.

Annikki glanced back at the house with its single, steady light. Even the sudden grandeur of the northern lights had not eclipsed it. She picked up the pails and entered the *sauna*.

The heat rose at once to meet her, and Annikki felt choked after the crystal clarity of the cold night air. A sudden faintness overcame her and she sat for a moment in the outer room. Presently, when she returned to the house, Erik noticed her pallor.

"The pails were too heavy," he said, but his voice was incredulous, for he had seen Annikki lift heavier things without effort.

"It wasn't the pails, but the heat. Suddenly I felt faint."

Erik studied her. It was a few moments before he spoke.

"Tonight you must not take your bath alone."

Annikki gazed at him levelly. She sensed that the moment was important for them both. He had never entered the *sauna* while she was in it. Such moments of intimacy between man and wife had never been theirs.

"It is for you to say, Vainen."

"It is for you, also. If you wish to be alone you must be alone. But your face is as white as cheese and you say it was the heat."

"It seemed to strike me when I went in after the cold outside."

"Then I will be with you and throw the water on the stones for you, and wield the birch twigs. When my first son, Kaarlo, was born, Kirsti was eighteen also. Surely I will do for you what I did for her."

"There is no need."

"There is need."

"Kirsti was . . . she was the wife you had chosen."

"So are you my wife. You were chosen for me."

Erik was trembling. The paleness of Annikki's face, her quickened breathing, the memory of her mouth, filled him with desire. An unclean desire. The memory of the gypsy's voice would never fade. *We will share her. She is ripe for the taking.* He had never looked upon the girl's body but now this he must do. She needed him in her weakness.

"Do not be afraid," he said.

"I am not afraid, Vainen. If I am afraid it is because you never say my name."

Erik drew a deep breath. "Old Akseli taught me that names have power. Perhaps we are all foolish, like children. But . . . once a name is spoken . . . it is spoken. Something goes out that cannot be recalled."

"I say your name. Vainen! Vainen!" she cried suddenly, passionately, and the echo filled the room.

"But that is no longer a name," he said gently. "It is a place. A promise. A region of the mind."

"You are a strange man," Annikki said slowly. Her glance was full of love.

"That may be so. But I have given you my protection and I swear that you shall never receive harm from me."

Yet he still trembled, Annikki saw, like a man who has been running hard. She came gently to him and put her hand on his arm. "I said to you once that I go where I am led. It is still true. Tonight, then, we will take our bath together. I know why you are trembling, Vainen, and why you look at me like that, as Arvo looked at me in the churchyard. It is nature. It is because you are a man, and I am a woman."

"A woman who is to have a child."

"One day the child will be born," Annikki said. "When it is born our lives will begin. Isn't it like that?"

They looked at one another. Erik's gaze was as level as Annikki's, as level as that of the girl who had seemed to grow from girl to woman before his eyes. When he thought of the girl who had looked up at him in the church, who had offered

the crumbs of bread to the gull, he knew that between that
girl and this the span of time had wrought great change. Yet
change had been wrought in him also, a change neither sought
nor desired. Kirsti had been his wife, his true love. To this
child he had offered protection. But the tender impulses of
pity and protection had shown another face. All his senses
throbbed with desire for her, and he thought, I am no better
than the gypsy.

Tonight they must sit naked, side by side. He would be
coiled in the shackles of his thoughts and his desires. His mind
turned wearily and as blindly as an animal seeking its lair,
to that lost darkness and silence at the heart of the whirlpool.

The dimness of the *sauna* received them both, hot, enfolding. They undressed together in the small outer room.
Annikki rose, tall and white and naked, and went ahead of
him. She turned in the doorway and Erik saw the young, full
breasts set high, the rounding belly, the long, silken thighs
gleaming in the candlelight. He rose, casting down his garments as if they were cerements, and followed her.

Annikki lay down on the lowest bench, raising her arms
above her head. Erik paused beside her and seized the dipper
and threw water upon the red-hot stones. At once the room
was filled with fiercely hot steam in which Erik stood enveloped, a man in full maturity, the powerful body covered
by unblemished skin. Annikki closed her eyes.

Erik climbed to the topmost bench and lay in silence for
some time. In the dim light Erik saw as in a vision, where
Annikki now lay, the slender form of that other companion,
the beautiful, cruel body with its sinuous, whipcord strength.
The candlelight glinted on whorls in the wood of the bench
as it had glinted on the small gold rings almost hidden in
the gypsy's ears, as it had glinted earlier on the silver buckle
of the belt which had held the gypsy's strange clothes together. Erik looked down at Annikki, lying motionless, with
closed eyes. The gypsy was still there with them, in spite of

the dark lake. There were three in that small room, together.

If Annikki knew what had taken place would she turn from him in horror? Would her eyes darken in fear, would she shrink from the touch of his hands? Erik lay silently, breathing deeply. There was silence and pervading warmth between them. Yet, though Annikki did not speak, it seemed to Erik that the silence itself had a voice, the voice of the gypsy, which spoke out of that resinous, smoky warmth.

Annikki sat up. She was sweating profusely and her fair hair, which she had coiled up, clung darkly to her head. Her young neck, with its purity of line, had a childish and immature appearance as it rose from the vulnerability of her naked body. Erik took the birch whisk and came slowly to her. The sap, and the aromatic scent, released in hot water, filled the room. He struck her lightly across the shoulders and thighs and Annikki turned and leaned gently against him. At the touch of her body against his own, at the sight of her head bent on its young neck, where the tender nape was shadowed by a strand of hair, Erik felt power go out of him and weakness fill his limbs. He, who had not wept since Kirsti's death, felt near to tears. Pity and tenderness welled up in him. Desire and lust drained away. He touched the young body resting against his as he would have touched the body of a lamb which the snow had imprisoned.

"Now you are feeling better," he said, when he could speak.

"Yes," Annikki said. "I feel strong and clean with so much sweating. I shall go and scrub myself now. I have had enough." She rose to her feet.

"Do you feel exhausted?" Erik asked.

"No. I have rested quietly, and made no effort. But now I shall go and wash."

"I will come later," Erik said. "I shall sweat and scrub and sweat again before I am finished."

Annikki went quietly from him, treading carefully on the hot floor. When she had gone Erik remained sitting on the bench. He heard the sounds Annikki made, the splashing of water, the little gasp when its coldness struck the heat of her body. The sounds were gentle and familiar. As he sat there in the warmth Erik felt that it might have been Kirsti who was splashing and singing softly under her breath, that, in a strange way, it was Kirsti, as though, for this moment, past and present and time to come had fused.

The girl, perhaps, was wiser than she knew. One day the child would be born and when it was born their lives would begin, she had said. But the girl saw everything in clear colors. Life was not so simple. Gentleness, kindness, compassion, at least she would know nothing but these from him. Life should be full of the sweetness of small things, he would give them to her with both hands. She would never know that the greatest gift was one he would withhold. Love was something he could never feel again. The deeper springs of his being, he knew well, had dried up with Kirsti. The girl who sang so softly and made gestures that were gentle and familiar was not Kirsti and never could be. That is why, Erik thought, I cannot say her name. Akseli would have known and understood.

Erik looked at the shining whorl in the wood beneath his bare feet where the glint of candlelight struck. He remembered suddenly once again the gypsy's belt with its silver buckle. When he had lowered the gypsy's body into the lake the belt had not been there. Erik caught his breath in sudden fear. He had not thought of the belt then, but now he remembered the looseness of the gypsy's clothing as the body had disappeared, taking everything with it.

There had been nothing left in the *sauna* when he had returned to look but the body of the hen, and at the time he had not thought of the belt. What had happened to it? Perhaps it had fallen into the boat or among the trees when he had carried the body from the *sauna* to the lake. Tomorrow he would search. If he found it, good. If not, well there must be more than one man who wore a belt with a silver buckle.

The following day Erik searched his boat and looked among the trees. But the boat yielded nothing and the snow lay thick among the trees. Nature herself had drawn a veil over what was past and so, surely, Erik thought, must man do likewise. He returned to the house and stood for a while surveying his small, cherished farm, his forest land. Standing there he vowed that if the child to be born should be a son, farm, house, and forest should be his. No man could tell the future or how his days would go. He, Erik, might beget a son by Annikki when day had followed day and life ran again into its immemorial grooves. But Anikki's first child, if it were a son, fathered by the gypsy, should inherit the farm. The thought brought cleansing with it. There was nothing more, he thought, that a man could do.

The lake had frozen to a depth of more than three feet and now they could go by sleigh across it whenever they visited Porvesi. Erik knew the currents which made it treacherous and so, also, did the horse. To drive now to the parish hall or to Margit's house for rehearsals could be done more quickly and Annikki was never tired of seeing the village come into view across the great white expanse fringed with dark pines.

Sometimes, when he had an errand to perform, Erik would ski across the lake and often the children came out on their skis muffled for the winter, and their shouts and laughter echoed on the breeze. It was hard, Annikki sometimes thought, to tell which were children and which clothes from the bundled appearance they would present until the spring. There was skating, also, and Elisabet Lahti came skating across the narrow end of the lake to see Annikki at Vainen.

They were placid, tranquil days, Annikki thought, and some instinct told her that they were days which she would remember. Since the night of the *sauna* a new spirit seemed to have entered the house. Erik's gentleness had grown, his care of her and consideration for her plucked at her heart, which was so full of love for him. Yet he did not touch her nor caress her, did not speak her name. There was an invisible barrier between them which neither of them must cross.

Annikki was certain that the barrier was the body in the lake. Often the words trembled on her tongue but she did not utter them. Of what use was it now to stir those deep waters? Time had covered that night as the deep ice covered the lake. Beneath, all was stillness, silence.

What she wanted most of all, Annikki knew, was Vainen's love. But this he withheld. Even their rehearsals for the play had, since that night, taken on a different character.

"We should play without fire or passion," Erik said. "This is a time when feelings would run deep and strong. We must make less ado, as people would."

Her mood had subjugated itself to his. In that scene with him Annikki began to show a depth of feeling, a restraint of gesture, which surprised Maia.

"Marriage has done much for the girl," she told Jussi. "The girl was right and I was wrong. She knew what to take from life as the animal knows what to take from the pasture."

"Now perhaps your mind is at rest," Jussi said.

"Yes, it is at rest," Maia told him. Yet when she fed the gypsy's horse Maia would think uneasily of the gypsy who had ridden the horse and gone his way. She would remember the way the horse had come galloping out of the forest and across the paddock to stand quivering and foam-flecked at the house.

"It's strange that nobody has ever claimed the horse," she said to Jussi.

"All the better for us."

"The creature has spirit," Maia said, "and I've grown fond of it." Though she would not have admitted it Maia loved the horse. It would come at her call and nuzzle her fingers and toss its head with the air of an animal that knows it is loved. It was gentle with Annikki also, when she approached it. Annikki liked to lay her face against it and stroke the soft neck and the horse would stand quietly under her hands. But always there was a light in its eye and a pricking of its ears as though it were listening for another footfall, a footfall which did not come.

Annikki no longer put on the birch skis which Erik had made for her, or skated with him, in case she should fall and and injure herself or the child. They did not speak of it from one day's end to another but the consciousness of it was there. It could not be otherwise. Once she had cried, *"I hate this child, growing in my body"* and when she thought consciously of it, remembering, her body seemed to contract, as though it would expel its burden. Yet for much of the time she accepted it, with courage. What was done was done and how could she know what she would feel when, finally, she held the child in her arms? Annikki did not know. Like Maia she too felt, in the recesses of her being, an unquestioning acceptance of what life might bring. And, whatever life might bring, somewhere, she was sure, would be found the strength to endure it. That was the way life was meant to be lived, and always would be. The rules were simple and, Annikki supposed, must have been made in far distant times when the earth was young. She realized that she, certainly, had never known any others. All her life till now must have been a preparation for this moment, just as this moment would prepare her for others to come. There was nothing to do but live and work and wait.

13

THE ARM OF THE LAKE which enclosed Vainen was alive with skaters. Everyone, obeying an impulse, had put on their skates, first the children, and then the mothers who feared the currents, and then, finally, the men, on this Saturday afternoon. Although skiing and skating were ordinary means of locomotion, the fact did not dim their pleasure now, and they wheeled and circled like earth-bound gulls, rejoicing in the rush of wind against their faces, the unconscious dexterity of their bodies.

"I started it," Elisabet Lahti cried, wheeling to a stop beside Maia and Annikki. "I set off for Vainen and nothing would do but that my big boys should come and then others followed and now all Porvesi is on skates." She looked at Annikki. "That is, except you and Maia and old Heikki and Fat Catherine," she laughed as she darted away.

Fat Catherine, muffled from her birdlike legs to her eyebrows, was walking with Heikki by the edge of the lake. Heikki wore his fur cap with the thick earflaps and failed to hear one word which Fat Catherine uttered in her thin, high voice. Their quaverings were carried on the wind like the querulous cries of distant birds. Presently Heikki tired of the struggle and returned to his Byzantium, where women were not allowed. Fat Catherine walked beside him, her watery blue eyes gazing ahead to some distant Byzantium of her own.

"Old Heikki can't last much longer," Maia said to Annikki. "He gets frailer every day."

"I think he will live longer than Fat Catherine," Annikki said. "*She* worries about *him*. He only worries about himself."

Maia chuckled. "There's sense in that. How do you feel now, girl? Nothing that needs the doctor yet? No sickness? No pains?"

"I never feel sick. I shan't go to the doctor, there won't be any need. When the time comes Vainen will look after me."

"We'll see about that. How often have I told you—women need women, and that's one of the times they need them most." Maia watched the skaters a moment, wheeling in ever-widening circles towards Porvesi. "You'll be on your skates long before this time next year," she said. "You'll be skating with Vainen with the baby on your back." She did not speak for a few moments and, used to her silences, Annikki did not speak either. She looked across at the frozen lake and thought of the depths where the water flowed, far down, and the fishes which swam there, deep under the ice. The fishes had swum round and under and over the gypsy long since. Her face paled suddenly.

"What is the matter?" Maia cried sharply.

"Nothing. Just this talk of being sick . . . and such nonsense. I never think of such things."

"Then don't think of them now."

"It was you who asked me," Annikki said. She was trembling.

"Perhaps women in the cities turn pale and tremble when they have a mind. This isn't Turku, girl, where you lived soft," Maia said roughly.

The long reeds at the edge of the lake were white and stiff with crusted snow which glittered in the pale sunlight. The wind whipped their faces and stung Maia's eyes until they

watered. "Turn back toward Vainen," she said. "I came to
see the house, and what preparations you've made for the
child."

"There's plenty of time."

"There's never enough time for anything. High summer it
will be and Christmas is long behind us. Full, high summer
with the long days."

"Perhaps sooner," Annikki said.

"Not sooner. Not before the end of August."

"Earlier—perhaps July."

"Can't you count, Annikki? You'll have time to act in the
play before you get too big. But for you to get too big is
what Iris Hassi is hoping for. Nothing will do but that she
must understudy you."

"She can play it if she likes."

"Where's your spirit? What you start you must finish. All
that Iris wants is to get up on that stage with Arvo Salonen
watching her."

"Arvo won't be back to see the play."

"He watched rehearsals, I noticed. Still, he's gone again and
won't be back till the summer and then you'll see Iris casting
glances from those slanting eyes of hers."

"I see no harm in it."

"Nor I. Except that the girl is a hussy and empty-headed
and Arvo is worth something better. Besides, if she prods
a man as Ulla prods, like as not he'll take her by the throat
and throttle her."

Annikki laughed. But she looked down at the reeds nevertheless, fearing the glance of Maia's sharp eyes. So little escaped Maia. Perhaps Arvo's deep, searching glance in the
churchyard had not escaped her nor her, Annikki's, knowledge of what it had meant. Arvo had made it very plain that
he liked her, perhaps more than he should like a woman who
was another man's wife.

Maia fell again into one of her silences. They walked
quickly because of the cold, skirting the lake where the reeds

stood so stiffly. Some were imprisoned in the ice, delicate
and cold, waiting for release.

Vainen was not far away. They could see the *sauna* and the
dark stump, white now with its blanket of snow, to which
Erik moored his boat. The boat had been freshly tarred and
pushed into the small boathouse beneath the trees.

They had reached the edge of the path which led from the
sauna to the lake, when Annikki stopped abruptly and stood
still, trembling, like a frightened horse.

"What's the matter with you now, girl?" Maia cried angrily,
her anger shot with sudden fear.

"A snake," Annikki whispered. "Oh, Maia, how horrible
it is. A snake, caught in the ice among the reeds. There, by
the lake's edge."

"A snake?" Maia echoed. She looked down, following Annikki's revolted gaze, and shivered at the long, black sinuous
thing, half coiled there, with its strange, shining head. She
bent closer.

"No!" Annikki screamed. "Don't touch it, Maia. Don't
touch it."

But Maia had bent down and wrenched the thing from the
grip of the reeds and the ice and dangled it before Annikki,
who covered her face with her hands, and shuddered, and
backed away.

"Don't be a fool, Annikki. What harm lies in this? It's no
snake, but a belt, a fine, long leather belt, with a silver
buckle."

Annikki knew. It was the gypsy's belt. The buckle had
caught the rays of the sun when he had flung himself upon
her. She looked at Maia and it seemed to Maia that the girl's
face had shriveled. Against her will Maia felt her own common sense ebb away under the influence of Annikki's terror.

She looked at the belt again and then at the girl and whatever fear it was that lay at the back of her mind rose suddenly and filled it. She said with forced calm, "You'll do
yourself harm if you let your mind play tricks. This is only

a belt. But," Maia said slowly as she examined it, "I've seen this belt before. It's the gypsy's belt," she said.

"Yes," Annikki echoed. "It's the gypsy's belt."

"You remember it, then? When did you see it?"

"Why . . . when the gypsy stood at Vainen's door. . . . When Vainen gave him the message."

Maia stared at Annikki, the hard, frozen belt dangling, half coiled as it had lain, in her hand. The silver buckle winked in the sunlight. "You have something else to tell me," Maia said, "surely."

"I? What could I tell you, Maia?"

"You are sure there is nothing you want to tell me? About the gypsy?" Maia's shrewd eyes narrowed to pinpoints in her white face.

"What is there to tell? I didn't like the gypsy . . . and the belt frightened me. I thought it was a snake . . . or something horrible. . . . I don't know what I thought."

"The gypsy was wearing this when I saw him," Maia said thoughtfully, "to keep his clothes together. It seems strange that he should have left it by the lake in the cold. It was the time of that early snow. The lake froze lightly that night and it was then that the belt must have fallen and been frozen among the reeds."

"Why then?"

"Because the gypsy hasn't been seen around these parts since. And he abandoned his horse, turned it loose, and the frightened creature galloped back to the house."

Annikki stared at Maia. "How can you know?" she said.

"I can't know. But that horse saw something which terrified it that night, or I'm no judge. Animals have senses, like us, and sometimes keener." Maia looked at Annikki for several seconds and opened her mouth to speak and closed it again. The two women stood with the belt between them. The cries of the skaters were no longer heard.

Maia forced a smile. "I'm a fool to be filling your head with nonsense," she said. "Who knows whether this is the gypsy's belt? Not I, nor you. So I'll take it home and put it away and say nothing. Who knows, I say. One day someone may ask about it. So there's a horse in the stable and a belt in the cupboard and nobody any the wiser." She put the belt in her pocket.

Maia took Annikki's arm and felt it shiver against her side. "I never knew such a girl for whims and fancies," she said irritably. "All our Porvesi women have stout hearts, like men, and Porvesi is no exception. You wouldn't see them trembling at a snake or a black shape in the snow."

"You didn't like it yourself. I saw your face go white."

"You're pert, girl, and saucy. I was frightened for you, and your vapors, not of the belt. Women here have borne sons and seen them go off at fifteen to defend their country. Boys with rosy cheeks, leaving their school satchels hanging on the nail. What sort of son will you bear?" Maia's voice was rough.

"It will be a son like its father," Annikki cried desperately. "Maia. Listen! When I married Vainen I didn't—I wasn't . . ." Annikki clutched Maia and then stopped abruptly, the words catching in her throat, for Maia had turned on her a face which was cold and white and hard.

"Stop talking! Stop crying! You weren't ready for motherhood, that's what it is, but it's come and you should be thankful. You knew what marriage meant. Let's hear no more of what you didn't want or what you weren't expecting." She took the girl by the shoulders and said quietly, "You'll have a son or daughter, whichever it is. Vainen's child. And there's no going back now."

Annikki stared into Maia's eyes. Did she know? Had she guessed? Or did the words mean no more than they said? Maia's face was cold and expressionless.

"How could there be any going back?" Annikki said.

"Vainen has pampered you. Don't think I haven't noticed. You shamed me that day in the forest, afraid to go here, afraid to go there. And now this, trembling and crying, because I was fool enough to tell you what passed through my

mind. Have done, Annikki. You'll have a dozen children before you're finished and Vainen won't be so ready to pamper
you with the next one."

They finished the walk in silence. When they reached the
house Maia herself set about making coffee and gave Annikki
a cup. "Say nothing to Vainen," she said. "If there's one thing
a man hates more than another it's a nervous, prattling
woman."

When Maia reached home she took the sodden belt out of
her pocket and hung it on a peg behind the door, out of sight.
When it was dry, she thought, she would put it away in the
cupboard in her bedroom. Aloud she said grimly, "And then
we shall see." She looked at the belt a long time. She was
angry with herself because she had shown anger so openly to
Annikki—anger which was the result of jangled nerves, anger
directed, partly, against herself. If only she could rid her
mind of thoughts of the gypsy! But he stayed there, obstinately, at the back of it. The picture was clear. The dark man
with his cruel smile, the dangling hen, the sudden fear in his
eyes. He had gone, out of sight, yet he had left tokens behind.
A horse, a belt, and a carved manikin. "We shall see," Maia
said again, "if ever he comes to claim his belt and his horse."
However, she did not think it likely that he would. If he
stayed away, she thought, he must have good reason for
doing so.

Yet, prompted, perhaps, by her own awareness, the moment
Jussi came in his glance fell upon the belt hanging behind the
door.

"That isn't mine," he said, taking it down. "Where did it
come from?"

"I found it today in the reeds by the lake. It has a good
silver buckle."

"It's a good belt of good leather and I've seen it before. I'd
know this buckle anywhere. I'll tell you whose it is, Maia. It
belongs to that gypsy."

"That's what I thought," Maia said carelessly.

"Well, if he went off without it I'd like to know how he
kept his clothes together," Jussi said. "It seemed to me that
the belt was all he had."

Maia shrugged. "They're a thieving lot, the whole pack of
them. Perhaps he stole this, along with the horse. Leave it
there to dry, Jussi. It went against the grain with me to leave
a good belt with a silver buckle rotting in the reeds."

Jussi put the belt back on the peg. "I'm hungry," he said.
"Is the food ready? Afterward there are the store accounts to
do—but you can see to those while I finish painting the backdrop for the play. And how was Annikki? She's been the
salvation of Vainen, if you ask me."

"And he of her, perhaps," Maia said thoughtfully.

Jussi's quick, darting gaze was on Maia's face. She turned
away and busied herself at the stove. Jussi said nothing. Maia
wondered why he did not jump, as usual, to defense of the
girl against the criticism implicit in the words just spoken.
That salvation, a new way of life, had been necessary for
Vainen, none would question. But Annikki? Still Jussi said
nothing, and yet Maia knew that if Jussi asked her what she
meant she would not know how to answer. What she did know
was that between Vainen and Annikki was something un-
spoken, some cord which bound them, some knowledge shared.
That, certainly, was true of all marriages but this, she felt,
had been true of Vainen and Annikki when they had scarcely
seemed to know each other. Well, Jussi was not going to help
her, that was clear. And yet, Maia thought, what troubles me
is not under my nose. Annikki has said nothing. Vainen has
said nothing either. But what was it that was unsaid? What?

She brought the meat stew to the table. Jussi helped himself, saying as he did so, "Everyone remarks on the change in
Vainen. He was more than halfway to being a hermit. People
went from one year to another, nigh on, without setting eyes
on him. But I've seen him stand in Porvesi and exchange
words with old Heikki and we all know he was at church on
Christmas Day, and is taking part in the play. As for Elisabet

Lahti, she could tell you everything there is at Vainen, from
floor to ceiling, she's been there so often. The man is an open
book compared to what he was. All he needed was a wife
about the place, to stop him from living with ghosts."

"Yes," said Maia. "A man who does that becomes a ghost
himself." She helped herself to the stew. There was plenty
to think of without thinking of Annikki and Vainen. There
were preparations for the weaving classes tomorrow, the final
rehearsals to think of, costumes to mend and press, not to
mention the store accounts and the rug she was making and
Jussi's new shirts and the cow barn to muck out in the
morning. A fine time to be fanciful, Maia thought. But as
she added up accounts Maia could see Annikki's terrified face,
hear the dread in her voice as she had looked down at the
belt in the reeds. *"Don't touch it! Don't touch it!"* she had
cried with horror. Twice Maia went in vain over each column
of figures, feeling the prick of unease in her mind like a thorn
in a finger. She jabbed at her disquiet as though it were a
thorn and suddenly it came to a head.

"Jussi," she said suddenly, "I don't think the child that
Annikki is carrying is Vainen's child. I think it is the gypsy's."

Jussi made a few, slow, sweeping brush strokes thoughtfully,
while Maia waited. She thought she had been a fool to speak,
but out it had come, and beyond her power to stop it. Jussi,
she knew, had had enough of her peckings at the question of
Annikki's marriage, like an old hen scratching bare soil. Jussi
rarely got angry but now Maia was certain that the storm of
wrath was coming. For the first time in her life Maia felt
afraid of Jussi. He was like his father, with the same sweet
good humor, the same patience, but it was his father, all the
same, who had once drawn a knife at a wedding, not too rare
a happening, perhaps, when drink flowed freely. Still, Jussi
was his father's son. Maia did not expect him to draw a knife
on her but she moistened her dry lips nevertheless, fearing
the sudden boiling up of his anger.

Jussi put his brush down finally and stared at her from the other end of the long table. "You think Annikki's child was fathered by the gypsy?"

"Yes," said Maia stoutly. "I do."

"Well," Jussi said, "and so do I."

Maia gasped, and half rose from the table. "How dare you sit there and tell me that!" She stood upright, gripping the edge of the table. "How dare you sit there, like an old goat in the bracken, and tell me that! Haven't I been fretting and worrying and my mind darting this way and that way—"

"Quiet, woman! Do you want Paavo and Riitta to hear you a mile away?" Paavo was the farm laborer who helped in the store and on Jussi's small farm, and who was at the moment trudging home in the moonlight. "Sit down," Jussi said quietly. "Now it's out we'll talk the matter over."

Maia sat down, as weak as a new-born calf. "We're man and wife," she said, "and have been for twenty-five years and to this day you've never kept anything from me."

Jussi bellowed like a bull and Maia cowered. "What have you been doing if not keeping something from me? Answer me that!"

"I wasn't sure. I only felt a nagging and a worrying, day in and day out. The marriage was so quick and the girl is really no fool. You can't convince me that she'd go rushing to Vainen like a brainless ninny. She wasn't afraid of *us*. No, she was afraid of something else, and what with the strange business of the gypsy—and *he* was afraid of something too— well, just now it all came to boiling point and I sifted off the scum."

"And there the truth lay below, simmering away like a fat capon," Jussi said. "Well, it's done plenty of simmering in my mind, I can tell you. I put two and two together when Vainen brought the girl back. I watched her, asking for permission to marry and squeezing out the tears and peeping through her fingers at me, knowing that here was a man she could twist to her way. The gypsy's had her, I thought in a flash, and how she's got to Vainen God knows, but here's Vainen willing to marry her and it's the finger of Providence!"

"And you said nothing?"

"What was the sense in trying to turn them back from doing something that could only bring good? The girl might need a husband, and quickly, but if ever a man needed a wife, the man was Vainen. So he'll father the child and least said soonest mended, thought I. But not a word goes out of this house unless you want to injure my own flesh and blood."

"Injure her? Injure Annikki? Do you think as little of me as that? Many a man has fathered a child not his own! If this child is the spit of the gypsy we can put his dark eyes down to yours. There are dark eyes right through in your mother's family. We must keep quiet, and we will."

"And not let the girl know what we know, either, for I'd stake my life that we're right. Think of her situation in a parish like Porvesi, with a pastor like ours! He's kept down what there is of drunkenness and there's no violence to speak of and as for a girl going astray—one look from Tuomas Palin and her feet would be back on the path of righteousness quicker than a man could flick open a knife. And as for—"

"Now you're wound up, Jussi," Maia cried. "Let's get down to practical matters. What happened to the gypsy? His horse is in the stable and that's his belt hanging there. Did he run off through the forest, dropping his clothes as he ran?" Maia's eyes narrowed. "Vainen and he had a fight, that's about it."

"I think Vainen surprised him with the girl and I'll take my oath that the girl was forced. Vainen acted quickly and as he thought best. If he'd brought the girl back we'd have seen what had happened. Yes," Jussi said thoughtfully, "it's clear. Vainen was capable of forcing the gypsy at gun-point to return and report on pain of handing him over to the law, and when the gypsy got back Vainen set about him. And when Vainen sets about a man—"

"Vainen has the strength of an ox. They say he heaved rocks with his bare hands—"

"I daresay he set about the gypsy in no light fashion," Jussi said grimly. "The horse must have bolted. The gypsy is lucky if all he left behind was his belt. The vagabond's gone for good, you can depend on that."

"But the horse. He might slink back for the horse."

"Let him take it in the night like the thief that he is. One thing is certain. He'll never dare show his face at Vainen. Set your mind at rest, once and for all. What's done is done." Jussi sighed heavily. "I took the girl into my care," he said. "She wasn't bold. Not that I know of. Would you say that she was flighty, woman?"

Dislike of Annikki and the trouble she had brought, welled up in Maia. But she said finally, "No, there was nothing at all bad in the girl, nothing bad or deceitful. Neither was she a fool. But there was something lacking in her. She had never been taught to think ill of another human creature."

"Is that a lack?" asked Jussi sadly.

"It's a weapon all women need. Better than her nails or a sharp bodkin. I daresay the gypsy spoke to her and she thought nothing of it. I remember now, she was out in the paddock with the dog." Maia paused, reflecting. "Yes," she said, "the dog slunk in later with his tail between his legs as though he'd been beaten."

"And he shot like a stone from a sling when the gypsy came next day to the door. I thought he'd had a kick from the man or a curse at least. Dogs don't relish being cursed, any more than we do."

"Well," Maia said heavily, "what now?"

"What now? Nothing."

"If only Annikki can hold her tongue. We all want the ease of confession, it's human nature, like putting your feet up at the end of the day. It was when she . . . yes, it was when she began to confess . . . if that's what it was . . . that some-

thing clicked into place in my mind. And if we wanted proof
we have it from her lips."

"She's *told* you?"

"As good as. Annikki knows the child will be early. She
knows it *now*."

"What's a month? It happens."

"You've counted too?"

"Yes. The thing has lain like a weight on me. She was in
my care, as I had promised. My word is broken."

"She's had nothing but good from you," Maia said sharply.
"And your word hasn't been broken, nor your kindness
changed by a hairbreadth. You acted without anger or mis-
giving. You followed the path that was clear." Maia drew the
account book angrily toward her. "Perhaps in future you'll
trust me."

"What is a man to do with a woman like you?" Jussi yelled.
"Have you trusted me? Why didn't you out with it in the
beginning?"

"I wasn't sure. I didn't know what it was that bothered me.
I only had my intuition to go on."

"Then *my* intuition was better than yours. It led me straight
to the point."

"But you couldn't tell me?" Maia, furious, said calmly.

"Least said soonest mended," Jussi said. "What Vainen and
Annikki know is between themselves from now on, as it has
been from the beginning."

"It's true, Jussi. We shall never know what took place
between Vainen and Annikki, what words were said that led
to marriage, or the promise of it."

"Two lives changed," Jussi said, "and all for a vagabond
gypsy. It's frightening, when you come to think of it, what
slender threads our lives hang on. If that gypsy had taken
another path, another fork in the forest . . ." Jussi sighed and
sat silent for a time. But it was not in Jussi's nature to be
silent for long. "Truth is out," he said, "and I feel the better
for it. It feels as though a weight has rolled off my chest.

A girl's reputation can run away as quickly as water in a
basket. But Annikki's is safe and what I say is, Be thankful
for the ways of Providence and let's have no more talk of it.
What's done is done." He got up swiftly and went to the little
corner cupboard behind him.

"This isn't a celebration," Maia said dourly.

"In a way it is. We'll drink to the first and last secret ever
to come between us." Jussi glanced back at Maia and then,
very slowly, took the precious bottle of *mesimarja* from the
cupboard.

"Not that," Maia said, aghast. "It's like drinking gold,
Jussi. And I know well you'll find any excuse good enough
for a celebration. But this time I won't join you."

Jussi looked at the rare, rose-colored liqueur. It was made
from berries which grow only in the far north and their rose-
colored flowers had ripened under the midnight sun. "I won't
join you, Jussi," Maia said again, and watched, her expression
cold and withdrawn, while Jussi sipped in silence.

"You're right," he said, putting the glass down and recork-
ing the bottle. "You're right, Maia. Somehow I don't seem
to have the palate for it, for the taste on my tongue is bitter-
sweet."

They looked at each other in silence.

14

THE SHORT, DARK DAYS grew longer imperceptibly. Children ceased gradually to go to school by moonlight, which fell cold and white over the silent forest and on the glittering lake, gripped by ice. The world was silent, a silence filled with the myriad tasks of living. It seemed to Annikki, during those winter days, that she had not been aware of the beauty of Porvesi in the early autumn, when she had felt, still, only the strangeness and loneliness of an uprooting. Those first days, which Arvo had recalled in the churchyard, had gone like the flash of a bird's wing, she would think, when the forest had blazed gold and red and green. Now, in this white intensity, her mind would feast on memories that she had not realized she had absorbed, memories of color, and its richness, under the sky.

Yet they were moving toward the halcyon days when spring would come overnight and the white forest would stir, and any moment, like a soft footfall, snow would fall gently from the branches, and the imprisoned brooks would flow again.

They were happy days, thought Annikki. Wild duck flew over the lake, soundlessly. In the morning hers would often be the first footfall to mark the snow on the porch. Silvi spent

lazy hours curled in milky contentment by the hearth while
Penna ran and barked joyously in the snow, his eyes bright,
his pelt vibrant. In the byre the cows turned their lambent
gaze on Annikki, fanning her with their warm, somnolent
breath as she went about her tasks. Erik gazed with new eyes
on his snow-covered land, on the hidden grain field rescued
from swamp and forest, and thought of the days ahead with
a strange, stirring sense of fulfillment. He thought, often now,
not only of today, which had for so long sufficed him, but of
tomorrow and the day beyond tomorrow. He was planning
as a man must plan on whom wife and child depend.

It had happened, as slowly, as imperceptibly, as the stirrings
beneath the soil, until one day he awoke and was aware of
some stupendous change. The dark, close roots of his being
had stirred and changed direction, tunneling deeper into him,
quickening him, as a woman quickens. He knew, now, that the
change, undreamed of, had taken place. That which he had
thought impossible had happened.

Slowly the image of Kirsti had faded and that of the girl
had taken its place; or rather they had merged, till the girl
who shared his life had become Kirsti, and Kirsti the girl.

He still slept alone in the small room he had built for his
son Kaarlo, and the girl still slept alone in the four-poster bed.
Sometimes, in the night, he wanted to rise and go to her and
take her in his arms, a woman, tender and warm, as Kirsti
had been, to know, not the desire, nor the lust, of tortured
flesh, but the warmth and tenderness his disciplined manhood
craved. But a deep-rooted male reluctance held him back.
Not yet, he would think, not yet. The time had not come.

To the girl he said nothing. Yet a deep, slow companionship grew between them as day followed day.

In February the play was performed in the parish hall.
"Just in time for me," Annikki said, "for if it had been much
later you could never have gone to Moscow leaving me as I
am. All Porvesi would be against you!"

Erik smiled, the slow, inner smile of the Finn. He smiled more often now and, Annikki thought, it is beginning to be a true marriage. She longed for some outward sign of affection from him but none came. Only in the play did he touch her and hold her close, and in her turn, Annikki clung to those moments to convey her love.

All Porvesi came to see the play. The presence of Vainen added excitement to the drama. The parish hall was filled, and while scene followed scene the room was as still and silent as the forest. Not a sound, not a murmur, came from an audience which gave itself wholeheartedly, with rapt attention.

Annikki felt the pathos and drama of her part sweep through her being. It was a woman, not a girl, who clung mutely to her husband, whose low-pitched voice, whose last cry, conveyed all the anguish of bereavement.

Ulla Hassi sat transfixed, her slanting eyes half closed. Elisabet Lahti held Lauri closer and cried silently with Annikki's voice, *Stay with me! Stay!* For those few moments the genuine accents of sorrow and despair filled the cold, bare room where the white night frosted the uncurtained windows.

Tragedy, which had touched all their lives, human endurance, with its bitter, satisfying savor, came to life on the bare boards, against Jussi's backdrop, came to life in the silence and the listening, and found an echo in every heart.

"The play was well chosen," Timo Vasola said afterward, scratching his head, "but who would have thought the girl from Turku had it in her?"

"And Maia. I've seen Maia act as dumb as that in life when nothing would make her say what she didn't want to. The police inspector got nothing out of her, not he," Veijo Lahti said proudly.

Performances were analyzed and judged, while Annikki stood proudly beside Erik in the brocade gown which, she was quite aware, contrasted with her white skin and set off her fair hair. She had a painful longing for Erik's admiration, for a word which would tell her that he found her beautiful.

It had not been hard for him to say such words in the play. She turned to look at him, all her love in her eyes, love which seemed almost to constrict her, seeking its release in words, in the sound of her name spoken as a man speaks the name of the woman he loves. She felt as though an unbearable tension were building up within her, and her eyes were very bright as the pastor paused beside them both in the rapidly emptying hall.

"Everyone belonging to the Dramatic Society is coming to my house tonight. You haven't forgotten, Vainen?" A flurry of snow whirled in as the door was opened. Maia and Margit and the rest of the women were already changing into their best clothes, the men into dark suits. It was an occasion for which Hilkka had been preparing most of the day and for which she had now hurried on ahead.

As Annikki changed her dress, shivering as she did so, she could hear a gentle drip, drip from the eaves. The snow was beginning to melt, here a little, there a little. This morning there had been a pale, February sun, with a faint warmth. Soon, now the long night of winter would be over.

Maia came to hook the back of Annikki's dress. The costumes used in the play had been heaped down in the small room, but her brocade dress, from which she had just stepped, stood almost by itself. Margit, the last to leave, had hurried out, bundled in layers of warm clothes. Maia said suddenly, "You think the child will be born in July?"

Annikki felt the sudden contraction of fear. She said, "Perhaps. Or perhaps later. Why worry? We shall know when the time comes."

Maia's hand rested for a moment longer on the girl's shoulder. Annikki waited for Maia to speak, but Maia did not speak. *She knows,* Annikki thought. She turned to face the older woman.

"Why do you ask?"

"No reason."

"You never do things without a reason."

"The child is not Vainen's."

"No."

"Whose, then?" Maia's breath was coming quickly. Her hand trembled on Annikki's shoulder. "Whose?"

"Why do you ask me?" Annikki said. Her eyes were large and brilliant. She in her turn trembled. With fear? With relief? She did not know.

"It is the gypsy's," Maia said.

"Yes." The word was a drawn-out sigh.

"Are you coming?" Margit called. "There's room for you both in the pastor's car."

"We're coming," Maia answered. She pulled the girl's dress into place quickly. "Jussi and I know," she said, "and we shall be as silent as the grave, what else? But tonight there was something in your face. You looked as though something had got to be said." She twitched the dress over Annikki's hips. "You looked like a person in delirium. Great eyes, you had, too bright."

"I'm not a fool, Maia, to speak to anyone of such a thing!"

"Tonight you worried me, all the same."

"How did you know . . . about the gypsy?"

"It was there, all the time, in front of our eyes. But we were blind at first. Then, suddenly . . ."

"Do you think others know it?"

"No. I'm certain of that. Keep your own counsel, girl, *always*. I'll be at hand, when the time comes. Quick—there's no time to talk now."

"Why don't you despise me? Berate me? It was your anger, and Jussi's heartache, that I feared."

"What's done is done. Vainen was your salvation. Be a good wife to him. No one will ever know." Maia gave Annikki a little push. "Keep a rein on yourself," she whispered, "and remember, what's said can never be unsaid. What's done can never be undone. Remember, girl, remember."

The words were echoed in the soft drip of the eaves. Soon the bare roof would be exposed as she, Annikki, was exposed,

everything melting, falling away, to expose the bare structure
of truth. What was there left to reveal of that body in the
lake? She shivered again and now her fear was real, it gripped
and held her, not as the first fear, a phantom which had
touched her and was gone.

"There's nothing to be afraid of," Maia said quickly.
"You're not the first and you won't be the last to go to your
marriage bed carrying another man's seed."

Annikki shuddered.

"Truth is as sharp as a knife, sometimes, girl. But neither
Jussi nor I judge you. We're sure it was none of your doing,
fool that you were. Smile, Annikki, smile," Maia said, as she
pushed open the door. Jussi was turning out the lights in the
empty room. "I thought you were never coming, or that
Annikki was sewn into her dress at least," he grumbled.

Outside, the sound of skis and sleighs hissed and crunched
on the snow. Harri Vasola's car had a full load, the headlights
gleaming on the road which had been cleared that morning.
On either side of the road the snow was banked high, the
drifts glittering in the light. The snow-covered pines caught
the bright, fugitive lights as they passed. Voices echoed across
the snow, and dark, heavily swathed forms were silhouetted
against it and then swallowed up by the night. Maia, with
Margit and Annikki, was seated in the back of the car. The
men had sped on their skis in the light of a pure, brilliant
moon. Maia's lips were set in a cold line and she glanced
sideways at Annikki's face with its chaste profile of youth.
Only the young could hurt so surely, so carelessly, she thought.
"Your anger. Jussi's heartache." So that's how the girl thought
of us both. There it was, in a nutshell. She sat silent. That
was the way of it and there was nothing to be done about that,
either. Maia had never lifted a finger for anyone's favor, certainly not that of this girl. She glanced again at Annikki, at
the cool sweetness of her cheek and throat. Jussi's heartache.
There was another side to it which the girl had not thought
of. Jussi was fiercely proud of his family, of which this girl

was part, and into which she had brought a strain of thieving, vagabond, gypsy blood. The girl would never think of that, but she, Maia, thought of it. If she shed a tear, let it be for Jussi.

The pastor's house was all that Elisabet had said, with its solid furniture, suggesting the Teutonic. The great sofa along one wall of the living room was upholstered in black horsehair, the wood smooth, heavy, and unadorned, as were the matching chairs, which looked as though they would defy generations of sitters. Tuomas Palin's family was an ancient one. In the seventeenth century, when Turku had still traded with the cities of the Hanseatic League, an ancestor had married the daughter of a merchant from Hamburg. The strain had cropped up, here and there, with Teutonic thoroughness. The pastor's uncompromising horsehair sofa, which had been his grandmother's, bore witness to it. The walls, in contrast, were made vivid with pictures by modern Finnish artists, a number of etchings and some brilliant *ryijy*, the hand-woven rugs made by the women of his family. There was a piano in the room, which was large and of rectangular shape, and a high and well-filled bookcase, the regular line of books broken by pieces of modern Finnish sculpture. The grandfather clock, set in one corner of the room with its rounded, almost feminine shape, should have looked out of place but did not. There was an affinity between the delicate, intricate designs which decorated it and the freer, bolder paintings on the walls. Though form and execution differed, there was something in both of vitality and harmony which sprang from the same creative impulse.

Hilkka came forward to supervise the shedding of warm outer garments and ushered the women in, to be followed by the men. Annikki, a little overawed by the greater formality of the pastor's house, stayed close to Vainen, but Maia unobtrusively drew her aside when the pastor had greeted each in turn.

"Let the men be," she said. "In company they like to keep together."

The pastor had greeted her as *Rouva* Vainen and the formal address had brought a flush of pride to her cheeks. Even Iris Hassi, who had acted as Annikki's understudy, had become *Neiti* Hassi, a subdued *Neiti* Hassi, whose slanting eyes looked demurely ahead. The men, as Maia had said, preferred to be together, merging into a dark mass at one end of the room, finding some topic of sudden, absorbing interest.

Presently Hilkka took a shining copper kettle to the dining room, in which were more books and another grandfather clock, and put it on the table, which was laden with cakes and little pies of her own baking. There all helped themselves and returned to the living room. Annikki drank her coffee and ate her *pulla,* glancing across at Vainen, deep in conversation with the *kirkkoherra.* People from Turku were considered, Annikki knew, to be stiff and unfriendly, but the pastor's expression as he talked was one of warm interest. Annikki saw, with surprise, that Vainen had brought Akseli's old *kantele* with its five strings. He had put it on the chair behind him.

The rugs on the walls, under the electric lights, blazed with color, woven in vibrant red and peacock blue and the leaf-green of young birch trees.

"Well," the pastor was saying between sips of coffee, "I hope you'll be prepared to join the parish council. Your name has been put forward by *Herra* Salonen. And by the way, there's an interesting article in one of the Helsinki papers about the murals. They were painted, it seems, according to a member of the Academy, by one of the monks with a great reputation for saintliness. I've often wondered where the line between saintliness and goodness is drawn."

"On the amount of charity we dole out to each other," Erik said. "By that reckoning old Akseli was a saint."

"The Lapp?" said the pastor. "He gave his life, didn't he, in a fruitless search for your son."

"That was the least of it. He was a saint in small things."

"Yet not a Christian."

"I am not close enough to Christ to know. But I know that he could tell of the ancient community of monks before the member of the Academy." Erik smiled.

"Akseli was a Lapp from the farthest north. In remote and silent places the senses of man must be keener," the pastor said reluctantly, for his nature, above all, was that of a realist.

"One can only tune a harp in silence."

"And I see you've brought yours," the pastor said, practically.

"It was Akseli's."

"You'll sing later, then? Good. *Herra* Vasola has brought his violin and *Rouva* Salonen plays the piano. *Rouva* Hassi is to sing.

"I shall do what is asked of me."

The pastor moved over to talk to Jussi. Conversation rippled among the women with rather more formality than that used in everyday speech. Iris Hassi came to Annikki and sat beside her with her laden plate.

"I thought you were like a real actress tonight, *Rouva* Vainen," Iris said. "When I join the Society I'll make them do *The Playboy of the Western World*. Have you read it? It is part of our course at school. I want to play Pegeen. So does Katri Niemi. But I mean to play it. One of the best lines goes like this"—Iris swallowed a mouthful of pie and her slanting eyes flashed scornfully—" *'You're making mighty certain, Shaneen, that I'll wed you now.'* I'd like to say that," Iris said, giggling, "to Arvo Salonen, the way he looked at me as though I were just waiting to be asked. Men are conceited when there are few of them about, don't you think, *Rouva* Vainen?" Iris chattered in her gay, laughter-filled Karelian voice, a heritage from a province she did not remember. Annikki sipped her coffee and listened silently and nodded, as befitted an older woman. Two years were all that lay between Iris and herself but now they might have been twenty, for here was Iris as

dutifully polite as an unmarried girl should be to a wife. While
Iris chattered Annikki looked across at Maia and thought of
the conversation they had had so short time ago. She was
filled with relief and fear. The voice of Iris Hassi dripped
softly, softly, with an occasional little flurry of laughter, like
the snow from the eaves. Suddenly Annikki could bear it no
longer and gave Iris her empty plate to take to the dining
room. Iris escaped with alacrity. Once you were married, Iris
thought, you became a quiet old woman, like Annikki Vainen.
She walked demurely across the room, her beautiful eyes
filled with sorrow at the words she was silently declaiming.
*"Oh, my grief, I've lost him surely. I've lost the only Playboy
of the Western World."* The words went to her head like
juniper wine and she did not see the rug on the floor till she
had tripped over it into an indignant Hilkka's lap.

The pastor paused by Annikki, who was gazing absently
ahead, thinking of the gypsy's belt which Maia had put in her
pocket.

"You are thinking of the city built on seven hills, *Rouva*
Vainen," the pastor said.

"Rome?" Annikki said vaguely, coming out of her reverie.

"No, no, no, your own city of Turku. Nothing was ever so
cool and so full of leafy green as Turku in summer. Don't
you agree?"

"I used to climb to the woods to look down on the river,"
Annikki said. "But it all seems a long time ago."

Maia came to her side. "Annikki has told me stories of her
childhood," she said, "and I've made her laugh with the tale
they tell of my great-grandfather. It might have been someone else's great-grandfather, for all that. We Tavasts," Maia
said, "can all tell a tale or two against ourselves." She looked
quickly at Annikki and felt that it would have been a relief
to prod, like Ulla Hassi, to emphasize her words. "Tell the
story, Annikki."

"The great-grandfather had a beautiful field of rye," Annikki said obediently, "but the field was placed just where it

was a temptation to take a short cut to the village. So, of course, somebody *took* the short cut, right through the field, and beat down the rye."

"So," said Maia, taking up the tale, "the angry old man fixed a big warning at the edge of the field, and since he had a violent temper, the warning was heeded. But one day great-grandfather himself was in a fearful hurry, and there was the field, and the short cut tempting *him*, and his rye standing that it was a pleasure to see. How to take that short cut with the warning about the trampled rye staring him in the face? Why, 'twas simple. He got two men to carry him through the field, shoulder high."

The pastor roared with laughter. "Ah, you vainglorious Tavast," he said slyly, "you're not the only one to know that our whole way of life is a balancing act."

When Hilkka had poured the last cup of coffee Margit took her place at the piano and Ulla Hassi stood up to sing. Though her voice was not true she sang without self-consciousness and with unforced pleasure, while Margit's work-hardened fingers ran swiftly over the keys. The song was about a *talkoo* for a widow. The widow needed a stable for her horse. " '*I have no man to build for me*' " Ulla sang, and the song went on to tell how the *talkoo* was called and everyone in the village came to her aid and worked as hard as they could till the stable was built and the roof put on. Then the widow made coffee and cakes and there was a feast afterward, with dancing in the barn. It was a long song with a chorus to every verse in which all joined with warmth and gusto and delight. The room was filled with a rich sense of living. Afterward Jussi played his violin, and when the last true notes had died away, the pastor put on a record of Sibelius. Now the room was filled with the power and majesty of Sibelius, the roar of the cataract, the silence of the forest, the stillness of the lake, and, beneath all, the deep, reverberating beat of the cosmic pulse of nature.

Annikki came back to herself, to the room, with a sense as

of coming from a great distance, and saw Erik take up his *kantele.*

"You shall finish the evening, Vainen," the pastor said. There was silence, and then the strange, almost metallic notes of the harp fell over the room. Erik was singing from *The Kalevala* about old Väinämöinen:

> In the dales he sowed the birch trees,
> In the loose earth sowed the alders,
> Where the ground was damp the cherries
> . . . Rowan trees in holy places. . . .

Annikki watched Erik as he sat, his fingers plucking at the strings as Akseli had taught him many years before. Erik's voice was deep and true. The *kantele,* so it was said in *The Kalevala,* had first been made by "the minstrel" from the bones of a giant pike, its pegs and screws from the gold and silver which flowed from the mouths of cuckoos.

There were giant pike in the lake, Annikki thought, as she watched Vainen, the light on his strong jaw, on his lowered head with the thick hair through which she wanted to run her hands. There were great pike in the lake. Sometimes, beneath the ice, a fish could be seen far below in that strange, shadowy world, silent, imprisoned, mute as a thought in the cells of the mind. But deeper, further, lay the bones of the gypsy, cradled in dark mud, unstirring, hidden, soundless as a thought. Annikki, watching Vainen, willed him to look at her. Presently he did so. Their eyes met, and Annikki felt confidence flow into her above the chanting song, above the plucked strings.

Turning away Annikki felt Maia's sharp gaze upon her, and smiled. Maia nodded briefly, satisfied.

15

IN THE EVENINGS when the day's work was done, Erik and Annikki would sit by the hearth. The stove glowed with fierce, banked-up warmth, the logs sending out their spicy, resinous heat over the whole house. The hearth was the all-embracing womb of the house, a place of security and sanctuary.

Soon, now, the ice would break, but the lake was still frozen. Together, Annikki and Erik drove in the sleigh across the lake, the air glittering like the icicles which hung from the pine branches, the horse's hoofs ringing, the sleigh bells sounding clear, toward Porvesi. Erik needed seed-grain and tools and other necessities. Annikki had said that as soon as the spring came they must make a swing seat for the garden, painted in bright red or blue, and some chairs.

"You have none of these things, Vainen," she said.

"Kirsti was dead before we had time to think of such things."

"We are not dead," said Annikki. "Our lives are before us, so we must begin now to have things ready for the summer. We will plant a little garden, with rose trees, like Maia's and Jussi's. Then we shall have roses for Kirsti's grave."

When Annikki had said the words she waited, scarcely

breathing, for she had trodden deliberately where no one else, perhaps, had ever trod. She knew where Kirsti's grave was. The last time she had gone to the churchyard with Maia she had seen fresh flowers there.

"One of the women has put them there. So it began in the beginning and so it goes on. Vainen never comes here. Kirsti lies near Eino Lahti, so Elisabet Lahti, I don't doubt, put them there," Maia had said.

Annikki waited for Erik to speak.

"It would be kindness," he said, "for you to put flowers on Kirsti's grave."

"And there should be more on the stone than just 'Kirsti.' Everyone else has his age, the years, the months, the weeks— even the days. To do as others do is good!" Annikki cried.

"I know Kirsti's name and age, that is sufficient," Erik said.

Annikki had spoken passionately. She longed, with what had become a fierce longing, to cross the barrier, to pierce Erik's inmost defenses so that he must yield, surrender to her his deepest feelings; she wanted to find the source of the hidden spring of his being. The tension was there in her always, beneath the surface, an inarticulate longing which had been conceived of her love and which grew within her as the child grew physically. Both were burdens which must find their natural release. Yet Erik would not yield. Annikki searched, in their deepest moments of companionship, for some sign beyond tenderness, something beyond protection, gentleness, and care; she longed for a sign of his love, a man's love for her, the woman. But Erik kept his inner self intact, kept his secrets. Yet Annikki, too, had hers. She did not speak of her conversation with Maia on the night of the play. She did not tell him that Maia and Jussi knew who was the father of her child, had, perhaps, always known. For Vainen to know this, Annikki felt, would make their unity, such as it was, less complete. Now, with a new awareness, she listened to every word he said, weighed it, remembered. Somewhere, she felt, she would find the key to his feelings for her and unlock the

inner silence, make herself free of it. Yet "freedom," Vainen
had once told her, "is emerging from a little prison into a
bigger one." Yet somewhere, Annikki knew, within that bigger
prison, lay what she sought. And to inhabit the bigger prison
with Vainen seemed sweeter than the freedom of the world.

Had she but known it, Erik, watching her, felt a strong,
quiet gladness welling within him. Annikki was maturing
slowly and certainly, a woman whose roots ran deep and were
slowly coming to fruition. Once the child was born a new day
would dawn for them both. What had been, had been. Justice
was done. It would be a life for a life.

When he looked at the pure curve of Annikki's cheek, at
the soft fullness of her lips, Erik thought of the days to come
and the happiness that lay in wait to take them both, as the
morning sun took the lake, light and water one and indivisible.

Meanwhile the life-giving air of winter revitalized them
both. It was a time when man and soil alike felt the slow,
inevitable stir of renewal.

"You look ten years younger, Vainen," Jussi said a little
enviously when he saw Erik. "So now it's a garden swing," he
grinned. "Watch out, or you won't be master in your own
house."

Maia came bustling in and cast a quick, experienced look
over Annikki's figure and face.

"I have news from Margit," she said. "Arvo is leaving the
sea and coming home for good."

Erik was running grain through his fingers. "A man has no
need of the sea when there's land for him to inherit," he said.

"That's what Eino felt when the boy went off. But he said
nothing."

"A man must make his own life," Jussi said. "It was a blow
to Eino when Arvo chose the sea, but now Arvo knows where
his heart lies and the farm will stay in the family. I daresay
Meri will marry, but land should go from father to son if
lasting good is to come of it."

"So your land is safe, Vainen," Maia said. She gazed straight and hard at Annikki, as though defying her to move a muscle.

"Yes, my land is safe. If this child is a boy the farm will be his, naturally."

"Let's drink to it," Jussi suggested, with a quick, sly glance at Maia.

"We'll drink to it," Maia said resignedly. "Be careful, Jussi, that you don't say *'let's drink to it,'* out of habit, when I breathe my last."

They went into the living room to the accompaniment of Jussi's laughter. He filled their glasses with schnapps. The frost had drawn leaves and ferns and scrolls upon the windows. Between the fronds the light came into the room diamond-sharp and bright. Annikki took off her heavy coat and gloves. She wore a dress of dark-brown wool against which her skin looked creamy white. There was a bloom and sheen upon her which took the eye, however ill come by, Maia thought. The girl looked as a girl should who was a wife with child and the long days of summer ahead of her. As Erik raised his glass, lifting it and his fine profile to the light, Maia thought that the ways of Providence were no easier to understand than they had ever been. There was something there in the room with them, something sprung from violence and fear, something with another name. It was happiness.

"To Vainen's son," Jussi said slowly and deliberately.

"To Vainen's son," Maia echoed.

They drank appreciatively. Moisture shone on Jussi's red, generous lips for a moment.

"What do you think of naming the child, Annikki?" Maia asked.

Annikki was looking out of the window toward the snowy paddock. She did not answer. Indeed, she had not heard Maia speak. Against the snow, she could see again the dark face of the gypsy.

"Speak, girl, speak," Maia cried. "Don't stand there like that French king who took a quarter of an hour to make his confession!"

"We haven't thought of a name," Erik said. "We must find the right one. There's such power in a name, more than we know, I think." He looked at Annikki.

"There *is* power in a name, Vainen," she said softly, and waited. She felt as though her throat would burst with longing as she looked at him, waiting for the word, the name. It had become, now, the fine balance on which their lives hung, the symbol of their love. Akseli had had a word to subdue fire and one word, one name, on Vainen's lips must subdue Vainen, find his hidden power, tap the undiscovered source.

"There is power in a name," Erik said again and drained his glass and put it on the table. Annikki pressed her hands together, aware of the silent struggle between them in which Vainen would not yield. The struggle was bound up with the child she carried and its bitter origin, bound up with that body in the lake, bound up with his past, his love for Kirsti, Annikki knew. To utter her name would be, for Vainen, to deliver himself utterly into her hands, to negate the past, to take the final, irrevocable step into the future. For this, Vainen was not yet ready. To do this, the man who had been Vainen must be transubstantiated, like a dead wafer, into a living body and blood, his past life the savorless wafer on the tongue transmuted into the richness of living bread.

What is there between these two, Maia wondered? She glanced at Jussi, always voluble, and now, with the schnapps, as ready to talk as a cock to crow. But there was nothing here which talking could better and plenty that it could worsen.

"I must get back to the larder," she said, "and you're wanted in the store, Jussi, by the look of it. Vainen hasn't all morning to buy his seed-grain."

She went out, beckoning to Annikki as she did so. "Put your coat on and come to the larder. You can help me move the beans."

The larder was as cold as the world outside, sunk into the ground and lined with snow. Annikki went down into the square well, with its sloping roof, and Maia followed her,

casting a shrewd eye over her stores of meat and butter, vegetables, and summer fruit. The air was icy and sweet. Together
they moved a tub of salted beans.

"Remember what I said. Keep your own counsel. And
another thing. If ever that gypsy comes looking for his belt
tell him he'll find it where his horse is," Maia said.

"I don't think he'll come."

"Nor I. And to tell the truth, I'd find it a wrench to part
with the horse."

"Is it still gentle?"

"As gentle as a lamb and as biddable as an old sheep. All
the fire gone out of him. You can tame any animal, however
wild, that eats from your hand. I sometimes wonder whether
it wasn't always meant to be so."

"No. There must be beasts of prey as long as men prey on
each other," Annikki said.

"You're right, girl. You know what they say?" Maia heaved
at a joint of meat and turned it. "If a man makes friends with
a man let him keep a knife in his pocket."

"And so . . . ?" Annikki asked slowly.

"And so nothing. The past is finished. There's nothing but
happiness ahead for you and Vainen."

In the store Jussi and Erik talked in level tones.

"I'm going to plant red clover after the rye," Erik said.

"There's nothing like it to improve the rye," Jussi agreed.
"Salonen got a fine strong crop with full ears last year, after
clover. And the scent of that clover. . . . I can smell it now.
It was intoxicating. I tell you, Vainen, I used to pass that
field singing at the top of my voice. Maia thought it was
schnapps and wouldn't believe me when I swore it was just
the smell of the clover."

"There should be plenty of wild strawberries in the woods,"
Erik went on. "I remember, the first year, how Kirsti and the
boy filled a big basket with them."

Now, thought Jussi, his curiosity whetted by this confidence,
Vainen will talk, for certain, he'll tell me what I already

know and there'll be an end of it. I would give a great deal, Jussi thought, to know just how Vainen and the girl came together.

Erik, however, drew out his wallet and counted out the marks from the little wad of notes and handed them to Jussi gravely, bidding him good day, and turned to go.

"No man," Jussi said to Maia, "will ever get to the bottom of Vainen."

"Perhaps Vainen hasn't got to the bottom of himself," Maia said.

"Only the girl can do it. Only Annikki. She loves that man."

"A woman will love any man who protects her. And at the time Annikki was hardly a woman, still a girl, even a child in some things. Yes, she loves Vainen. But there's something fevered in her love. And little wonder."

"They don't sleep in the same room, or the same bed. You saw that for yourself, and we know why. Vainen has never touched her. He'll never touch her till the child is born and the past is the past. No man or woman born will stir Vainen from his own way of thinking. But then, it's the way I'd feel myself. The way I'd be."

"You?" Maia said. "Perhaps not, Jussi. That much of iron may not be in you. You're a strong, good man, none better. But the mold that made Vainen is bigger than the mold that made you."

Jussi took Maia's arm and drew her to the window. He pointed to the garden, where an aspen tree stood cold and still in the snow. "Come the summer," Jussi said, "that tree will be quivering under its leaves, sighing and rustling this way and that with the sun combing it with great gold fingers as a girl combs her hair. But underneath that tree . . . do you remember?"

"The great granite boulder. Yes, I remember."

"That's the mold that made us all, woman. That's our matrix. Granite."

"But I see your summer leaves sighing and rustling clearer

than I see Vainen's," Maia said obstinately. "There's a bit
more of the granite there than in any of us. And sometimes
I wonder . . ." Maia turned from the window. "Sometimes
I wonder for Annikki and Vainen . . . how it will all end."

"It *has* all ended. What comes after is a beginning. Not a
soul in Porvesi knows the truth except you and me. And remember, the child Annikki carries is half hers. And, by God,
that makes it something of mine, too. The time has come to
stop your frettings and teeterings like a hen on a roof. The
course is set fair. Keep a tight mouth and follow it. Woman,
ask yourself, when you think of this violation of Annikki, ask
yourself, what is life? I'll tell you. It's a narrow ledge between
two precipices. The end is not seen. One must keep on walking. To turn back is to perish. One must keep on walking."

16

SPRING CAME OVERNIGHT. The snow melted, the forest brooks ran, the white land of the frozen lake which had borne man and beast became water again in which dawns and sunsets and tall pines were reflected. The young grass grew, there was the sound of birds singing, the air was soft, pure, blowing across the forest, new colors came to the land. The young birches put out their tender green, the dark pine and spruce glistened with their renewed, aromatic oils. Here and there a juniper stood, blue-green, and the good smell of growing things was carried on the breeze.

"I must paint the house this spring," Erik said, looking at the soft, muted color of the walls which had once been ocher-red. "The shutters, too. You can hardly tell they were once green."

Annikki would bear her child in some three months but she stood tall and upright with her burden. Her skin had a silken sheen. The fine golden down on her arms shone in the sunlight which grew stronger every day. "I will help with the potato planting today," she said. "I can follow you with the basket of seed potatoes and drop them into the furrows, as Kirsti did."

"The work is tiring."

"Not as tiring as for Kirsti. Food was scarce in those days. I eat well. I haven't known what hardship is."

"Why do you talk of Kirsti?"

"Because you think of her."

"I haven't forgotten her, if that's what you mean. I haven't forgotten my son, I haven't forgotten other springs either, springs like this. But life goes on."

They stood together in front of the house, the forest about them astir with life. The long barn gave out its own vibrations of life. The cows moved restlessly now, sniffing the sweetness of the air when Annikki opened the door, turning their great soft, inquiring eyes upon her.

"It's warm enough to let the animals out," Erik said. Penna came barking, making little dashes at the horse which was waiting, harnessed to the cart.

"We shall hear the cowbells again." Annikki smiled. "And the hens clucking about. I shall hunt for eggs—and they will be *our* eggs, wherever I find them. All this is yours, Vainen, and now mine as well." Annikki bent down and picked up a handful of soil. "It's when the spring comes that the earth seems real. Isn't it strange that human beings can own the soil? Can own it as they own the things they build?" She held the moist earth to her cheek. "I am glad I am alive," she whispered.

Her face had something of the soft, sensuous tenderness of the morning, making her one with it. How is it, Erik thought, that good can come out of evil? He glanced away toward the lake. There was the sibilant murmur of ripples against the reeds at its edge, where the little path led to the *sauna*. Annikki followed his gaze. She put her hand on his arm and looked into his eyes, and trembled suddenly. The words she wanted to utter froze on her tongue. *There is nothing left now of the gypsy in the lake,* she wanted to say. She felt the child stir within her and stood very still.

"What is it?" Erik asked.

"I felt the child move again."

"That is natural. But you were going to speak, to say something else."

"Only . . . only that you promised to make a little jetty so that we can dive into the lake after the bath. And I was going to say . . ." her voice trailed into silence.

"What were you going to say?"

"To make it a little higher up, on the other side, where the water is not so deep. Then, when the child comes, I shall not worry when he is out of my sight."

"You were thinking of little Kaarlo. You trembled," Erik said.

"I was thinking . . . how easily . . . a body can disappear in the lake."

Erik's eyes, deeply set and intensely blue in the clear morning light, narrowed suddenly as though the limpid sunlight was too strong. He touched the hand that lay on his arm with a touch so light that Annikki wondered whether she had imagined it.

"You trembled for my son," Erik said.

A cuckoo called suddenly with a note, clear and evanescent as quicksilver, across the lake.

"The first cuckoo," Annikki said.

"Soon they will call to each other all day across the lake."

"But this is the first cuckoo."

"*The cuckoo called when I was born,*" the gypsy had said. As he had replied then, Erik found himself replying now.

"A bird of good omen."

"Yes. A bird of good omen. Do you remember, in *The Kalevala,* when Ilmarinen asked for the lovely maiden of Pohjola? She said that if she sought a foreign country the nightingales would migrate and the cranberries vanish and all the cuckoos vanish with them. Think of a summer without cuckoos!"

"The cuckoo will call when our son is born."

"*Our* son?"

"Our son. But the cuckoo will be at the end of his song by then." Now, thought Annikki, Vainen surely will touch me, take me in his arms, give me a sign for the future. The cuckoo called again, a pure, heartless note out of the silence, leaving silence behind. Erik went back to the cart. "We must finish the potato planting," he said. "I want to whitewash the byre too, as soon as the beasts are out."

"I'll clean it out as soon as it's empty," Annikki said.

It would be hard work, and satisfying, like a renewal. Everything was being renewed, the earth, themselves, most of all themselves. *"Our son"* he had said. But so, also, had he said *"I will marry you,"* as one accepting his fate. I was young then, Annikki thought. I did not know then how a man can trap himself by his own words, his own nature. She went to the cart and climbed in beside Erik. As they drove, Annikki looked at him, recalling him as he had been that first day in the forest. Imperceptibly, day by day, change had come to him also, as well as to herself. He held the reins lightly and gazed about him now intently. His face would never lose its inward, contemplative look, but the subtle difference was there. The past had laid its imprint on him but the intentness of his gaze was directed at the future.

"There will be clover there this year," he said pointing ahead. "And I am thinking of clearing some more forest land to extend the farm. As it is it would not suffice a family for a living. My wants were few and easily satisfied but as the family grows so must the acres."

"Will you work alone, as you did in the past?"

"There is casual labor to be had. Jussi's man, Paavo, would be glad of extra money. Veijo Lahti, too. They're hard put to it sometimes, I think, with three growing boys."

The future began to take shape before Annikki's eyes, a future fashioned for her by Vainen's quiet voice. The months are slipping by, she thought; the pattern is formed. Vainen will never tell me that he loves me as men in the beginning tell their wives. We have had no beginning. It was like coming straight to a new country without seeing its borders. We crossed the borders with our eyes closed and so, she thought with clarity, there is no wonder, no expectancy. The country we inhabit is not new and strange. Its climate is a steady, settled affection. So I have begun where Kirsti left off.

She looked at Erik and tried to imagine him in his youth, hot-blooded and eager, unabashed by the words of courtship, of love, of passion. I shall never know them, Annikki thought, from a man who never speaks my name.

The cuckoo called again. The pure, silvery, heartless cry echoed across the lake. Annikki's eyes filled with tears. She was filled with anguish for what had never been. She wanted to weep for what she would never know.

"I shall get good hay from this field," Erik said. "It lies in the path of the wind and the eye of the sun. At harvest time I shall buy another horse."

Annikki caught her breath. She thought of the gypsy's horse, its gentleness, its beauty. Maia loved the horse. But . . . you do not kill a man and take his horse. The horse, with all his fire gone from him, would grow old in Jussi's service. From what far place had he come that day, through the white forest?

"Eino Salonen will sell me a horse," Erik said, "if need be. And at a fair price. Eino drives a hard bargain but a just one."

Annikki crossed her arms over her body. "This child may not be a son," she said thoughtfully.

Erik sat silent, thinking of the gypsy, of the hard, slender body with its urgent life. He had caught some of that urgency in the carved figure. The wood lived, and had become a man. But Annikki did not know that he had finished the figure. It stood in the woodshed in the darkness.

"It will be a son," he said. "I am sure of it."

"You should hate the gypsy," Annikki cried passionately, "as I do."

"I did hate him," Erik said, "I hated him to the death. But

men do not think as women think. No man will ever know
what it means to a woman to be forced." He turned from
Annikki as the horse stopped of its own accord at the potato
field and dismounted, leaving her to follow. The words she
had been about to utter died on her lips. *"You killed him,
Vainen, you killed him."* They were wild words, perhaps they
were not even true, perhaps she had never seen that dark
form on Vainen's shoulder, never heard the midnight splash
in the lake, she thought feverishly. She took the full basket
which Vainen had filled from the sack and followed him as he
harnessed the horse to the plow.

"Work with me till the sun gets warm," he said, "and then
you must rest in the shade."

There was silence as they worked except for the sudden
flight of a bird startled from a furrow or the sound of wheels
on the road, the voice of Veijo Lahti calling a greeting, and
once again the cry of the cuckoo across the lake. It had an
unearthly sound, a spirit with a sudden echo. Faint and far
away was a tinkle of cowbells.

"Jussi's cows are out," Erik said. "That echo came from
the edge of the forest." He began to sing softly and the horse
pricked up its ears and listened. The sun grew steadily
warmer with the promise of summer.

The spring sowing was finished. The days lengthened steadily. Now there were fresh fish to be caught in the lake and
cooked and eaten at once, full of richness and savor after the
salt fish of winter. There were no fresh vegetables yet, since
there could be no winter sowing, but berries and fruits were
ripening and bloomed, as Annikki bloomed, during those
golden days.

"Soon," Annikki said, "they will be lighting the bonfires
for St. John's Day. Midsummer will soon be here."

They were sitting on the shores of the lake in the cool of
the night, the day's work done. The day had been hot, as hot

as July, though it was still June. The sun shone with a serene
and gentle radiance over lake and forest, over the homestead
and the cattle which sat so tranquilly in the meadow chewing
their cud, their breath flowing softly on the still air. The
strangeness of the light, the light of the midnight sun, gave
the scene on which they gazed the quality of a dream, a dream
transmuted into memory. The silence was the silence of a
dream. The stillness and the magic of the light produced their
own vibrations and within them the universe seemed to hold
its breath.

Erik spoke softly.

"I remember as a youth jumping over the bonfires on St.
John's Eve. I remember dancing in the woods as they dance
now, all night long."

"I remember dancing among the trees. The nights were hot,
but the breeze was cool. Everything seemed to smell so sweet,"
Annikki said dreamily. She closed her eyes and the strange
light touched her eyelids. A fish jumped in the lake, sending
up a shower of quicksilver. No sound came from the quiet
cattle or from the little horse peacefully grazing, flicking its
tail at a fly or mosquito as it browsed. The pines and birches
were reflected in the lake, their reflection no more dreamlike
than the trees themselves, which stood unstirred by any wind.
All was softness, and mystery, sunlight and peace, in a day
which had begun long since but which would never end,
simply melting imperceptibly into the next.

From Porvesi could be heard faint, distant sounds, once the
ring of a hammer or an ax, where Eino Salonen was putting
up a barn. Faint as the sounds were Erik heard them. No man
could waste the long, precious hours of sunlight. It was not yet
two o'clock. Eino's ax would be heard a little longer yet.

Annikki sat with her hands folded in her lap. She moved
a little more slowly now and often fell silent over the knitting
or the sewing which had grown slowly between her fingers. In
Kirsti's linen cupboard she had found a store of baby clothes

and Maia, thriftily, had urged her to use them for the child.
But Annikki had put them back in their folds of paper.

"I will use them for Vainen's child," she had said, "when
that day comes. This child is mine alone."

She opened her eyes now to find Erik looking at her. Like
her, he was tanned by the sun. As soon as they had felt its
summer warmth they had started to bathe in the lake, flinging
off their clothes in the *sauna* and running swiftly across the
sandy sedge to plunge into the gleaming water, drawing in
their breath sharply as they were enveloped in its pure, sting-
ing coldness, their solitude complete. From head to foot their
bodies were brown and resilient. Annikki stretched now as
luxuriously as a cat, the sun hot on her face.

"I'm going to swim," she said.

The golden light restored to the world its first peace. Silently they undressed and slid into the water, moving in it
almost soundlessly, floating, their faces to the sky, an infinity
of clear light. Neither spoke. Annikki half closed her eyes
and dreamed of a field of buttercups in which the horse and
cattle grazed, moving delicately between the golden flowers.
That morning she had plucked a bunch of marsh marigolds.
Even the shadow they had cast upon her hand had been tinged
with gold. There were flowers everywhere; pale harebells grew
in the woods, the scent of heather and clover was borne on
the wind. The cows were warm and somnolent when she
rested her head against their sides to milk them. Soon the hay
would be fully ripe and piled, cone-shaped, onto the drying
poles. The rye was pale gold in the field. The little farm
throve. But Vainen was right, Annikki thought. It would not
suffice a growing family. Next year there would be other voices,
Veijo's, Paavo's, the voice of a child. This was the last of their
solitude. Annikki closed her eyes but the light still shone
against her dazzled eyelids.

Erik swam slowly and effortlessly to the shore and stood a
moment in the sunshine before drawing on his clothes. An-

nikki followed him, her full, naked body gleaming and beginning to dry immediately and almost imperceptibly in the
warm air.

Erik did not look at her, yet delight filled him. This was
Kirsti, coming up sun-browned and serene from the cold lake,
carrying her child. This was Kirsti, yet it was not Kirsti but
the girl, a woman who came toward him bringing with her
peace and fulfillment. The child she carried was as much his
as any man's. He, the girl, and the child were one with the
eternal renewal of nature.

This was fulfillment and peace. This, truly, was the heart
of the whirlpool.

17

THEY WERE DANCING at midnight in the summer woods, all the boys and girls of Porvesi. A wooden platform had been built in a clearing among the trees and on it they danced tirelessly, music and laughter echoing between the trees under a lambent sky. Morning was approaching without sign, night and day one, fusing and melting into each other. The air was sweet. Birds began to stir. On the bright green moss which grew beside the rivulet the dew clung in minute globes of light.

Iris Hassi was dancing with Arvo Salonen, who had come out to join the dancers. He whirled her this way and that so that the full, red skirt which Iris wore petaled out like a flower. The glance of Iris Hassi's slanting eyes was triumphant and a little mocking as she whirled past her friend Tyyne, dancing with Farmer Vasola's eldest grandson. She, Iris, was dancing with the pick of all the partners, a man to their silly boys. If only Annikki Vainen could see her now! Once, long ago, at the beginning of last fall, she had heard it said that Arvo Salonen had made up his mind to marry Annikki. That was the trouble with a little place like Porvesi, Iris thought. Old Heikki had once said that at the other end of Porvesi they knew when he turned over in bed.

The breeze fanned Iris's hot cheeks and she smiled up into
Arvo's face, into the gray eyes with their dark, thick lashes.
Arvo was singing gaily as he danced. His mother had said
that all the modern dances had a lot in common with the old
country ones she had danced as a girl. "Face your partners . . .
turn about, over-arm, under-arm, nothing ever changes," Margit had said. Iris Hassi's soft mouth looked inviting beneath
his own, Arvo thought. She was a baggage, but, as yet, as
sweet as well water. The violin played faster, feet flew, skirts
rustled, laughter echoed in the leafy woods.

"I'm going to give you a name, Arvo," Iris cried. "It's 'The
Playboy of The Western World.' I think he was like you,
I do really."

"I'm not a playboy, I'm twenty-five, settled and serious,"
Arvo said teasingly. "Besides, that's a bad choice of name.
For you see yourself as Pegeen, I don't doubt."

Iris tossed her long brown plaits and her eyes sparkled. This
was life; she was living in the way she had always dreamed,
dancing and talking, and yet, flirting, with a man like Arvo
Salonen. Her breath came quickly, eagerly; color came and
went in her round, soft, innocent cheeks.

"You're going to stay in Porvesi for good, aren't you?" Iris
said, artlessly, her feet moving nimbly.

"Yes. I'm going to be a farmer. I couldn't stay away any
longer from the farm—or the girls of Porvesi," Arvo teased.
The music came to a stop. Arvo looked with laughing eyes
into the young face below his.

"Another long summer night is nearly over, Iris. Now you
must dance with little farmer Vasola over there. He is nearly
as old as you, fifteen, I think, and he has been looking at you
all night and hoping for a dance." Arvo gave her a brotherly
pat. "Here he comes to ask you for one. If you want to be
a woman of the world, Iris, you must learn to be gracious,
though chagrined."

Iris moved away, not quite certain whether she was being
laughed at or not, and smiled graciously at the little Vasola.

When he took her hand in his, however, she wrinkled her
nose in disdain and all her worldliness vanished. "You're hot
and sticky, little Harri Vasola," she cried. "If you want to
dance with me, go and wash your hands in the stream."

She tossed her head and undulated away, affecting not to
hear Arvo's laughter.

"I can do the quickstep," said little Harri defensively, "and
the cha-cha."

"Then cha-cha to the stream," Iris said, fluffing out her
skirt, "and cool your hands. Then perhaps I'll dance with
you."

Still laughing, Arvo turned away and took out a cigarette.
He had come out on an impulse to join the dancers as he had
done as a boy. There had been boys and girls then who had
since gone away, as he had gone, passing their examinations,
going on to university, perhaps, if they were lucky and suc-
cessful, always with a goal: to learn, to work, to *do*. They had
all been gay and lighthearted, celebrating *Kesäkuu* as it would
always be celebrated, dancing and singing and visiting around
Porvesi, when they had won their students' caps, as these boys
and girls would dance and sing. Of them all, Arvo thought,
Iris Hassi stood out, with that little aura of difference which
might one day mark her for success. There was just that
touch of ruthlessness about her, also, he thought, which might
make that elusive goal certain. Arvo drew on his cigarette,
watching the dancers in the soft light which touched the
young, unmarked faces gently. It was good to be home again,
to feel the soil of his own farm beneath his feet, to breathe the
forest air. Perhaps, subconsciously, he had always known that
it would call him back. But there had been another call, deep
and almost unacknowledged, perhaps the call of something
stronger than himself. It was only when he had made the
decision to return and had come back to Porvesi that Arvo
had known why he had been drawn back. It had been partly
the pull of the deep roots of his family background, partly
because he had fallen in love with Annikki Berling.

He had seen her a few times only, talked with her twice, a short enough time, Arvo had thought, in which a man might surrender something of himself. But it had happened. Something in the girl's quiet beauty, her inexperienced youth, which yet had in it a sense of awareness, had stirred a deep chord in him. He had not forgotten her. She had filled his mind, the memory of her had had power to stir him. It had not been her beauty alone, a beauty of soft white skin, fair shining hair, long smooth limbs. Other women had these also. In the long summer nights and days the women of his country bloomed, Arvo knew. It was a fresh, glowing beauty, born of air and sunshine, wind and water. No, he had fallen in love with Annikki, and that was all there was to it.

He had returned to find her, swiftly and unaccountably, married to Vainen and already to bear a child to a fine man, young and vigorous still, in the prime, perhaps, of his years. But one could not speak of such things. A few words in the churchyard, a moment filled with an almost unbearable sense of loss when he had seen the color run up in her cheeks, her full, soft mouth tremble—that was all there was to that, also. His mother had guessed, Arvo knew, doubtless knew also, how deep and strong his feelings had run. But there was an end to it. There was nothing to be said or done. One day, perhaps, the void would have to be filled. A man must raise up sons for the land. Arvo stood apart, the smoke from his cigarette curling on the soft, pure air and felt, for the first time, the loneliness of life, asked, for the first time, the eternal questions a man must ask when he has come, finally, to maturity.

The sound of wheels, of subdued voices, made him turn his head. In the distance, coming leisurely down the forest track, was a man riding a horse, and behind him a cart in which another man and two women were seated, one old, one young. The old one was driving.

Gypsies, Arvo thought, rogues and vagabonds all, and he thought suddenly of his bicycle, propped against a tree at the edge of the forest, where it could have remained propped for

a week, if need be, in the ordinary course of things. But gypsies were another matter. One of them, probably the man in
the cart driven by the old woman, would almost certainly
make off with it, and a few old sacks would be thrown over
it on the floor of the cart.

The sound of wheels and hoofs drew nearer. There were
usually more of them, Arvo thought, when they moved from
place to place. Perhaps these had come on ahead to find a
good camping ground. If so, the farther from Porvesi the
better, or no one's chickens would be safe. Perhaps, Arvo reflected, they were not as bad as they were painted but they had
been known as rogues and thieves by all ever since he could
remember. To give a dog a bad name was to hang him, as far
as Arvo and his neighbors were concerned. The ins and outs
of any depredations had never concerned them. A bad name
was its own justification, as well as a good one.

Arvo waved a brief good-by to Iris Hassi who was dancing
vigorously, a head taller than little Harri. The clear gold
morning sunlight, stronger, less mysterious than the sun of
night, was bathing the trees, slanting through the branches on
to the little cavalcade. The man who rode was not young, a
stocky, thickset man, his dark eyes set in a sallow face. He was
bareheaded, his black hair grizzled, but in spite of the summer heat he wore a greasy coat. His horse was a roan with a
pale-colored mane. The man in the cart, Arvo saw, was young,
probably this man's son. He was dark-eyed, with pale, pock-
marked skin which would turn sallow as he aged, and he
appeared taller, as well as considerably slighter, than the
older man. As they approached, Arvo, from his point of van-
tage, looked at the women. The older one was a crone, but
the younger a woman of surprising beauty.

Arvo stood a moment gazing at the pure, oval curves of her
face, at her liquid dark eyes and the black, silky hair falling
to her shoulders. Then he remembered his bicycle and began
to make his way through the trees to the forest edge. He would
swim before breakfast and the day's work, he decided. The

lake would be at its most beautiful, sapphire blue, reflecting
the colors of the sky and the newly painted red walls of their
sauna set at its edge.

The gypsies had almost reached him, and the older man
called some greeting, and beckoned. Arvo stood still, ignoring
the gesture, and waited without appearing to wait, for the
man to approach. He came close and drew rein and the cart
halted behind him.

"*Hyvää päivää,*" he said ingratiatingly.

"Good day," Arvo replied. The horse nuzzled his shoulder
and the old man reined it in with a jerk. The man behind,
and the two women, watched intently.

"I am looking," the old man said, "for something. For a
belt which," he smiled craftily, "my son lost last summer. A
belt like this. Have you seen it? Or heard, perhaps, of such a
belt?"

The man's voice was old and guttural, Finnish and Swedish
mixed. It rasped on Arvo's nerves. He was about to walk on
with a shake of the head when the old man suddenly dangled
a belt in front of him, startling the horse as the leather swished
through the air. Out of politeness Arvo looked at the belt. It
was of good leather with a shining buckle, chased and polished.

"No," Arvo said. "I know nothing of it."

"Such a belt is worn by all my sons," the old man said. "The
buckles are made by our tribe. See, these are the markings.
And the buckle is silver." He pointed with a black-nailed
thumb at the buckle.

"I know nothing of it," Arvo repeated. The sound of the
violin came to them on the breeze and then a sudden burst of
laughter. The old man turned his head to listen. The younger
man and the two women listened. Even the two horses pricked
their ears and listened.

The old man smiled. "They are dancing, the young people."

"Yes. And they know nothing of the belt either," Arvo said
slowly, thinking of Iris Hassi and the young man in the cart

who might intercept a glance from those strange eyes of hers.
"No such belt has been found here. If it had I would have
heard of it. Belts with silver buckles don't grow on the trees."
He turned to go. "Keep on your way," he said. "Keep on going. Good day."

"We are on our way," the old man said. "Yesterday we
passed through Vituri and spent the night in the forest. Nobody in Vituri had found a fine belt. Today we reach Porvesi." There was a strange menace in the ingratiating smile.
The younger man and the two women sat silent.

"Keep on going," Arvo said again. "You're not welcome
here."

"We must pass through Porvesi," the old man said softly.
"It is on our way. This is the way my son went . . . by all
accounts."

"Keep your hands off our hen roosts then," Arvo said. "I'll
warn our neighbors."

The old man smiled. "We are not looking for chickens,"
he said.

Arvo struck off to the right to take a short cut. The gypsies
moved off and Arvo turned to watch them. The younger
woman's eyes met his and she spoke. "We are not looking for
chickens," she said, and smiled.

Arvo waited till the gypsies had disappeared down the leafy
forest glade, past the dancers who were already, he saw, beginning to disperse. The sound of hoofs and wheels died away.
Arvo ran through the forest to his bicycle and mounted it
and rode back in the full light of morning to the farm. Margit
was out emptying a bucket of pig swill into the iron trough.
The air was sweet as honey.

"Keep an eye on the fowls," Arvo said. "I met gypsies in
the forest on their way here."

"Now what can they want," Margit said crossly. "I suppose
they'll be camping in the forest and lighting their fires and
laying their thieving hands on all they see. Take the billhook
to the tool shed, Arvo. That shouldn't be lying about here."

"The old gypsy is looking for a belt—so he says."

"A belt?"

"Yes. With a silver buckle. He showed me one like it."

"He might as well look for a flea in a haystack."

"That's what I thought."

"Arvo," Margit said abruptly, "tell your father I want to speak to him."

"He's bringing in the hay."

"It isn't a life sentence. He can still come. You take his place."

"I was going to swim first and have some food before starting on the hay."

"Tell him, there's a good lad."

"But why the hurry, Mother?"

"There's something . . . I have a feeling about these gypsies."

Arvo grinned. "Are you going to barricade yourself in?"

Margit waited for the pigs to come squealing to the trough before she spoke. "The truth is, Maia has a belt with a silver buckle hanging behind the door."

"What harm is there in that? If it belongs to the old man's son she will give it back."

"We want no truck with them. The last time a tribe of them passed this way a batch of new bread and a whole side of bacon passed with them. All of it managed as neat as a cat's mouth. Before you were grown, lad, they were trading stolen ration books while honest folk starved."

"Where did Maia get the belt?"

"She found it by the edge of the lake. Stuck there in the reeds, frozen."

Arvo shrugged. "I still see no reason to call Father."

"Very well. Take your bicycle and ride over to the store and tell Maia the gypsies are looking for the belt."

"It sounds mighty important."

"It could be. I have a feeling."

"Oh, you women and your feelings." Arvo smiled.

"All the same . . . it's *my* feelings, and not your words, that tell me you'd give your right hand for Annikki. Isn't that so?"

"Something like it."

"Men should listen to what goes on inside them, as well as women. The world will be a better place when we get back, every now and then, to living by instinct rather than reason."

"Like the pigs?"

"We are not pigs. That is the difference."

"Instinct tells me to go indoors and get a hunk of bread and cheese before going to the store."

"Listen to instinct, then. But go, all the same."

Margit had noticed the belt hanging behind the door. Maia had spoken of it briefly. There had been nothing remarkable about that, nothing remarkable at all. But people who live close to each other, Margit thought, understand each other's silences. That belt, the gypsy, Annikki's sudden marriage to Vainen, there was a connection somewhere. A gypsy who came to bring an innocent message would not be likely to leave his belt behind. He would not be likely to swim in the lake under a coating of ice and lose it there. Annikki had been missing during the sudden snow which had come earlier than usual, unseasonably, and which had run to slush under a warm sun which had brought a sudden burgeoning with it before the real onset of winter. Now, it seemed, the old gypsy had come looking for the belt. Perhaps he was looking for more than the belt, Margit thought.

When Arvo returned from the house Margit asked, "Who was with the old man?"

"A young one, and two women in a cart."

"Then it will be the young one who passed this way last year."

"I never saw him. This one was pock-marked."

"Then it isn't the same, for I saw the other riding by. A handsome devil, I thought, with red lips, who looked as though he'd be interested in something beyond a hen roost."

Arvo looked up suddenly and met his mother's direct gaze.

Neither of them spoke, nor seemed able to break the silence.
Finally Arvo said slowly, "I'll be on my way to the store."

The gypsies continued on their way through the woods. The
sunlight fell through the trees on their path, checkered by the
leaves. The old man in front sniffed the air, sweet and rich
with the oils and saps of the trees, as an animal sniffs, his
dark eyes narrowed as he glanced about him. Birds flew,
startled from the undergrowth at their feet, across the head
of the ridden horse. Once or twice the old man leaned over
and whispered into the horse's ear, pulling it fondly, and
when the fondling and whispering had ceased the ear remained pricked, alert. The old woman and the younger one
sat silent, as did the man. The creak of the harness sounded
above the twittering of birds, the sudden scolding of squirrels.
The young woman pushed back her long, glossy hair as the
morning heat of the sun made itself felt. Her neck was long
and full, the skin glowing with health and cleanliness. Her
tribe, long ago, had hailed from Russia, as had that of the old
man. Their origins were forgotten. They were, and had been
for centuries, Finnish gypsies, reputed to be as clean as their
unwilling hosts.

The old man rested his hand proudly on the horse's mane
every now and then, and rode with the air of a king riding
through paltry dominions as they neared the edge of the
forest and glimpsed the smoke of a distant, small homestead,
the smoke of men earth-bound, imprisoned between four walls.
They themselves had descended from birds, at a time when
the earth was young.

Presently they emerged from the forest and came upon the
lake and a *sauna* set among birch trees at its edge. The distant house with its curling plume of smoke stood out clearly
with the sunlight on its walls of faded red and on the traces
of green in its shutters. A woman, heavy with child, came out
of the *sauna*. It was Annikki.

The old man reined in his horse in front of her and greeted

her as he had greeted Arvo. The cart with the three people in it had come to a halt. Annikki looked from one to another of them and felt a sudden coldness run over her body, like a snake.

She returned the old man's greeting levelly.

"I am looking for a belt," the old gypsy said, smiling.

Annikki trembled and could not take her gaze from that of the younger man. Pale, pock-marked as he was, there was something frighteningly familiar about the bold gaze of his liquid dark eyes. The coldness crept to her heart. She turned swiftly to go.

"Like this," the old man said, and with a sudden swish of leather dangled the belt in front of her.

Annikki, half turned from him, stiffened, and instinctively crossed her arms over her body in a gesture of protection. The old man moved his horse lest her shadow fall on his path and defile it.

"Have you seen such a belt?" the old man asked softly. "It was lost by my son in these parts, last summer."

The young woman's eyes traveled slowly over Annikki's body. The old woman spoke for the first time. Her voice was deep, commanding, like a man's, a strange voice to come from that shriveled crone's body. "The woman is near her time," she said.

"I have seen such a belt," Annikki said. A powerful, instinctive emotion, stronger than herself, had prompted the words, a powerful instinct to protect the life inside her threatened now by this extremity of terror. Whatever the life was, it was life, sacred. She looked up at the old man and saw there in the lined face traces of the face which had hung perilously over her own in the winter wood: the red lips, the sly, predatory smile, all the terror, none of the obscene beauty, all the menace, all the absence of pity. The child she carried was of this man's blood. There and then Annikki wanted blindly, savagely, to bear it, to leave it there upon the ground, but her arms covered her body in a wild, overriding impulse of protection. "Go to Porvesi," she cried, "over there. The village lies over there. There is a belt like yours in the village store." She clutched at the memory of Maia's words as though they were the only realities in the world, as indeed at that moment they were. She had one driving impulse at that moment, to rid herself of this smiling, menacing old man, to see them all move away from Vainen which held all that was dear to her.

"Over there," she cried again. "Porvesi lies over there. You will find nothing here."

The younger man's glance ran up and down Annikki's body and lingered on her face. "We are looking for a horse that was stolen."

"You will find the horse there too. But it was not stolen. It came out of the forest and was taken in and given shelter and fed all winter. The horse was not stolen." She turned and walked swiftly away, holding herself upright, across the sandy shore of the lake, back to the house. As she reached it Annikki turned for a moment and saw the gypsies in conclave but even as she watched they began slowly to continue on their way. She ran into the house to the accompaniment of Penna's joyous barking. Vainen, then, was somewhere near. He came in almost immediately, carrying a hay-rake, which he put outside the door.

"What is the matter? I saw you from the workshed, running. You shouldn't run, just now."

Annikki swung around to face him, her eyes dilated in terror.

"The gypsies have come. Two men and two women. They're looking for the horse and the belt—"

"Did you tell them where they could be found?" Erik asked slowly.

"With Maia and Jussi at the store," Annikki said. "Maia found the belt in the reeds last winter."

"Maia found a belt?" Erik echoed.

"Yes. Yes," Annikki said, frantic with impatience. "Yes. They're on their way to Porvesi now."

"So . . . Jussi will hand them over. And Maia can have her fortune told by the women." Erik smiled into Annikki's ashen face. She moistened her lips.

"Vainen! You know what they're looking for! They're looking for the gypsy," Annikki cried and held her hands away from her body in a gesture of helpless terror. "They're looking for the gypsy."

"He isn't here," Erik said calmly. "Who can tell where he is now? To find him—who knows? They may have to ride many days and nights."

"Into the lake? Will they ride into the lake?" Annikki came close, whispering, and clutched Erik's arm. "I know," she said hoarsely. Her eyes searched his.

"You know . . . what?"

"I know that the gypsy's body is in the lake. You killed him, Vainen, you killed him."

"How long have you known this?" Erik said.

"Always. From the first night. I awoke in Kirsti's bed. It was moonlight. I saw your two shadows. I heard the splash in the lake."

"That is why you knew he would never come back?"

"Yes."

"That is why you stayed?"

"Yes. Because the gypsy's death bound us together. Oh, Vainen, speak! You did it for me. You killed him. After that I knew that there was no going back. How could there be? It was just you and me and this child. Did you kill him to silence him?"

"Yes," Erik said heavily. "That is why I killed him. To silence him. I had not meant to do it. But the youth was evil. His words and his thoughts were evil." Erik stood, silent, thinking of the gypsy.

"He spoke evilly . . . of me?"

"Yes."

"And so you killed him," Annikki said softly. She felt submerged by gratitude and love, as by a warm tide. Her clutch on his arm loosened. Now, at last, when they stood revealed, one to another, when the last pretense had been stripped away, Vainen must speak. Annikki waited as a man dying of thirst waits who sees the cup within his reach, waited for the healing words of love. But none came. Vainen looked at her levelly, steadily, and tenderly, and she felt her own eyes dilate with tension and longing and fear.

"What are we going to do?" she gasped.

"Nothing can be proved," Erik said. "Nothing."

"They will prove it, if it takes a lifetime. A gypsy will wait a lifetime for vengeance."

"Let them go! Let them spend a lifetime proving it! What is that gypsy's life? Did he care about yours? Did he care that you wandered about half crazed and would have frozen to death if it hadn't been for the shelter of the ruined church?" Erik turned swiftly.

"What are you doing? Where are you going? Vainen!" Annikki cried.

"I'm going to Porvesi, to the store. I shall sail the boat across the narrow neck of the lake. I can be in Porvesi in little more than an hour, with a good breeze."

"The currents are dangerous there. You've never sailed across the neck! Nor has anyone."

"No harm will come to me. I must go. I'll bring Margit back with me. The time has come for you to have a woman near you. As for this gypsy, justice has been done. It was a life for a life."

"Then why must you go to Porvesi? The gypsies can take their horse and go."

"It is not for Jussi and Maia to finish my business for me. In all innocence."

"They know who fathered this child," Annikki said. She looked desperately at Erik to find the moment's weakening, the pause, which would bring them at last into each other's arms.

"You told them?" he said slowly, incredulously.

"No. They guessed. Everything was so quick. One thing led to another—"

"I might have known that a woman's wits would put two and two together." Erik put his hand gently on Annikki's shoulder. "It is better so. You have had trouble and sorrow, and I am glad there's a woman to share it with you. The worst is over. Soon the child will be in your arms and the gypsies gone and all this nothing but a dream. The body will never be found."

"But . . . if a gypsy waits, as they say, a lifetime for vengeance . . ."

Erik shrugged. "What comes tomorrow is better left till tomorrow. Stay here quietly and cook the meal. I'll leave Penna with you. I must go before the breeze changes."

They looked at one another for a long time without speaking.

"Poor child," Erik said. "The choice was taken out of your hands. As it was taken out of mine."

"I'm not a child, but a woman, Vainen. And now there are no secrets between us."

"Yes. You are a woman, and a brave one." He touched her cheek in a fleeting caress and turned slowly and left the room. Anniki rushed to the window and watched him as he pulled the boat out and ran up the sail. The world was as luminous as a great pearl, floating in the firmament. The air shimmered with a summer haze, the sky was cloudless. A soft breeze rippled along the surface of the lake and turned the moist green blades of meadow grass so that their undersides shone, silver-gray. The tinkle of a cowbell sounded on the edge of the forest. The little boat moved swiftly across the narrow neck of the lake. Penna came padding across the room and put his nose in Annikki's hand. Then he stiffened suddenly, and whined.

"Down, Penna, down," Annikki whispered. She felt her throat constrict with fear. Soundlessly, on small, light feet, the pock-marked gypsy had come up from the direction of the *sauna* and was moving stealthily toward the outbuildings. Transfixed with fear, Annikki watched. Penna's tongue lolled, his eyes snapped dangerously, but Annikki's touch and voice held him against the pull of scent and sight and muscles straining toward their prey.

The gypsy entered the workshed and came out with something held beneath his coat. Then he went soundlessly to the woodshed and for a little while was lost to view. Presently he came out and held an object to the light, an object clearly visible to Annikki crouching at the window. It was the carving of the gypsy at which the intruder gazed, running his hands over the wood, tracing the outline of the features with his forefinger. Penna whined and snapped and broke free, racing toward the gypsy with fangs bared. In a second the man had turned and run like a hound to the shelter of the forest. Penna stood on the confines of his own territory, yapping and whining. Presently he came back to the house.

Annikki was gutting and cleaning a trout which Erik had caught that morning. She worked mechanically, raising her eyes to the shining trunks of the birches, white against the green of their branches. But she did not see them, all her being concentrated on the faint sounds from the forest, sounds which seemed to grow clearer and could not have been part of her terror and fear. The sounds were of people, voices raised distantly in laughter or song, and mingling with them the sound of a flute. The remainder of the gypsy caravan was on its way to camp somewhere in the forest.

18

WHEN ERIK REACHED the store he heard voices from the living room on the right and pushed open the door. At first the room seemed to be filled with people. Then he saw that there were five seated at the table—Jussi and Maia, Margit and Eino and their son Arvo.

"Good day," Erik said. "I thought you were at your hay-making, Eino."

"And you, for that matter, Vainen," Eino said.

Jussi got up. "We were talking of you, Vainen. Come in. There is a small matter to be talked of and done with."

"It's about that I've come." Erik glanced at the belt on the table and then at Jussi. "The gypsies have come for the lad's belt," he said.

"Yes. Arvo brought us the message and then Margit and Eino followed," Maia said. "They were ahead of you by five minutes."

"The time has come to talk," Erik said. "All of you here know why I married your young cousin, Jussi."

"We know, Vainen. But Margit here . . . we're not sure . . ." Jussi looked doubtfully at Margit.

"Do you think Eino and I were born yesterday?" Margit

221

smiled. "The girl came to some harm at the gypsy's hands, so we thought." She glanced at Maia. "What better way to put a matter right—if need be—than finding the girl a husband? You fought the gypsy I don't doubt, Vainen. But, whatever happened, the gypsies are looking for more than the belt—so it seems to us. It's likely they're looking for you."

Arvo was gripping the edge of the table. "What's the truth of this matter, Vainen?" he asked quietly.

Erik turned to look at the young man. "The girl was raped," he said, and saw Arvo's face whiten suddenly, "by a gypsy fleeing from his tribe. I found the girl sheltering in the old church and took her back to Vainen. The girl was ruined, or thought she was, and I . . ." Erik paused. "How can I explain? It seemed to me that a charge had been laid upon me and I accepted the charge. That's the truth of the matter."

"And a truth good enough for us," Maia said stoutly. "There would have been other ways of dealing with the matter but you chose yours out of hand and that was that. If need be I'd have taken the child myself and reared it. Find me a home within twenty miles without an orphan in it and I'll find you a flea in a haystack. And here was one without the pastor's blessing—child I mean, not flea—and what was that, here or there, to make a coil about?"

"Since the girl married Vainen you've never stopped talking, woman," Jussi growled. "Get to the point, if there is one."

"The point," Maia said, "is what the gypsies are getting to. Here's the belt. But where is the gypsy?"

"Where was the belt found?" Arvo asked. His fingers still gripped the table and his eyes were fixed on Erik.

"Frozen in the reeds by the lake," Maia said.

"Did you fight him there, Vainen?" Jussi asked.

"I killed him there," Vainen said.

"Killed him?" Jussi echoed. "That's another matter altogether. Killed him, you say?"

"If you make friends with a gypsy keep a knife in your

pocket," Maia said. "But, God help us man, did you have to use it?" she cried.

"He slandered the girl. I strangled him," Erik said.

"Then he's in the lake," Margit said.

"At the bottom," Vainen said.

They sat silent for some moments, dour-faced, tight-mouthed, considering.

"Murder is a matter for life," Eino said. "They can imprison you for life, Vainen, if the gypsies bring you to court for it."

"Wait, wait, wait," Maia said. "Not so fast, Eino. There's a good lawyer in Vituri, Matti Nestori—"

"Not so fast either, Maia," Erik said. "First find the body. Then the lawyer."

"Vainen's right. Shall we have a word with the pastor over this?" Jussi asked, after a pause.

"And burden his conscience? Hasn't it enough to carry with the weight of all the sin there is hereabouts?" Maia demanded. She got up and banged the table. "Get up, any man or woman of you, who has known a good gypsy."

"They're rogues and vagabonds," Margit said. "Thieves and sorcerers. Good-for-nothing lay-abouts who think they own the earth. There are sorcerers among them, it's well known. Never cross swords with a gypsy. If one has gone, then that's one less to worry about."

"But he is the father of Annikki's child," Arvo said. "A thief, a sorcerer, a vagabond lay-about—"

"Vainen will bring up the child in the way it should go," Margit told him. "Let's get back to facts, lad. You say the gypsies have been inquiring in Vituri and now they're on their way here. We'll give them the belt—"

"And the horse," Jussi said.

Maia sat down suddenly. "The horse. I'd forgotten it. So the horse must go too."

"Do you think we're thieves?" Jussi asked, outraged.

"No," Arvo said. "Only murderers."

"If you had seen the girl as I saw her and heard the gypsy's foul words as I heard them, you would have done what I did, Arvo. Your hands would have been round that gypsy's throat as mine were," Erik said quietly.

"You're right, Vainen. I would have done it. But they say that you have the strength of ten when you're roused."

"The girl is safe as she has been since I found her. She is my wife. The child is ours, born as it will be in wedlock. Isn't that as it should be?" Erik asked.

"True enough. And the half dozen of us here are the only ones who know the truth or ever will know," Margit said.

"I saw the hand of Providence in it from the beginning," Maia affirmed. "Vainen, it's been the making of you, having a wife to care for instead of living like a ghost."

"But . . . a gypsy brat," Jussi said heavily.

"You said yourself it was half Annikki's and that made it yours. Life is life, however it starts. A child is a child. There are bigger things to cry about. What must be done now is to send the gypsies packing with the belt and the horse and forget the matter. What do you say, Vainen?" Maia asked.

"What is done is done. The gypsy has been eaten by the fish long since and who is going to recognize a bone? I did what the hour called for. If there is to be judging I will judge myself in a balance of my own making. Putting me in prison will not bring the gypsy back. It's the living who must be thought of. The girl and the child. Which is the greater sin? To take innocence or to take life? I tell you, I will be my own judge."

"Why was the gypsy fleeing?" Eino asked, after a silence.

"He had insulted the woman promised as his wife. Insulted her by rejection. He fled on a stolen horse—that horse out there in the paddock grazing like a lamb."

"Then the truth is that the woman's kinfolk were just as likely to put a knife in his back," Maia said, "as you to strangle

him. He got justice. Rough justice, if you like, but there's
many a good man under the soil who died without it. What
are we wasting words about?"

"Does Annikki know," Jussi asked, "that you killed the
gypsy, Vainen?"

"The girl knows. She has always known. She awoke in the
night and saw and heard. And said nothing."

"Then it's a matter between man and wife and not for us
to meddle with. Vainen will live with his conscience and
Annikki will live with Vainen and neither of them, if you ask
me, could make a better bargain."

Arvo sighed heavily. "You acted quickly, Vainen, marrying
her."

"There are times when a man must—or forfeit action for
the rest of his life." Erik turned to Margit. "The girl is getting
near her time. I thought you might come back in the boat
with me, Margit."

"I'll come gladly. Eino, you can fend for yourself for the
next few hours, and you too, Arvo."

"No. I'll come with you. To Vainen."

"You? To Vainen? Why?"

"Listen," Arvo said. "Listen."

They listened. Faint and clear on the breeze could be heard
the sound of the gypsy caravan, a distant susurration from the
woods of voices and singing.

"The whole tribe is passing," Maia said. "Tomorrow they
will be gone."

"No. They're camping. Pitching tents. They sound halfway
between here and Vainen. So I'll come and keep an eye on
things while Vainen brings in the hay," Arvo said.

Erik smiled. "It's your mother the girl needs, lad, not you.
There's your own hay to be got in and your own farm to
look to."

Maia got up and walked heavily to the window and looked
out. "There's nothing more to be said, the thing is done,"

she said dourly. "A gypsy dies and a gypsy is born and there's
an end of it. Anyone who thinks differently, let him speak
now."

"There's an end of it," Eino said and the others echoed him.
"There's an end of it."

Arvo turned stubbornly to Erik. "So it was a forced marriage for Annikki? A forced marriage, Vainen."

"It was the girl's choice. Who are you to question? Sometimes the path is marked clear and there's nothing to do but
follow it."

"By God, I don't see the end of this one."

"The end is never seen," Jussi said. "You keep on walking."

Margit got up and put her hand on Arvo's shoulder. "Jussi's
advice is good," she said. "Follow it. Annikki is Vainen's wife
and all of us here stand by Vainen. Now take your bicycle, lad,
and go to the farm, and get me the case I packed just for this.
I'll sleep the night at Vainen and keep Annikki company.
It isn't the time for her to be there alone, listening to the
singing in the forest. She'll imagine things that will never come
to pass."

"That old gypsy man means business," Arvo said.

"How can he when he has no proof of anything and never
will have? And one thing is certain, he won't be in a hurry
to go to the police, and neither will we. It's a pother about
nothing, a stew without meat."

The gentle radiance of the midnight sun shone over lake
and forest. Within a clearing in the forest the gypsies had
pitched their tents and made their fires. The smell of wood
smoke drifted toward the lake. The gypsies were restless, un-
sleeping, playing their flutes and guitars, dancing and singing.
The music and voices were haunting, like the voice of the
forest itself.

Annikki, lying sleepless in bed, listened to the faint yet
compelling melody, and her very skin seemed to contract with
fear. It was as though those haunting, plaintive voices were

calling to her and to the child within her. She would start up in bed in the cool, clean room with its freshness and simplicity, to see the serene light of the sun streaming in and shining on the pale tiles of the stove, start out of a strange nightmare of dark faces, red lips, sly smiles and cruel, pinioning strength.

Once, Margit, dozing by the stove in the living room, came hurrying in at Annikki's sudden cry.

"I was dreaming," Annikki said. "I wish those gypsies would stop singing."

"Tomorrow they'll be gone. Go to sleep, Annikki. If I'm not mistaken you're going to need all your strength tomorrow."

"Is Vainen asleep?" Annikki asked.

"Sleeping as a man should who's worked since dawn. It took all his strength and knowledge to get the boat across the neck, let alone a day's work after it. Once or twice I thought we'd both be at the bottom of the lake with that gypsy."

Annikki gave a little gasping cry. "How can you say such things, Margit?"

"Secrets are like an overflow of bile," Margit said with rough kindness, "and bile has to come up—or else poison you. The time comes when knowledge has to be faced. Are you going to cry and shudder every time you look at your child? In this life you have to be strong, girl. You'll never get to the end of it, otherwise."

"I'm afraid for Vainen. I read once of a gypsy who spent his whole life looking for the man who'd killed his brother. Every day he practiced with a gun till he could—"

"He had proof, I daresay. All that the old man knows is that his son passed this way. And tomorrow the old man and the tribe will pass this way and be gone. Go to sleep and save your strength for what lies ahead, don't waste it on what's past."

Annikki lay down again beneath Kirsti's covers and closed her eyes. Margit went back to the rocking chair by the stove but she did not relax, sitting there, watchful and tense. The sounds from the forest were strangely menacing. They brought with them an undertone of restlessness and fear. I'm as bad as the girl, Margit thought, to be so nervous. For there was nothing in the world to connect Vainen with the gypsy's death. Nothing could be safer than a few white bones lying far down on the mud of a lake till Judgment Day. If every good lad, Margit thought, who had been killed on the soil of the land had had his avenger they would come marching in an army thicker than the trees of the forest. You had to be strong, she had told the girl, to get through life, and not only strong, but keep a sense of proportion.

The luminous night wore on, and Margit slept.

At noon the following day the old gypsy on his horse and the two women in the cart with the man pulled up at the store. The old man secured his horse and approached the store. Elisabet Lahti was just leaving with a full basket in one hand and holding Lauri with the other. She glanced curiously at the gypsies. She saw them glance in turn at the child beside her and at the wooden manikin in Lauri's fist. It was his favorite toy and served admirably to cut his back teeth on. The pock-marked man, who had dismounted from the cart, snatched the manikin from Lauri's hand and the child set up a howl. Angry and frightened, for stories of the evil eye might have a grain of truth in them, Elisabet snatched the toy back. In the ensuing commotion Maia and Jussi came out of the store.

The gypsies were talking excitedly among themselves while Elisabet comforted Lauri and without a backward look, in case worse befell, hurried away.

"Those are the toys my brother carves," the pock-marked man said angrily to Maia. "He's been here, that's certain."

"Likely enough," Maia said, "if he's the one who lost his belt and left his horse for me to feed all winter." She turned to the old man. "They say that's what you're looking for. Wait."

She hurried indoors and returned with the belt. "Take it and go. The horse is in the paddock, well fed and cared for."

"So my son passed this way," the old man said softly.

"On the run," Maia said. "He was on a stolen horse or I'm no judge."

"If you were decent folk I'd expect pay for feeding the horse all winter," Jussi said. "But seeing you're what you are, take it and go. I've worked the horse besides, so we'll say no more."

The young woman leaned over swiftly and snatched the belt from Maia's hands. Her eyes had a hard gleam. "It's his," she said. "It's my bridegroom's belt."

"We'll find the bridegroom," the old woman said. "Patience."

"That you won't, not here, at any rate. He took to his heels and was never seen again," Maia said, "in these parts."

"Or heard of, either," the old man answered. "The trail ends here, in Porvesi."

"Do you want your horse or don't you?" Maia asked. "Take the animal and get out. And if you keep up the noise your tribe made last night we'll have a word with the police."

The old man's eyes narrowed.

"You're rough with an old man looking for his son. When a woman is rough it's because of fear."

"Fear?" Maia laughed. "Fear it is. For our chickens, for one thing, and your fires, and your noise and your dirt. The horse is in the paddock. Your troubles are your own. Don't come here plaguing Christian folk."

The old man turned and ran his hand over his horse's mane. "We'll go," he said in his soft voice, "but not far. My son came as far as this and unless he's dead he must be hiding somewhere about. The boy can't live without his tribe unless someone is sheltering him."

"He's dead," the young woman said somberly. "He's dead. I feel it."

The old woman spoke suddenly from the cart in her commanding voice. "We must know whether he is dead and if so how he died. We will seek him for the rest of our lives. We will never leave Porvesi. We will camp in the forest. Some will go, some will stay, turn and turn about, but always some of the tribe will stay here, in Porvesi."

"Your troubles are your own," Jussi said. "But if the boy is dead what's the use of staying here?"

The old woman opened her eyes till they seemed to burn in her face.

"We must find his grave," she said slowly. "We must find his grave and visit it and take food to it so that he may die completely, unforgotten, vindicated."

Maia gaped. "What heathen belief is that?"

"Woman, there are beliefs older than you," the old woman said contemptuously. "There is knowledge that you and your kind, held prisoner between walls, have never been given. My grandson's spirit will put on flesh and blood and come to denounce us, otherwise. If he has died he has died here. And if he has died at some man's hand it is here, in Porvesi, he will come to call us. If he is dead it is here we must find his grave and set his spirit free."

Maia shrugged. "We're busy folk," she said. "Tell us, if you can, how this belt came to be found on the shores of the lake and how the horse came galloping here out of the forest. We're practical people. We fed the hungry animal and put it to the plow and thought no more of it. But we're not thieves. Take it and go."

The old man gave her a long look and then mounted his horse and walked it a few yards down the road. He looked over the hedge, his gaze on the tussocky meadow bright with summer flowers. He sat motionless, waiting, as did the two women in the cart. The pock-marked man stood silently. Maia felt the skin crawl on the back of her neck. She glanced at Jussi, who stood as silently as the gypsy beside him. It was as though they were all imprisoned in silence, like an invisible shroud.

Maia moistened her lips, which had gone suddenly dry.

"What fools we are," she said, "to be standing meekly here while others of these vagabonds are raiding the hen roost."

The old man raised his hand. There was a gentle snorting, the soft thud of hoofs on the springy turf, and then the horse with the white star on its forehead came into sight in the clear morning sunlight. It came swiftly and almost soundlessly and stood motionless on the other side of the hedge. The old man leaned over and caught its forelock and whispered softly. Then he turned away and rode on. The pockmarked man climbed back into the cart and took the reins and followed the old man.

The horse remained looking over the hedge, its pale mane bright in the sunshine. Then, with its ears pricked and alert, it took a flying leap over the hedge and cantered down the road till it reached the cart. The pock-marked man handed the reins to the old woman and sprang from the cart onto the horse's back. Twisting his hand in its mane he rode up by the side of the old man.

Maia and Jussi watched them out of sight and then Maia glanced down the road in the opposite direction, narrowing her eyes anxiously for the sight of curious faces at the windows of the scattered houses. None was to be seen.

"The whole thing couldn't have taken more than ten minutes," she said thankfully to Jussi, "but I feel that I've been here all morning. It was strange the way the horse came without being called."

"It saw and heard the other horses."

"Heard perhaps," Maia said doubtfully, "but it couldn't have seen them. It was far away grazing in Eino's field on the other side. It must have gone clean over that hedge, too, without a word spoken."

Jussi shrugged and said nothing.

"A lot of rubbish they talked," Maia said, "about finding the grave. It'll be a fine thing if we have to call in the police to move them, Jussi."

"People do say," Jussi said thoughtfully, "that gypsies believe their horses have their own familiar spirits."

"And they know how to talk to them too," Maia added.

"Well, that's that, Jussi. We'll hear no more of it! I must get
on with the washing."

"I wonder how Annikki is?" Jussi said.

"Margit's with her. She knows what's to be done and has
never failed yet, and the girl's strong and healthy. We'll hear,
in good time."

Jussi turned back into the store and paused on the threshold. "It's all been easy," he said uncertainly. "Too easy."

"No," Maia said, standing rocklike in front of him, her
arms folded, "it hasn't been easy, man. Nothing is easy when
it's a matter of conscience."

The gypsies continued slowly down the road, the old man
and his son riding in front, the women in the cart behind.
The horse which the pock-marked man rode walked softly
and proudly, picking its way delicately. There was an airiness,
a lightness, about it. The brown hand of the man seemed to
be twisted in a mane of gossamer. Once or twice the horse
pricked its ears and turned a lambent, interested eye upon its
rider and upon the other horse; but it continued to walk
gently, delicately.

The old man spoke after a while. "It's clear," he said "that
we must go back."

"To the house, you mean? To the farmhouse on the opposite side of the camp?"

"To the farmhouse. That is where you found the carving
of my son. We are fools. The boy must have stayed there
many nights to have been carved so surely."

"That is where we shall find the answer," the pock-marked
man said.

"And perhaps the grave," the old woman said. "Yes. That is
where we shall find the grave."

The young woman shuddered. "If I am to have peace the

grave must be found. If I am ever to marry another it must be found."

"His sin would have been forgiven him," the old woman mused. "He would have paid, one way or another, and it would have been wiped out. But if he has met his death, been killed by one of these knife throwers"—the old woman spat—"then we can never rest till his grave is found and his death avenged."

They rode on in silence. Presently they turned off the road and into the edge of the forest at the point where the young gypsy had galloped the stolen horse. It now pricked its ears, snorting, as the cool green glades of the forest enfolded them.

Between the trees a frail old man wandered, carrying an osier basket. It was old Heikki, looking for wild strawberries. "But they are not out yet," he quavered. "All of them still hard and tight and green among the leaves. I shall not live to see them."

Fat Catherine, sitting beneath a tree, went on with her knitting, but looked up when the gypsies approached. Old Heikki glanced up also, for a moment, where he stood, a little apart, in their path. The gypsies reined in.

The foremost gypsy pointed to old Heikki. "Ask him," he said to his son. "Show him the carving."

The pock-marked man drew the carving from inside his coat. It was about a foot long and showed the figure of a naked man. Life breathed from the wood. The face was alive, the carved eyes seeking.

The pock-marked man held the carving in front of old Heikki. Fat Catherine watched and then got up and came nervously toward the little group.

"Old man," the gypsy said, "this is the carving of a man. Look at the face. It is a good likeness. Have you seen this man?"

Old Heikki lifted his eyes from the ground again and looked at the strange group and the carving held in front of him, the wood warmed by the sunlight. His eyes went incredulously to the two horsemen, the women in the tumble-down cart, the wild, dark faces. He thrust his hands into the sleeves of his jacket, the osier basket dangling from his elbow, and strange, confused images passed through his tired brain. These wild dark men, these silent women, what were they doing with the carved figure? The sacrilegious ones, they were holding the carved figure of Christ!

The green colonnades spread away from them like the great aisles of a church. The music of wind and bird song rose about them, swelling like a choir in old Heikki's ears, an ancient, eternal chant, a haunting paean of prayer.

"Yes I know the Man, sacrilegious ones," he quavered. "Where have you stolen the sacred figure, if not from a church?"

The old gypsy laughed. The pock-marked man struck old Heikki a glancing blow which almost sent him reeling. Fat Catherine ran forward and steadied him.

"Thieves! Vagabonds!" she cried in her thin, high voice, rocking on her birdlike legs.

The gypsies touched their horses and moved forward, laughing at old Heikki's amazed, quivering face.

"You are full of sin," he said sorrowfully. He raised his arm and made over them, slowly and reverently, the sign of the cross. He made it twice, once for the men, once for the women. They rode on and disappeared into the rustling, leafy woods, under the sacred sign.

19

THE FOLLOWING MORNING Annikki rose as usual and dressed and found Margit dozing in the rocking chair. She awoke with a start at the sight of the girl.

"You look as fresh as the morning, girl. What's the time?" Margit looked at the china clock on the wall. "Past seven. Vainen must have gone out long since without disturbing me."

"I heard him outside an hour ago," Annikki said. "You rest, Margit, while I get breakfast."

Margit got stiffly out of the chair. "So you slept well, after all, in spite of keeping me up half the night," she said crossly.

"I'm sorry. But in the night things seem worse. One dreams in the night, never in the day." Annikki went to the window. "Even the sound of the gypsies isn't so frightening in the morning. They're kindling their fires, as we are, and cooking food, and later on we shall hear them moving away. I'm right, Margit. Tell me that I'm right."

Margit went to the window. There was nothing to be seen but Vainen's land and outbuildings, Vainen's *sauna* and the lake beyond. It was a day like any other except for Annikki, standing beside her, fresh, young, heavy, with no trace of the night's fears on her face. Yet from the woods, in the silence, came the sound of a voice, the ring of a hammer, the occasional whinny of a horse. There was life in the woods.

"How clearly the sounds carry," Margit said. "But of course you're right, they'll move camp soon. Always wandering, never a place to call home. Such folk aren't human. You get breakfast, Annikki, while I go and wash. Then we'll put everything ready for you and the child. It's a fine, sweet morning for a life to come fresh into the world. Think of it. By nightfall, if I'm any judge, there'll be a child in your arms."

Margit left the room and Annikki stood a moment longer by the window. A thrill of excitement and fear, pleasure and repulsion ran through her. The door opened and Erik came in. The open door seemed to bring all the life outside into the room. Cool and clear came the sound of cuckoos calling across the lake.

"Are you all right?" Erik asked.

"Yes. Margit thinks the child will be born today. Yet I've had no pain—or so little that I would hardly call it pain."

Erik came closer. "That's because you are young," he said, "and so there's nothing to fear. Margit is with you and she's experienced in women's matters."

"What's that you say, Vainen?" Margit asked, coming into the room. "Experienced? Well, I should be. Before I married Eino I was a nurse, and trained as a midwife to boot. That's the sort of skill you never lose." She looked sharply at Annikki. "Haven't you put the coffee on? This is a day to keep busy. Stay a moment, Vainen, and drink some coffee with us."

Annikki busied herself. She said, with a smile at Erik, "I think, if you scratched Maia, you'd find Margit underneath."

"You're saucy," Margit said, not ill-pleased. "I think Annikki has spirit, Vainen. There were times when I wondered. She'll make you a good wife yet."

"The girl suits me well enough," Erik said gently, but he looked at Annikki as he said it and his eyes held hers a moment. The old tension rose in Annikki, the longing to hear what had never yet been spoken. This was a moment when, if Margit had not been there, he might have taken her in his arms. She felt restless suddenly, and got up.

"I don't feel like food or drink," she said. "I'll go and put out the towels and things you want, Margit." She went out of the room to the linen chest in her bedroom.

"Go after her, Vainen," Margit said. "This is a time when a wife needs comfort."

Erik followed Annikki. She had opened the chest and was looking in it absently. She turned as Erik entered the room.

"Kirsti was young," she said accusingly, facing him, searching his eyes with hers, as though by the words, the sound of Kirsti's name, she could tap the secret spring of his love and tenderness and slake her own thirst.

"Kirsti was young. But she had already borne a child and used her strength in work, and besides, there was no woman to help us. We were alone, Kirsti and I, in the *sauna*."

"It is Kirsti you would like to see before you now! This child—Kirsti's and yours. I know it! I feel it," Annikki said wildly.

"No, you are wrong. Kirsti belongs to the past. All that is over. You are my wife. Dry your tears. Now you need strength, not weakness."

Annikki drew herself up and looked long and proudly at Erik. I could cry out, she thought, *I love you! I love you!* But she knew that the words would match her weakness against his strength. She wanted to batter herself against whatever it was that was rocklike and unyielding in this man's nature. She longed with passion and intensity to feel him tremble against her in an anguish of longing, hear her name on his lips: *Annikki! Annikki!* But instead she heard her own voice crying out: "Vainen! Vainen!"

He came close and took her gently in his arms so that she rested against him for a moment. His voice was calm, strong, tender. "You will forget all this when the child is born," he

said. "It's natural to feel weak and afraid. Dry your tears. It's
Margit you need, not me." His arms were strong and enfolding, his heart beat steadily against hers. What is it that I
want? Annikki thought desperately, and knew that it was the
last stronghold, the moment of weakness and power, the ultimate surrender and union, her name on his lips. But something held this man that was stronger than himself. He would
never, now, surrender his will, or any part of it, into the power
of another.

Annikki dried her tears with the back of her hand. "You're
right, Vainen. This is my moment of weakness. I'll go and
help Margit. She'll soon put an end to it."

In the doorway Annikki turned back, waiting for Erik to
follow her. He was listening to the sounds from the woods.
Annikki realized suddenly how her awareness of him had
grown, subtly and imperceptibly, over the past months. She
was intensely, now, aware of his grave handsomeness, of the
extraordinary sense of life and vitality he gave out in spite
of his strange quietness. The blueness of his eyes, with their
gaze at once searching and withdrawn, the carriage of his head,
the low tones of his voice had fused in her mind into the image
of something unattainable. He was the first man she had
known, the first man she had loved. Vainen had created a
world of his own, and, Annikki thought, some part of me
will live in that world forever.

"Are you listening to the gypsies?" she asked him.

"Yes."

"The air is so clear you can almost hear them talking."

"I think," Erik said, "they are on the move, coming this
way."

Margit looked out of the window and saw Arvo. "Bother
the lad," she said to Annikki, "he needn't have come out
here. But he fusses over me. 'A man only has one mother,' he
says, and there are times when I like it. But not now."

"Why has he come?" Annikki asked. She was sitting in the rocking chair, her face a little drawn with the pain that had come and gone. Color crept slowly back into her cheeks and she got up and went on trussing a boiling fowl.

"He thought that Vainen would be busy getting in the hay and if I needed a man to fetch and carry he'd be the one." Margit rapped on the window. "Fill two pails with water," she called out, "since you are here."

Arvo came to the doorway and opened it, filling the threshold with the sudden, dark bulk of his body. His eyes and Annikki's met over Margit's head.

"Why have you come, Arvo?" Annikki asked.

"We've got our hay in, got it yesterday. Vainen's singlehanded. And there's a pack of gypsies on the road who might be better for the sight of a man about."

"I suppose it's safe to put the milk churn out," Margit said, and bustled off to do it.

"If there's anything I can do for you, Annikki," Arvo said, "I'm here to do it."

"I have a husband, Arvo."

"Yes. And a good one."

"Well?" Annikki said. She went on trussing the fowl. Arvo stood watching her. There was a sudden tension in the room. From outside came the clatter of the churn, and then the sound of sheets flapping in the wind as Margit hoisted the sagging clothes line.

"This isn't the time, I know, to say what I must say. But I know everything, Annikki. I was at the store when Vainen came over yesterday."

"Then there is nothing more to be said. Keep your own counsel."

"There's this. When I spoke to you that day in the churchyard I didn't know how everything had come about. But I think there was no shame in an honest man trying to tell an honest girl that he loved her."

"All that was over, Arvo, before it had begun."

"I knew it then. I was not trying to come between you and
Vainen. I'm your friend, and his."

"How much do you know, Arvo?" Annikki asked. She did
not look at him, her head bent over the fowl on the table, her
hands busy.

"I know that Vainen killed the gypsy. And why."

"A man must do what he must."

"Yes. Vainen said that he did what the hour called for."

"The thing is over and done with, surely," Annikki said.
"And Vainen is the keeper of his own conscience. As I am of
mine."

"True enough. But if you want to know why I'm here it's
because I respect Vainen and I love you and I'm not ashamed
for either of you to know it. Besides that I have a good pair
of fists and ready to use them if need be."

Annikki looked full at Arvo. "Do you think there will be
need?" she asked quietly. "Listen, Arvo. Vainen was right.
The gypsies are coming this way."

"They're just heading for Vituri. They've got the gypsy's
belt and the horse he left behind him and as for the rest, why,
it's any man's guess. So you bear your child and think no
more of it, and let men deal with men's matters."

Arvo smiled and his smile was full of confidence. Annikki
looked into Arvo's face with its square chin like Margit's,
into his gray eyes with their thick, dark lashes. She remembered the churchyard, Arvo's smile, a moment of delight, the
knowledge that somewhere still was light and gaiety which she
had almost forgotten. She gave Arvo a faint smile now.

"You haven't filled the pails."

He took them from under the sink and went off. Annikki
watched him go toward the well. Silvi, her coat sleek and
shining, came out of the woodshed toward him, licking her
whiskers. She paused beside Arvo, arching her back and
purring. The little cat was filled with voluptuous well-being.
She raced toward the young birches, scratching her claws on

the silver bark, making the green leaves quiver about her.
Margit was right, Annikki thought. It was a fine, sweet morning to bring a new life into the world, with the dazzling
warmth and the fullness of harvest and the late cuckoos calling. She finished the fowl and put it into the pot. There was
nothing, Margit had said, like a good chicken broth to give
her strength afterwards.

When Margit came in later Annikki said, "The room seems
to stifle me, Margit. I'm going out for a while."

"Yes. Go out and walk about in the sunshine. There's no
way of hurrying Nature, and why should you. There's all day
before you."

Annikki went out and walked toward the hayfield, where
Vainen would be working. She felt consumed with restlessness
to which Arvo's arrival had contributed. Why had he come,
if he did not expect trouble of some sort, or danger? The
gypsies were incalculable. No one could say what was really
in their minds. They were suspicious and seeking, malevolent,
giving the impression that they knew more than they would
say. It was nearly a year since the gypsy youth had left the
tribe, and so, Annikki thought, their lives and journeyings
must move to some sort of rhythm, some plan or design. If the
youth could not be found now they would surely conclude
that he was dead. How did they know that he had passed this
way? What were their tokens, their secret knowledge? They
were closely knit—parent, son, sister, brother, husband, wife—
bound, seemingly, by closer ties than ordinary beings, a race
apart, answerable to none but each other. You could see it
in their eyes, their faces, Annikki thought. Perhaps that was
why they endured.

She thought of the gypsy's death and now horror no longer
rose in her; not horror, nor dread, nor fear. He might have
killed me, she thought, with cold fury; he could have killed
me. I might have frozen to death that night. His death was
just.

She stood still, feeling the sudden drag, the ache, deep in-

side her, and sat on a sawed-off tree trunk on a piece of land
which Vainen had begun to clear. She could see his distant
figure against the light.

The pain was not strong and soon subsided. I should feel
horror at this, Annikki thought; but she did not feel horror.
For now, somewhere at the back of her mind, half forgotten,
half realized, was a memory of the smiling gypsy in the paddock, a confused memory of something free in him, a sort
of wild innocence, at one with Nature.

It was only afterward that the obscene horror had descended. It was afterward that she had tried to scream, voice-
less, in the forest.

Yet, somewhere, she felt confusedly, somewhere in this spark
of life which he had kindled, must be that freedom, that wild
innocence. When pain descended in its extremity she would
think of that.

She looked up and saw Vainen coming toward her. His feet
were planted surely, steadily, as he walked toward her against
the light. There was something hard and strong in the set of
his shoulders as he approached. Like a rock, moving, Annikki
thought.

She got up and went toward him. He put his hand on her
shoulder, feeling its warmth beneath her thin, cotton dress.

"What are you doing out here?" he asked.

"I felt restless. And Margit said that it's good to walk about.
There's plenty of time."

"Yes," he said, as Margit had said. "It's something that can't
be hurried. But go back to the house. Stay near Margit."

"Arvo is here too, did you know?"

"He offered to come yesterday. He thought there might be
trouble."

"What sort of trouble?"

"Who knows, when a camp is on the move? A pig stolen,
the hay fired by some careless fool."

"Once they've gone it will be for good, I'm sure of that,"
Annikki said. "We'll be left in peace," she added desperately.

"Go back to the house now," Erik said gently. He looked away beyond the farm toward the forest and began to walk in that direction.

"Where are you going?" Annikki cried.

He turned back and said slowly, "There are some things that have to be finished. All night long I lay awake, thinking."

"Thinking of what? What? Oh God, Vainen, what?"

His gravity, his steady gaze, filled her with sudden terror. She knew then that she had no more power over this man than a blown leaf has over the wind.

"Why does a man work, suffer, endure?" he asked, as though there were all the time in the world to consider this.

"Ask the pastor! Ask the pastor!" Annikki cried, between sudden pain and anger. "Ask him, not yourself, not me. We work and endure and suffer," she said through gritted teeth, "and that's all there is to it. All I want is to be happy, happy. Yes, even with this." She rocked a moment while the pain ebbed away and faced him with blanched cheeks.

"Animals work and suffer and endure," Erik said, "and they don't know why—"

"And we don't know why, either."

"It comes back to a matter of human dignity. If I let those gypsies pass without a word—"

"Without a word? What do you mean?"

"They're coming this way. They may be coming here or they may be going on to Vituri. But they are not going to pass Vainen without speech with Vainen."

"What do you mean?" Annikki asked, every word coming through clenched teeth.

"I will see the old gypsy, tell him what happened. Vengeance is not justice, and justice is not one-sided. It is his right to know where the gypsy lad is and I will tell him."

"Vainen, you fool! You're weak, weak, you can't live with your conscience. They'll set on you, kill you. Have you thought of me? Alone here? Vainen!" Annikki clutched his arms. "Vainen, I love you. I love you. I won't let you do this. Now,

when it's all over, when we're safe. . . . Can you bring the
gypsy back? Don't go near them! Don't speak! What you did
was done in righteous anger. The pastor says that God is
merciful. God will judge you, God, not a vengeful gypsy."

"God does not seek to be man's judge," Erik said. "Man is
his own judge."

Annikki stepped back and stared at him. She echoed incredulously, "God is not man's judge?"

"Man is his own judge. By his own self-judgment man stands
or falls. I have weighed myself in my own balance and I know
that the gypsies are not going to pass Vainen without speech
with Vainen."

"They'll kill you. Knife you. Shoot you."

"I'll take no risks. I'll speak with the old man alone. I'll
stand trial, as the dead man will stand trial. There are laws
for us as well as for them. They know that if one of them
shot or knifed me he'd be tried for it. The world is not a
jungle."

"It sounds like one," Annikki said fearfully.

The gypsies were coming nearer. Now the sounds they made
rang confusedly on the air.

"It's like the sound of an army moving," Annikki said.

"An army of tinkers and horse-dealers."

"And silversmiths. I remember that chased silver buckle."
Annikki stood close to Erik. "We are speaking empty words,"
she said. "You know, and I know, that you'll risk your life
if you go to them."

"It is not a very big risk but I must take it. It is better to
go to them than have the whole tribe here, prowling around.
Is this a time for it?"

Annikki shuddered. Then she flung her arms around Erik,
pressing the bulk of her heavy body against his. Her face,
uplifted, was desperate, tender, imploring.

"Vainen, I love you. Now is the time to tell me what I have
longed to hear. Hungered to hear. I love you. Tell me you
love me. Give me strength to go on with our lives together."

He looked down at her steadily, his blue gaze level and compassionate.

"There are many kinds of love. Once I lusted for your body. I was no better than the gypsy."

"And now? And now?"

"It is not like that any more. A man and a woman grow together. There are bonds between us. There are many kinds of love."

"There is only one kind," Annikki cried, "between a man and a woman, between man and wife. You will never break that rock inside you, Vainen. You will never yield to me as you yielded to Kirsti, call my name in love or passion or longing as men do. I am a woman now, Vainen, not a girl. I know how a woman feels, how she longs—" Pain gripped Annikki and she gasped. "I am torn, Vainen, I am a woman in labor—"

"Gently, girl, gently," Erik said softly and bent to lift her into his arms. "I will carry you to the house."

"No," she cried passionately, "no, don't touch me. The pain is gone for the moment but others will come and in the end my body will give up what it holds in spite of me, in spite of itself." She reached up and gripped his shoulders. "Is there such strength as yours, Vainen? Break as I break, yield, cry out, tear down the last stronghold, find your moment of weakness and power, *speak my name*. To speak my name is to give up your years of struggle and loneliness, the years when you forged the iron in your soul to help you to endure against man and Nature."

"Quiet, quiet, you will hurt yourself and the child. I tell you there are many kinds of love—"

"Keep them all and give me only one! *Speak my name!*" Annikki gasped. "When you have done that you will be absolved from the past, from that body in the lake, from your bitter memories of a dying Kirsti, from all the bitterness and strength that holds you rooted in one spot. 'There is power in a name,' you said. There is power in my name, power that

you fear. Akseli was right. Once my name is spoken it is
spoken. Something goes out that cannot be recalled."

"Akseli was right," Erik said heavily. "And I cannot yield."

Annikki beat frantically on his shoulders with her clenched
fists. "What goes out will be your deadening hold on the past,
its hold on you, the iron will that held you together—fear,
lust, love, and death—all those things that are bound up in *me*.
Yield, Vainen, yield. You love me. Say it. Break yourself as
the pastor breaks the sacrament, as the plow breaks the soil."

She was sobbing wildly. They stood against the skyline,
a man and a woman who might have been lovers, held in
each other's arms.

"You will be my care while life lasts," Erik said, "I swear it.
When the child is born our lives will truly begin. There are
many kinds of love."

Annikki gave a great cry and ran from him. Erik stood a
moment, watching her go, then turned and walked toward the
road, toward the edge of the forest, toward the advancing
gypsies.

Near the edge of the forest the old gypsy who led the caravan turned on his horse and spoke rapidly. Then he beckoned
to the pock-marked man who rode behind him and to the
two women in the cart.

"Wait," he said to the rest of the camp. "Wait and watch.
If I give the signal you will follow me."

Some were on foot, some in caravans, men, women, and
children exuding a sense of urgent, powerful life, watchful,
alert.

The old man, his son, and the women rode out of the forest
and gained the road. Ahead of them, on the left, the farmhouse with the faded red walls stood in the full noonday
sun. Every leaf on the birch trees seemed to quiver with life.
Smoke rose upward, plumelike in the still air, from house and
sauna. The lake was translucent, its calm, clear reflections

showing another world of sky and reeds and trees quivering on another vibration.

The old man rode silently, the pock-marked man beside him, his hand twisted in the pale mane of the unsaddled horse. Its airy, delicate motion was still apparent. Its ears were pricked, its hoofs shone, its grace was that of a horse reflected evanescently in water.

"That is the house," the pock-marked man said, "where I found the carving." He gestured with his free hand. "Over there, in that shed not far from the *sauna.*"

The old gypsy narrowed his eyes against the sunlight.

"There is a man coming toward us," he said. "We will ask him."

They continued to walk their horses in silence for a few moments, the cart creaking behind them. The little cavalcade moved more quickly than the man, who walked purposefully.

"It will be a long walk." The pock-marked man smiled. "If he is going into Porvesi."

They continued in silence. The horses' hoofs stirred the dust on the sun-baked road. The smell of heather mingled with the smell of horse and leather, and a tangy, animal smell from the gypsies themselves.

They were lessening the distance between themselves and the man. Now the farmhouse stood out clearly. They could see its shutters of faded green and the two women and the man busying themselves about it. One woman stood motionless, shading her eyes with her hand, looking down the road at them.

The old woman in the cart spoke. "That is the woman we saw yesterday. The one who told us where to find the belt. We were right to come here."

"She hasn't given birth yet," the pock-marked man said.

"It takes longer with *gorgios,* who live in houses, like rabbits in hutches," the old woman answered.

As the man, who was Erik, drew abreast of the gypsies, they

halted their horses. The pock-marked man drew from under
his coat the carving of the gypsy and held it up suddenly in
front of Erik as he had held it in front of old Heikki.

"This is the carving of a man," he said. "It is a good likeness. Have you seen this man?"

Erik looked at the warm wood, of which his fingers knew
every line, remembering the moment when the wood had
come to life and the body had taken on the strength and lines
of a man. The sunlight filled the empty, searching eye sockets,
giving them the illusion of sight. It was as though the young
gypsy were before him.

"Yes, I know the man," he said calmly. "He came to my
house nearly a year ago." Erik turned and pointed in the
direction of the farmhouse.

The pock-marked man twisted his hand more firmly into
the mane of his horse. The horse pranced, arching its neck,
its nostrils dilating, its ears set back.

"Why did he come?" the old gypsy asked.

"For shelter. I took him in, fed, and rested him. But that
was not all."

"What else was there?" the old man asked softly. Behind
him the women sat motionless and silent as though they, too,
were carved out of wood.

"My house is over there, as I said. Ride there and we will
talk the matter over," Erik said. He gazed at the old man
levelly. The pock-marked man breathed heavily as the horse
beneath him pranced and reared. Suddenly the old woman
gave a hoarse cry, like a wild lament. In the same instant the
horse reared high up and screamed, a sound to rend the
nerves. Its nostrils were red and dilated, its ears set back, its
shining hoofs flailed the air, then suddenly, murderously, a
gleaming hoof cut a great scimitar of light and clove its way
through Erik's skull.

Even as he saw it coming, in that one stark, eternal moment,
before he sank to the ground, Erik gave a great, anguished cry
from the depths of his being.

"Annikki! Annikki!"

The cry echoed across the sky, across the forest, across the lake, across the farmhouse and *sauna*.

"Annikki! Annikki!"

Annikki heard it.

In that cry she heard the storming of the last stronghold, it was the moment of weakness and power, the ultimate surrender and union, her name on his lips.

Annikki heard it.

Margit and Arvo heard it and came running to Annikki, who stood transfixed.

"God in heaven, girl, what was that?" Margit cried.

"It was Vainen," Annikki said. "It was Vainen."

"It was the cry of a man in his death agony," Margit said. The sweat of fear stood out on her face. "I've heard that cry once before, when a man gave up his soul."

Annikki stood, looking straight ahead, unseeing. "It happened so quickly. So quickly," she whispered. "The gypsy's horse . . . there . . . in the road. It crashed its hoof through Vainen's skull."

Margit and Arvo looked fearfully toward the road. They saw an old man on a horse, a cart, and a horse with a pale mane galloping riderless. The old man made a sign and out of the woods a strange cavalcade swept, whipping on their horses, gaining, gaining momentarily on the dark shadow lying on the road.

Annikki swayed and Arvo caught her before she fell.

"Did you hear?" she asked. "Did you hear?" Her eyes had a strange, transfixed look as of one in ecstasy.

"Annikki. Annikki," she whispered.

The cavalcade of gypsies swept by. The riderless horse swept by, leaving death behind.

"She's out of her senses," Margit said, "with shock and grief."

"That's Vainen out there on the road, Mother," Arvo cried. "That's Vainen. Don't you understand?"

Annikki suddenly broke free and ran, in spite of her burden, out of the gate and down the road and sank to the ground beside Erik and took his head on her lap. The dust where he had lain was dark with his blood.

When Arvo and Margit reached her she looked up at them with her unseeing, transfixed gaze.

"He called me," she said. "At the last moment he called my name."

"It's what a man would do in his last moment," Margit said, weeping. "He'd call the name of his wife, the woman he loved."

In Annikki's mind the great cry still echoed. A veil had been rent in twain, her whole being was flooded with a sense of release. All the anguish, all the yearning, dissolved like mist, disappeared like Vainen's blood into the dust.

She turned to Margit. "He broke himself as the pastor breaks the sacrament. As the plow breaks the soil."

"Lift her gently, lad," Margit said, through her tears. "She's out of her mind with grief. Carry her to the *sauna*, it's quicker, and there's water and warmth in there. There's no time, no time, the child is coming. She'll have to have the child in the *sauna*, where it's sweet and warm, as Kirsti, God rest her, had hers."

Arvo lifted Annikki up in his arms.

"But Vainen, Mother. Vainen. We can't leave him here."

"Carry Annikki to the *sauna* first and then come back here. I'll go to the girl afterward. You've got shoulders on you like a bull. You must carry Vainen to the house." Margit wiped the blood from Erik's face and closed his eyes. "A life has gone and a life is coming," she said to the dead face. "Vainen, you were your own judge but none of us will ever know the rights and wrongs of it." She sat dry-eyed now beside the body on the deserted road.

When Arvo came back Margit went to the *sauna* and bent over Annikki, lying with her eyes closed.

"You've nothing to fear," she said. "All is going as it should.

You mustn't fear and you mustn't fret. You've got your life before you."

"He called my name," Annikki said, and clenched her hands joyfully against the pain.

"It's something to remember," Margit said.

The great cry still echoed in Annikki's mind. Her name had been called with a great, anguished cry across the sky, across lake and forest.

She felt free, suddenly, of doubt and fear, as Vainen was free. She heard the sound of footsteps and with a great effort raised herself and looked out of the small window of the *sauna*.

Arvo was carrying Vainen's body over his shoulder, back to the house. Their shadows on the ground were dark in the sunlight, like those other shadows on the moonlit snow.

The reality of death filled Annikki. She would never see Vainen again. All that was left to her now was her name on his lips.

She lay back again, her eyes closed.

I am free, she thought, Vainen has given me freedom. But it was a freedom of the mind, the soul. In the end he had broken himself for her, cleft the iron rock of his will, torn himself free. The dead wafer on the tongue had become living bread.

The moment of death had been their moment of union. He had freed her as he had freed himself.

Yet Vainen had said that freedom was emerging from a little prison into a bigger one. Annikki opened her eyes, her body held in a vise of pain, and looked through the small window to the infinity of the sky.

Was that the bigger prison, so wide, so beautiful, so limitless? What was the compass of man's soul?

Not yet, she thought, not yet. Neither Vainen nor I will know it yet.

She felt Margit beside her while she lay in a confused blur of pain. In the silence Annikki heard a cry, not her own.

"Your son is born," Margit said. "And listen, a cuckoo is calling in the woods. A cuckoo called while your son was born. They say it is a bird of good omen."

Annikki opened her eyes and looked at the child. This child was hers. Life was waiting to be lived. There would be other winters, other springs.

When Elisabet Lahti heard of Vainen's death she wept. Veijo stroked her hair clumsily. "Don't cry for Annikki, the poor lass," he said. "She has her child, and perhaps in time she'll have her man as well. They all say that Arvo Salonen loves her."

"I was crying for Vainen," Elisabet said.

"His death was sad. But no man lives forever."

"I loved him," Elisabet said and looked up quickly, fearful, but Veijo went on stroking clumsily.

"We needs must love goodness when we see it, lass. Vainen was good," Veijo said simply, "and perhaps goodness is the only thing that lives forever."

ABOUT THE AUTHOR

Flora Sandstrom was born and educated in England, and now lives in London. She has traveled extensively in France, and received high critical praise for the authentic feeling of Normandy and of its people which she conveyed in both of the novels which were published in America—*The Midwife of Pont Clery* and *The Virtuous Women of Pont Clery*. The setting for *Other Winters, Other Springs* stems from a long visit to Finland and an admiration of its countryside and of its rugged people.

ABOUT THE AUTHOR

Flora Sandstrom was born and educated in England, and now lives in London. She has traveled extensively in France, and received high critical praise for the authentic feeling of Normandy and of its people which she conveyed in both of the novels which were published in America—*The Midwife of Pont Clery* and *The Virtuous Women of Pont Clery*. The setting for *Other Winters, Other Springs* stems from a long visit to Finland and an admiration of its countryside and of its rugged people.

THIS BOOK WAS SET IN

BASKERVILLE AND CAROLUS ROMAN TYPES BY

HARRY SWEETMAN TYPESETTING CORP.

IT WAS PRINTED AND BOUND AT THE PRESS OF

THE WORLD PUBLISHING COMPANY.

DESIGN IS BY LARRY KAMP.